Where the Willows End
by
Bernard Pearson

Published by Leaf by Leaf Press 2021
www.leafbyleafpress.com

Copyright © Bernard Pearson 2020

Bernard Pearson has asserted his right to be identified as the
author of this work in accordance with the Copyright, Design and
Patents Act 1988

ISBN 978-1-9993122-3-7

Printed and bound in Great Britain by Clays Ltd, Elcograf S.p.A.

BERNARD PEARSON

After 30 years in Social care working for and with people with a learning disability Bernard now concentrates on writing. He is a published poet, biographer and prize winning short story writer. his work has appeared in many publications, including *Aesthetica Magazine* and *The Edinburgh Review*. In 2017 a selection of his poetry 'In Free Fall' was published by *Leaf by Leaf Press*. He won second prize in *The Aurora Prize 2019* for poetry.

Acknowledgements

There are many people who have helped me in writing this book . My thanks go to my good friend Joe Powell for his insight, Monty Dart and Helen Baggott for their practical help with earlier drafts. I am also grateful to The Oswestry Writers Group for their fellowship and friendship; Kirstie Edwards for her superb copy editing skills and for helping me every step of the way; all the other Leaf by Leaf members Ron Turner, Trixie Roberts, Vicky Turrell, John Heap Wendy Lodwick Lowdon for their unstinting support and expertise. I also wish to thank Reg Turrell for his wonderful Front cover;. The United States Holocaust Memorial Museum whose website has provide invaluable background information and last but not least My beloved family Alwena, Jessica and Matthew for their forbearance and love.

Where the Willows End

by

Bernard Pearson

CHAPTER 1

November 2016

Tom Bradshott, up until now, had always had a way of landing on his feet in life and hence his mistress's nickname for him, 'Kitten'. He was taller than average, with dark hair succumbing to grey in places, little boy lost blue eyes and a lopsided grin; his looks had certainly opened a few doors in the past. Tom had a mostly genial disposition, apart that is from two areas in his life. On occasion, when dining out he could be extremely waspish about a fellow chef's fare and when driving he could become a kind of malevolent 'Mr Toad', spitting venom at other road users.

He was on his way to a pre-meeting concerning a forthcoming episode of *Family Matters*, the genealogy show made for Sunday night TV by Janus Films. The programme was really an updated version of *This is Your Life*, with a bit of juicy family history thrown in.

'Frankly there's far too much news on television at the moment, people have had enough of it,' the show's producer and chief executive of Janus Films, Barry Goldwing, had told him when putting forward the idea of Tom being a subject on the show. 'We need more Sunday night wallpaper and less from our embedded correspondent in Aleppo. That's where *Family Matters* comes in and snuggles the great British public under its duvet again a bit like your own show; what's it called now? *Let's Do Lunch*? Only without the politics.'

Tom put his foot down and his Jensen Interceptor responded. He had a weakness for classic cars and had given the Jensen to himself as a reward when he got his first cookery show on television. His hands-free phone started flashing and ringing in a slow dull tone. That's all it did: no music to herald the entrance of the Queen of Sheba, no theme from the *Waltons* or the Dambuster's March. People with elaborate call alerts on their phone irritated him. They were people who had accepted that they were less interesting than their handheld devices. They hid their lights under the darkest bushel allowing their phones to take all the applause. Tom's musings didn't make the call terminate, so he eventually answered.

'What's your ETA, Tom?'

'How the hell do I know?' barked Tom. 'The traffic is appalling. How they let half these people walk the streets, let alone get behind the wheel of a car, I'll never know.'

'Excuse me,' said the person at the other end. The voice sounded eastern European with something of an affected mid-Atlantic overlay. It was Kat Kowalski, Tom's agent.

'Tom, I need to know when you're going to get where you're supposed to be going. It's important,' said Kat, as if she was talking to a seven-year-old.

'Just about then, darling,' said Tom. 'It's what my mother says. Mind you, her idea of timekeeping is arriving for an appointment in the right week.'

'Okay, listen up, Mr Big Shot. You need this gig; your career, right this moment, is as vulnerable as a soufflé with the oven door open. Barry Goldwing is hot in TV-land right now and if he likes what he sees, a whole world outside of the kitchen may open up for you – like property shows, quizzes, anything. Your portfolio could be huge!'

'I thought you said it was big enough as it is,' quipped Tom.

'I am being serious, Tom,' said Kat.

'Alright, sexy, don't get your knickers in a knot, or not at least 'til I get there... Prick!' bellowed Tom as a lorry hogged the lane in front. The driver gave him a stately finger.

'Still making friends and influencing people, eh Mr Bradshott.'

'There are some fuckers out there who frankly should have been sink fodder on the day they were born,' Tom retorted.

'Now, now, "Mr Sunday Roast... Never mind the food. Tom's good enough to eat", says *OK!* magazine,' teased Kat, reminding him of his 'lovable rogue', public image.

'With any luck I should be there in half an hour or so... Pillock!' yelled Tom.

'Charming,' said Kat. 'Remember, Tom, we need you to do this show. Call me when you get there.'

CHAPTER 2

Down in deepest Berkshire in the pretty little village of Willows End complete with its ancient church and babbling stream, the Bradshotts did themselves pretty well in respect of a des res, reeking as it did of all that the comfortably off took for granted: beamed reception rooms aplenty; en suite for every bedroom; indoor pool and a country style kitchen made for any self-respecting TV chef. However, it was Mrs Bradshott who was presiding over it that day.

Bonnie Bradshott was small, but stood well; a pair of spectacles peeked out from her blond hair, which tumbled down loosely to her waist. She dressed purely for herself, in the way that only very beautiful women do. Perched on a paint-spattered stool, Bonnie was half reading a book she had lost interest in about twenty pages ago. She was trying to put off the reality that she herself had a book to write and her publisher was getting fractious. Evie, her daughter, was at the other end of the room, busying herself with various kitchen utensils looking up earnestly now and again at her father on the television screen.

'Take the mixture and ensuring you have thoroughly greased your ramekins with butter...' said the voice on the TV.

On hearing this, Evie took her bowl and greased it vigorously.

'Use the fine side of your grater, being careful to avoid the fleshy pith.'

Evie made as if she were grating. At the other end of the kitchen, Bonnie answered the house phone.

'Hi there... no, I'm sorry, I have no idea where Tom is. I guess if he says he'll be there, he'll be there. Yes, he should have his phone I think but whether he's got it switched on, that's another question. His agent Kat has probably got more of an idea of his movements these days... Have you got her number? ...If you can hold?'

'Pop it into a hot oven at 180 degrees centigrade.'

4

Evie watched her father on the TV and took her bowl with the mixture over to the oven, which was already on.

'Hey, excuse me, don't you people listen? I'm his wife, not his warder... you got a problem with that?' said Bonnie, whose patience was running out.

Evie had reached the oven and opened the door. She bent down hands on knees and peered in.

'Ooh!' she exclaimed.

Bonnie spotted what was going on and rushed across the kitchen, sweeping the little girl up in her arms.

'Hot, Evie! Too hot!'

Evie turned to her mother, grabbed Bonnie's glasses from her head and put them on, then she said sternly,

'You are silly, Mummy!'

Tom Bradshott grinned cheekily from the television screen.

'Next week, how to cook ham hocks; the secret of the flavour is all in the bones.'

* * * * *

Kat Kawalski had bought her north London flat during a rare slump in the market. It was part of what had once been a match factory. The decor, what there was of it, was minimalist in tone, save for a few expensive pieces of installation art. The bed on which she and Tom Bradshott were making love looked more like a piece of gym equipment than somewhere one might get a decent night's sleep.

'Do you ever buy any food at all?' said Tom getting up to look hopefully into Kat's fridge.

'Yeees, but I forget to sometimes, okay! Besides, you go home to your fat American wife for that. Now are you coming back to bed, Kitten?'

The meeting with Barry Goldwing had gone well, despite Tom arriving half an hour late. Work had already begun on the episode of *Family Matters* and Goldwing had agreed on the fee for Tom that Kat had been negotiating for him. It was modest but the press explosion that Tom would get from the show would ensure he remained in the premiership of celebrity chefs for another season.

Tom looked at Kat, lying naked across the bed; her black, Pre- Raphaelite, crinkle cut hair falling neatly across each small breast. She was reaching furtively into his jacket for a cigarette, like a Victorian street urchin picking the pocket of a country gentleman.

Kat had been born in Poland, but moved to England with her parents in her teens. Her father was a self-made man in the shipping business and her mother a GP. They lived in Southampton, but relations between them and Kat had become strained over her 'in their opinion' strident political views and her lapsed Catholicism. As a result, Kat's visits home were becoming more and more infrequent.

'So how's the stopping smoking going?' said Tom, closing the fridge door and returning to the bed with a barely edible apple he had found, lurking at the bottom of what he hoped was the fruit bowl and not an expensive piece of art.

Tom and Kat had been lovers for three months now, but this was the first time they had used her flat. Mostly their affair had been carried out while on location with Tom's cookery show, *Let's Do Lunch,* in local country inns involving much creaking of floorboards and four-poster headboards.

'Christ I'm late; she'll kill me!' exclaimed Tom.

'Screw Bonnie!' Kat responded. 'Today, you are my Tom Kitten.'

'I'm talking about my mother, not Bonnie,' replied Tom tersely.

'Well screw her too!' said Kat, drawing on the cigarette.

'What a little charmer you are,' said Tom tucking his shirt into his trousers. 'I'll call you.'

'And screw you too!'

'You just have,' said Tom. 'Now eat something!'

Tom slipped out of the apartment block and strode off in the direction of where he'd parked the Jensen, stopping for a bacon baguette on the way.

'Hey! You're that Tom Blackburn,' said the girl at the café.

'Bradshott, Tom Bradshott,' corrected Tom. 'Easy on the brown sauce, if that's okay.'

'Do you really do the cooking like?' asked the girl.

'No, we have chef doubles for that,' said Tom.

'You what?'

'Look, I'm sorry, I'm in a bit of a rush. Do you want me to sign something, paper towel, burger box?'

'No, you're alright,' said the girl slapping the baguette into Tom's hand. 'It's our busy time, see.'

'Right, I'll be off then. Have a nice day.'

CHAPTER 3

Heidelberg was, according to its website, a cosmopolitan, culturally diverse, student orientated town, at the heart of the Rhine Neckar triangle.

Chloe Whiting sat in the back of the taxi, hypnotised a little by the block after block of almost identical flats flashing by. Perhaps it was the sleety rain and the gun-grey leaden skies, but the town didn't appear at its best.

This was her third trip away, researching for the series, *Family Matters*. The other two had meant weeks in Jamaica and Florida and had certainly not involved her mother's old pair of leggings and an itchy, woollen, Peruvian bonnet. Perhaps this TV malarkey wasn't as glamorous as she had been led to believe. Chloe had been lucky to get a job so soon after leaving university. Her interview with Janus Films had been nerve-racking but she'd managed to convince the panel that there were transferable skills from a degree in criminology that she could use as a television researcher.

The car pulled up outside one of the more dilapidated blocks.

'*Danke*,' said Chloe, paying the taxi driver, before looking up at the flats. She wanted the eighth floor and was surprised on entering it to find the lift working perfectly and smelling not unpleasantly of disinfectant. She knocked at number seventy-nine.

'Herr Rohmer, Heinrich Rohmer?'

'*Yah.*'

'My name is Chloe... Chloe Whiting... we spoke on the phone.'

'I don't remember,' said Rohmer.

Herr Rohmer was a tall man with quite a pronounced stoop. A pair of spectacles dangled from a chain around his neck; he was dressed in a pair of cords, a checked shirt and a faded green fleece and walked with the help of a stick.

'It's about your nephew, Tom... Tom Bradshott,' explained Chloe. 'I've come over from England. We spoke on the phone.'

'Yes, that is right, he is my nephew, but we have not even met. I do not really know how I can help you.'

'You've never met Tom?' said Chloe.

'No, but I have seen him on the television of course.'

'You get Tom's shows in Germany?' queried Chloe.

'Yes, we have our passion for celebrity chefs over here you know. How remiss of me, come in, come in, let me make you some tea, after coming all this way. It is the least I can do. But as I say, I know very little about Tom.'

'It's the family history I'm really interested in, in particular your brother Gunther Rohmer,' said Chloe, as the old man ushered her into his sitting room. There was a piano laden with photographs; the furnishings were faded, but a number of colourful throws and cushions suggested an artistic eye, as did the abstract pictures on the wall, remnants of a more affluent time perhaps.

'Ah, the past... something we're not very keen on here in Germany. I have loose tea, or teabags, which ever you prefer.'

'Whatever is easier; Tom's grandfather; what are your memories of him?'

'Memories, why would I want memories of that time? I would prefer to remember where my keys are and what day I need to collect my pension, but memories of Gunther... By the way, have I asked you if you would like tea?'

'Yes, thank you, that would be lovely. We know quite a bit about his life after the war in England.'

'Yes indeed, he became a very well-respected Englishman of course. He needed a new name. George Roberts, Sir George Roberts in fact, Chairman of Roberts Road Builders, pre-eminent among your civil engineering companies.'

'It's really about his time in Germany that we want to know,' explained Chloe. 'The family seem to have very little information.'

'I have been on my own for many years now so you must forgive me when my manners slip a little,' said Heinrich softly.

'Oh, please don't worry.'

'In my student days we used to hold the best parties in town.' Heinrich smiled.

'Do you mind if I ask what happened?' asked Chloe.

'Separation is what happened, Miss Whiting,' said Heinrich, his eyes moistening.

'Oh, my parents are separated,' said Chloe.

'Not I suspect by a wall that ripped flesh from flesh; sinew from sinew, but it is not old Heinrich you've come to hear about, it's George, or should I say Gunther of course. Apologies for when I digress, Miss Whiting.'

'Tom has told us that your brother won the Iron Cross and had a distinguished war record.'

'Distinguished? So you think war is distinguished do you, Miss Whiting?'

'I think it is what it is, Herr Rohmer,' said Chloe. 'Can you tell me what your brother was like when you were children?'

'No, not really; you see he was twenty-four when I was born, but in my early memories he already seemed middle-aged, more like an uncle than a brother. To begin with I was in awe of him, but as I got a little older and wiser he struck me as a stuck up prig. He always looked like he had a knackwurst stuck up his arse. Forgive me, I am being crude I think,' said Heinrich

'Not at all, your English is very expressive. By the way, did I mention the fee in our phone conversation?'

'Oh yes, Miss Whiting, I remember now, you did. Otherwise you might have found me not at home to visitors today,' smiled the old man.

CHAPTER 4

Pink Cottage, Trotfield St Giles, was just as the name might suggest, a chocolate box idyll, set deep in the Surrey countryside. Tom's mother and father had moved there in 1997, on his retirement as a partner in a firm of chartered accountants in Haslemere. Two years ago, Tom's father had gone upstairs for a nap after Sunday lunch and had not come down again, a typically understated death. If there was one thing Roger didn't like, it was a fuss, apart, that is, from where his wife was concerned, on whom he lavished gifts on any and every occasion. No birthday or anniversary was allowed to pass without Phyllis being showered with what he called 'a little something'.

Regarding not wanting to make a fuss, Tom even wondered whether Roger had timed his own demise to avoid 'all the palaver', as he would have put it, of the millennium.

Tom had been quite fond of his father and the feeling was, at times, reciprocated. Conversations were limited to safe topics, like the Test Match score and the vicissitudes of the British weather. His father made little secret of the fact that he didn't think much of Tom's chosen career in 'cookery', as he put it. He had hoped that two stints in the kitchen with some chap down in Padstow would put the boy off, but it had had the opposite effect.

The camera crew of *Family Matters* were just setting up for some external shots and were purring with delight as a gentle, sunny, morning light bathed the garden of Pink Cottage. Multicoloured leaves remained on many of the trees even in early November. Meanwhile, Phyllis Bradshott was now in her late sixties; she was still solidly built and expensively dressed. Striding up her garden path came Tom with a bouquet of flowers in one hand, while swatting good naturedly at the make-up girl with the other. He had learnt, over his relatively short television career, that it paid to keep the make-up girls onside, as their patience would occasionally wear thin. What began as a mere gentle caress with a powder brush would descend by the end of a shoot into a cursory slap around the chops, which in most courts in the land would be classified as common assault.

Phyllis Bradshott snatched the bouquet brusquely from her son's hand.

'What were you thinking of? You look a mess,' observed Phyllis acidly.

Callum, the young director of *Family Matters*, hurried over to Phyllis and Tom. Callum was an earnest character who longed to cut his teeth making gritty documentaries. He was an ardent fan of the director, Ken Loach.

Callum dressed in the hipster uniform of smartly pressed jeans, lumberjack shirt and sported a well-trimmed beard and horn-rimmed spectacles. He had just entered into a civil partnership with Oliver and they were buying a large flat off the Edgeware Road. Oliver worked in fashion and their joint income gave them an enviable lifestyle and holidays anywhere from Hawaii to the Maldives. Callum was very aware of being one of the 'haves', hence his devotion to social realism films. Oliver's approach to life, on the other hand, was that of the entrepreneur, who had worked bloody hard for what he'd got and was bloody well going to enjoy it. As far as a family was concerned Callum longed for children, while Oliver couldn't see himself ever being a father.

'I think we are ready for a take now, Mrs Bradshott.'

'Dear Callum, your wish, is our command!' She smiled sweetly at the young man.

Tom wondered how he would get through the next hour with his mother being so unctuous. His relationship with his mother had never been good. He had never been able to shake off the feeling that he was viewed, especially by his mother, not as a precious only child but as something of a gooseberry interfering in their marriage. When he was younger, he used to suspect that perhaps he had been adopted, something he knew many children felt. It had come up during one of his therapy sessions as an explanation for his predilection for infidelity. He felt slightly disappointed on coming across his birth certificate in his father's office proving, as far as these things do, that he was the product of his parents' loins.

'Darling Tom, how wonderful!' exclaimed his mother (for the camera).

They went into the cottage followed by the cameraman, soundman and make-up girl. Tom and his mother sat at the dining room table for the next shot. The table was spread with photographs and various family certificates and documents.

'Hello, Ma. I was hoping you'd help me find out more about your side of the family,' said Tom.

'Darling, I think it's a wonderful idea,' cooed Phyllis.

Callum had been distracted by his mobile phone.

'Did you get all you needed from us there, Callum?'

'Err, I'll tell you what, what if we give it one more go, but you were terrific, Mrs B.'

'Oh, you really are a sweetie, Callum.'

'Now, I wonder if you would be kind enough to tell us a little about your father, Mrs Bradshott?' said Callum.

'I will make some tea,' said Tom, glad to excuse himself from the mutual love fest.

'Daddy was a marvellous man, could turn his hand to anything, came to England with practically nothing and built an empire.'

'And your mother?'

'She came from one of the oldest, aristocratic families in Britain, but was always, how shall I put it... mentally delicate.'

'Were you and your father close?' asked Callum.

'Oh yes, we were, I adored him.'

'Spoilt you rotten I reckon, Mother,' said Tom coming in with a tray of tea.

* * * * *

Jubilee Park was a five-minute walk from Tom and Bonnie Bradshott's house. It was situated behind the cricket pavilion, where in the summer Bonnie and Evie would come down most Sundays to watch Tom play cricket. He was a top order batsman of God-given power and grace, who might well have made a career in the first-class game, had it not been for his dislike of net practice.

Today Bonnie was sitting on a bench, by the side of the children's playground, with her head as usual in a book. There was a thin drizzle in the air and the wind was beginning to whistle across the open ground. Two dogs were careering together through a pile of ribbon like leaves under the willow trees that marked the course of the village stream. Bonnie looked up to see Evie playing with another little girl.

'Is that your daughter? She's very pretty,' commented Bonnie, to a woman sitting on the next bench. The woman was dressed in a sleeveless padded jacket, an expensive pair of slacks and fur boots. She was fiddling with her mobile phone.

'Have you seen the news today? Apparently Brexit doesn't mean Brexit. God, I don't believe this country sometimes!'

'I was saying your daughter is a real sweetie.'

'Yes but they do seem to grow up so quickly, don't they... Oh, I'm sorry I didn't mean...' said the woman half watching as Evie blew an enormous raspberry, while the other little girl pushed her round on the roundabout.

'No problem. I'm Bonnie by the way, Bonnie Bradshott.'

'Pamela Richards, nice to meet you and of course your husband is the one on the TV, the chef – is that right? I seem to remember him being a bit of a dish himself; better than that awful old tranny they had on the telly when I was a child, yuk! Must be difficult to get out of bed in the morning when he's at home.'

Bonnie had put up with women talking about her husband this way for years. It always struck her as odd that the women most likely to talk like this were the ones first to the barricades when some nubile, star-struck nineteen-year-old pulled her designer tee shirt up for the red tops.

'Seren, that's my daughter's name,' said the woman. 'It means 'star' in Welsh you know. Well she's our little star anyway. Do you know, from the moment she was born she hasn't given us a moment's trouble? "Our little princess" her father says. She sings with the voice of an angel and has just passed her first ballet exam; her teacher says all the other girls love her. Do you know I filled forty, yes forty! goodie bags for her birthday party?'

'My Evie loves parties,' commented Bonnie.

Pamela Richards continued her monologue while still fiddling with her mobile phone.

'Oh, look at the time, her brother will be coming out of school... home for his tea, then football practice, then Scouts. Not enough hours in the day. Anyway, must fly, nice to meet you.'

She looked across at Evie, squeezed Bonnie's hand and gave her a pitying look.

Meanwhile Evie was at the top of the slide, enjoying the wind streaming through her hair. She beckoned for Bonnie to join her, which she did and they slid down, both screaming their heads off defiantly. Pamela Richards coughed nervously and took her daughter's hand and walked off without a backward glance, unaware of the two little girls waiving vigorously to each other.

* * * * *

That afternoon Callum had arranged to see Bonnie for the forthcoming episode of *Family Matters*. What the viewers liked was a bit of mushy romance, so a set of questions by the show's narrator were about spouses and partners.

'So, Bonnie, where did Tom take you on your first date together?'

'As matter of fact he took me to the Ideal Home Exhibition and bought himself a new set of knives and a wok.'

'And what did he buy you?'

'A ginger beer, I think; I was the driver. He got very drunk as I remember and tried to get off with a girl selling power showers.'

'Not a very auspicious beginning,' said the interviewer off camera.

'I guess not, but I just thought things could only get better.'

'And did they?'

'Well, we're still speaking,' said Bonnie.

This wasn't exactly what Callum was looking for and it would need some creative editing if they were to use any of it in the programme.

At this point, Evie came in from the garden, carrying a large slug.

'Look, Mummy, a homeless snail. Can it come and live with us?'

'Hello there,' said Callum. 'You must be the Evie, who I've heard so much about.'

'Do you like snails?' said Evie.

'Er, yes,' lied Callum.

'Why?' asked Evie.

'Well, they're not going to take you by surprise,' quipped Callum.

Evie looked at him with good humoured forbearance before placing the creature in Callum's hand.

'But I think that's a slug we've got there.'

'It's still coming to stay with us. Isn't it, Mummy? After all, with Daddy away there's plenty of room. What's your name by the way?'

'Callum.'

'Mummy, can Callum stay for tea?'

'Well.'

'Please.'

'Honey, he may have other plans.'

'Pleeease.'

'Could you spare the time, Callum?' said Bonnie tentatively.

'It would be a pleasure,' said Callum. 'Now, Evie, have you thought of a name for this slug of yours?'

* * * * *

Back in Germany, Heinrich Rohmer shuffled into his sitting room carrying a large brown leather suitcase.

'This is all I have of his. He visited me after the war to tell me of his plans to move to England. He asked me to look after it because he wanted to take nothing of his life in Germany with him. He didn't want reminding of too many ghosts, me being one of them, I think. He said I was to burn it in the event of his death.'

'Quite a strange thing to do, don't you think?' said Chloe.

'That was Gunther for you.'

'Did you ever talk about the war at all?'

'No, he was barely at my house for ten minutes. That was the last I ever saw of him. Oh, his parting words were, "Exercise and keeping busy, Heinrich, that's the secret to a happy life," and then he bowed in that way of his, clicked his heels and off he went.'

Chloe took the case from the old man.

'Forgive me, Herr Rohmer, but you and your brother, is there, or should I say, was there some kind of problem?'

'It's not something I want to talk about really, Miss Whiting.'

'There'll be no mention of this in the programme. We are only interested in Tom's forbears, in terms of what they did and how life treated them,' explained Chloe.

'Very few of us ordinary Germans were treated fairly back then, Miss Whiting. We were all victims of our political masters at the time.'

Heinrich started to wheeze badly and Chloe helped him to his chair.

She began to worry that this was all taking too much out of him. His blue eyes had a milky quality to them and his complexion was of high colour.

'No, it is nothing, I shall be fine. I have prepared some food for you,' said Heinrich rising slowly from his chair. 'It's not much, I'm afraid, I get so few visitors now. You are very welcome to look through the case. Gunther is long gone and it is difficult to upset the dead, I think.'

'Thank you, Herr Rohmer,' said Chloe

'I am afraid my brother didn't think much of me. Gunther had very high principles you see. Old frosty drawers we used to call him, behind his back that is,' said Heinrich, stumbling into his small kitchen.

CHAPTER 5

Tom was quite new to the whole book tour thing, but Kat had got him a slot at the Hay Festival earlier in the year. With her usual panache through networking at Hay, she had also managed to secure him a book signing at the Reading Reader, a new, independent bookshop in the centre of the Berkshire town. It was a light and airy building, with a coffee shop area at the front and bookshelves above, set out on two floors. Last week it had hosted a book launch by Jeffrey Archer and next week there was to be a poetry reading by the Poet Laureate, Carol Ann Duffy.

Tom hadn't been sure about the Hay Festival site itself, finding it all rather odd. To his eyes it resembled a field hospital and the tent where the authors did their signings had been curiously soulless. The place was full of young female PR types, striding around in their Barbour jackets and skinny jeans and old men in leather jackets and Palestinian Liberation Front scarves searching for 'anything by Tariq Ali'. These old class warriors had been brought back from the dead or from their organic allotments by the rise of Jeremy Corbin. Tom was basically apolitical in his views; however, he knew what to say depending on whose company he was in.

Tom found the town of Hay more to his liking with its higgledy-piggledy streets and its rather spooky castle. His talk had gone down quite well in the morning and in the afternoon, he had time to explore the town. In a book shop the size of an aircraft hangar, where even the walls seemed to seep intelligence, he picked up an Elizabeth David book on French cuisine and a biography of Ian Botham. The woman at the till gave him a pitying look. She obviously did not recognise him, probably Tom mused because she looked the kind of woman who would rather have Satan, Baal and Beelzebub sat on her sofa than allow a television over her threshold.

He had managed to escape his mother's clutches sooner than he thought was possible this morning. Phyllis had been too busy flirting with Callum to notice her son making his apologies to the rest of the film crew. He now found himself ensconced in the minstrels' gallery of the Reading Reader, signing copies of his latest book, *Zest of Life*.

'Have you come far?... Thanks... who shall I dedicate it to?'

A middle-aged couple in matching green fleeces were standing in front of Tom's desk.

'Ralph and Shirley, if you don't mind. We've come down from Kidderminster. Never miss your shows. We like Jamie and the black girl and Gordon of course, before he thought that having a mouth like a sewer was clever, that is.'

'There you go, have a great day.'

Tom took another copy of the book without looking.

'Hi. How far have you come today? Who shall I dedicate this to?'

'To a friend would be good, I guess,' said Bonnie Bradshott.

'Bonnie!' Tom exclaimed.

'And Evie,' said Bonnie.

'Oh yes. Hi Evie.'

'Daddy!' The little girl dived across the desk to embrace her father, knocking a pile of books flying.

'Tom, I need to leave Evie with you for a couple of hours.'

'Yes, that's fine, when?'

'Now.'

'Now! Bonnie, you can see I am a bit tied up.'

'Yes, I can and you probably want to know what my reason is.'

Evie had placed a copy of *Zest of Life* on her head and started to sing 'God Save the Queen' at the top of her voice.

'Hey, can we keep it down a bit, Evie? So what's so important?' growled Tom.

'That I leave Evie with her father for an hour? I'm sorry I didn't make an appointment. I guess I'll leave you to work that one out... Evie sweetheart, you stay with Daddy.'

'Daddy, will you do some cooking? Daddy, will you do some cooking?' demanded Evie.

'Bonnie... God you can be such a...'

At this point Kat Kawalski arrived, threw her handbag on the desk and took Evie in her arms.

Kat and Evie had got on like a house on fire from the moment they first met. Kat had driven down from London one Sunday afternoon earlier that summer with the publishing contract for *Zest of Life*.

Tom was playing cricket and he was batting well, so Kat had to wait until the tea interval to get his signature. Bonnie was sat outside the pavilion in a deckchair in a white lacy summer frock and enormous straw hat looking like something out of the film, *A Room with a View*.

'Excuse me, are you by any chance Mrs Tom Bradshott?' Kat had asked.

'Yes, that's right and you must be Carol? My husband's new agent.'

'It's... um Kat actually... Kat Kawalski.'

'Right! Well, Kat, you may have some time to wait. My husband is the batter right now and he's usually out there quite a while.'

'I never really understand cricket,' said Kat.

'Me neither; it's that bozo with three hats on his head doing a kind of dance in slow motion I don't get.'

'He's the umpire, I think,' said Kat.

'But why are there two?'

'The other one's apparently the square leg umpire.'

'If you say so, honey,' said Bonnie. 'Sorry, this is our daughter Evie. Evie, this is Katy.'

'Call me Kat, Evie; most people do.'

'Kat. That's a funny name for a person,' said Evie.

'Well some people think I'm a funny person,' said Kat.

'Would you like to take me to the swings?' asked Evie.

'Well sure, if that's okay with your mummy.'

'Oh, it's okay,' said Evie. 'She had her turn earlier.'

'Is that okay, Mrs Bradshott?'

'Of course, but do me a favour, Kat, don't call me Mrs Bradshott. It makes a girl feel over a hundred.'

* * * * *

In the Reading Reader, Evie had her arms around Kat.

'Hey Tom, it's cool. Hi Bonnie, my you look good. So, Evie, you want to hang out with me for a while?' Evie started to play with Kat's hair.

'It seems you've got two fans in the Bradshott family,' said Bonnie, peering over her glasses.

At this point a middle-aged woman in very sensible shoes strode up to the desk.

'Excuse me, but we've been queuing for three quarters of an hour and this lady just pushed in!'

'Okay, lady, keep your hair on. Want to know a little secret? That was no lady; that was his wife.' Bonnie turned and walked slowly out of the shop.

* * * * *

In Heinrich Rohmer's flat in Heidelberg, Chloe had begun to sort through the contents of the brown suitcase. Amongst various military and legal documents, Chloe came across a copy of *Mein Kampf*, the middle of which had been hollowed out; in the cavity was an Iron Cross and a small leather-bound notebook.

CHAPTER 6

March 1941

In large, well-fortified barracks on the outskirts of Berlin, General Major Gunther Rohmer was busy giving orders to his staff. He was a tall man with a silvery tinged beard and moustache, who walked with a slight limp.

He looked out from his office window to the street below; gaggles of people were busily buying provisions which seemed surprisingly plentiful, given that it was wartime. Most of the shops were full apart from an empty shop front, on which 'Judenscheisse' had been scrawled in red paint. In the barracks car park, SS officer Oberscharfuhrer Pieter Von Geysell was getting out of his staff car. All the staff apart from Gunther made sure they were busy. A few moments later, Von Geysell entered Gunther Rohmer's office with a peremptory knock.

'My dear General Major Rohmer! It is good of you to see me at such short notice.'

Von Geysell was fifteen years Rohmer's junior, the age difference accentuated by his bad case of acne and wispy adolescent attempt at a moustache. He wore a pair of tinted glasses and flapped a pair of black calf leather gloves nervously from hand to hand.

'Not at all; I had a message to say it was urgent,' said Rohmer.

'Urgent? Well only in the sense of asking your forgiveness. Your name has unfortunately been left off the guest list for a reception being given by the High Command tonight. Everyone still hopes you can make it.'

Gunther had known about this event for some time but had assumed that he had not been invited, which suited him very well.

'Well I am honoured of course but...'

'There is a rumour going round that the Fuhrer himself will be popping in. I know he would be very disappointed not to see one of the Fatherland's favourite sons.'

Von Geysell impatiently beckoned for one of the junior staff to bring him a seat. He threw himself into the chair, growing in confidence and enjoying Rohmer's discomfort.

'Of course, in that case,' said Rohmer.

'Good, good; the matter is settled then. I shall not hold you up any longer. Shall we say seven for seven-thirty? Heil Hitler!'

Gunther Rohmer gave something of a desultory salute as Von Geysell left. Then he watched as the young SS officer walked out into the car park, inspecting his staff car meticulously for scratches.

'Pompous little man wouldn't have lasted five minutes in France in 1916,' muttered Rohmer.

* * * * *

Later that day in Gunther Rohmer's large, detached house located fashionably off the Alexanderplatz, he paced up and down in his living room.

'What am I to do? If that common little painter and decorator turns up and I am not there, there will no doubt be hell to pay.'

Ingrid Rohmer handed her husband a glass of schnapps in an attempt to calm him down. She was small and delicately boned, with large, blue eyes and raven coloured hair. Her husband, fifteen years her senior, towered over her.

'Gunther, this has been arranged for weeks. Dr Albrecht is a busy man and Freddy has been told he is coming now. You know how he hates change,' said Ingrid.

'There is nothing for it, you will have to see Albrecht, find out exactly what it is he is proposing,' said Rohmer.

'Very well, but I do think you...' said Ingrid.

'Look,' said Gunther. 'The old days are gone now. We are all at the whim of people who in times past we would only have let in at the servants' entrance... I am too old for the Russian front and besides I need to be here in Berlin. The place will need rebuilding once these fly by nights in their pretty uniforms are run out of town.'

For a moment, Gunther turned, worried that one of the servants, none of whom he trusted, had overheard his little tirade. He closed the sitting room door and saw Freddy, his son, standing at the top of the stairs flapping his hands while rhythmically humming to himself. Freddy was eight years old with dark chocolate coloured eyes and tousled black hair. He had yet to speak and spent much of his life in the nursery.

'It's okay, Freddy, your father has to go out now,' said Ingrid reassuringly.

'Why does the boy always look at me as if he had never seen me before?' said Gunther, brushing his uniform in front of the mirror.

'He looks at every one that way. That's why we need Dr Albrecht's help so desperately. They say there's a clinic where children like Freddy have made tremendous progress.'

'Well, get the details. I will pay whatever it costs to rid the poor boy of this curse.'

'It is not a curse, Gunther. Freddy is just different; it's a condition, an illness if you like... Oh, I forgot the Rohmers don't get ill,' said Ingrid sarcastically.

Gunther replaced his monocle.

'Well, I will leave it in your hands, as you always seem to know best where the boy is concerned,' snapped Gunther.

'Your son's name is Freddy and he is waving to you.'

On the landing Freddy had raised one hand and was watching his fingers cast a shadow against the wall.

Gunther Rohmer was already out of the front door before Ingrid had finished her last sentence; a car was waiting for him.

He was driven at high speed through the blacked-out streets of Berlin to one of the larger government buildings in the centre of town. The room was filled with military top brass. Pieter Von Geysell made his way towards Rohmer.

'Why, General Major Rohmer! So glad you were able to make it.'

'Your invitation was hard to resist,' replied Gunther.

'It's this damn war, makes such a mess of one's social life don't you know. Were it not for the fact that our English cousins are now the enemy, I would be on a grouse moor in Yorkshire as we speak.'

'I understand Herr Hitler has many friends among the English aristocracy. I am sure after the Reich's glorious victory you will have many more invitations. Now, if you will excuse me, I think I need a little fresh air.' The words stuck in Gunther's throat, even as they were uttered.

He made his way out onto one of the garden terraces and looked across the city. A few searchlights shone out in the distance and the low throb of aircraft could be heard. No air raid warning had been given, so the party went on regardless.

'Grouse my backside! The man has never shot a grouse in his life.'

Rohmer saw his old comrade Conrad Meyer coming towards him. Meyer and Gunther Rohmer had served together on the Western Front during World War One. Meyer had put on about forty pounds since those days and lost most of his hair.

'Conrad! How good it is to see you!'

'Well, Gunther, my old friend what is it all coming to eh? I think we had a better time on the Somme.'

'You need to be a little careful in what you say, old chum, they have snitches everywhere,' cautioned Gunther.

'Oh, do not concern yourself, Gunther, the Nazis need old dinosaurs like us, at least for the moment. They will keep us in their tent until one night when we will wake up with our throats slit!'

'Hard to do, I think... wake up, with your throat cut,' Rohmer smiled grimly.

'That is why instead of minding our Ps and Qs some of us think we should wake up now,' said Conrad, smiling politely at Von Geysell who was just out of ear shot.

When Gunther Rohmer returned later that evening, he was not in a good mood, having spent more time than he cared to in the company of the SS; thankfully Herr Hitler had failed to turn up, so Gunther was able to make his excuses and leave. But not before Von Geysell had a final word.

'Back to the bosom of your family, dear General Major. They are why we keep fighting. So precious families, some of us old war dogs are the only people who understand this, that one moment we have them and then the next, puff they are gone.'

Old 'war dogs' thought Gunther; the only people Von Geysell had ever taken arms against were defenceless labour slaves and Jewish families, who he had prodded onto trains at the end of his bayonet and sent God knows where.

As Gunther opened his front door, a maid was showing a short-bearded man in a grey overcoat and brown homburg out.

'Ah, you must be Dr Albrecht. Good evening! I am so sorry to be arriving just as you are leaving. Have you had a successful visit? May I offer you some schnapps? I know that it is March, but it is still cold out there.'

'Thank you, General Major,' said Albrecht, peering at Rohmer through the gloom. 'But no, I must be going. Unfortunately, you may find your wife a little upset. You see, we are unable to help with your boy at present.'

Gunther made his way through the house to a small room they used as a snug, where he found Ingrid; she'd been crying.

'Oh Ingrid, do not upset yourself; there are other clinics.' Gunther took his wife in his arms for a moment. She struggled like a small, feral animal and then seemed to collect her thoughts.

'Yes, I am sure you are right... other clinics, why of course,' she responded.

'He seemed pleasant enough, Dr Albrecht I mean,' observed Gunther.

'You will have to excuse me, Gunther, but Freddy will not go to bed until he has done his routines.'

'Go to the boy; tell him his papa says night-night... It has been a long day... good to be home... I am sorry you had to deal with Albrecht, I know how trying you find it meeting new people.'

'It is not that I dislike meeting new people, but while caring for Freddy, I never really get the chance and then when I do...' Ingrid started to shake.

'When you do what?'

'Oh, it's... By the way, did you see Herr Hitler?'

'No, our beloved leader failed to show up, but I met up with Conrad Meyer. He is just the same, you know. You seem a little upset, my dear,' commented Gunther, who didn't like too much emotion getting in the way of the smooth running of his household.

'It's nothing. Now fix me a drink while I tend to Freddy; you know, one of my favourites and then you can tell me all about Conrad. Does he still wear that ridiculous toupee that makes him look like a cockatoo? Or has he let nature take its course?' said Ingrid.

CHAPTER 7

In Heidelberg, Chloe Whiting closed Gunther's notebook with a smile.

Heinrich refilled her cup of tea and passed it to her.

'Don't tell me you've found old Gunther had a sense of humour after all?'

'Oh, I'd love to hear more. The notebook is fascinating.'

'Which is more than you can say about the man, God rest his soul.'

Outside Heinrich's house the snow had started to fall. Silky flakes soon began to cover the drab uniformity of the blocks of flats, giving each a new identity. Washing lines struggled under the weight of clothes and new snow and the few trees that there were took on a spectral quality amidst the gloom.

'The trouble with Gunther was that he never knew when he had a good thing going. He was a great military strategist, but human nature was a complete mystery to him, as I'm afraid was his son. Although I suspect he loved the boy more than he let on. Here, I have packed you some sandwiches, but I think you'd better go now; the weather is closing in and I am very tired. All this socialising; I usually see no one, one week to another. Come back soon and we will continue. Oh and don't forget the fee; fifteen hundred wasn't it?' queried Heinrich.

'A thousand, I think we agreed,' corrected Chloe.

'Oh yes, you'll have to forgive me, my memory is terrible these days. I think you asked when it was that he was awarded the Iron Cross. At the beginning of 1916 my brother was assigned to a unit with responsibility for tunnelling under enemy trenches and blowing them up. But as casualties rose during the Battle of the Somme, he was reassigned to above ground duties and put in charge of a group of men. Losses were so high on both sides that age meant nothing; he was twenty and an officer. Within only a few days, Gunther and five of his men were trapped in a foxhole. The silly idiot took four stick hand grenades, got out of the foxhole and started lobbing the grenades in the general direction of the British trenches. In open ground, he then collected ammunition from both the German and British corpses and returned to his men, who, with the new armaments were able to hold their position until reinforcements came. That's where he got his nickname, "Elster". Magpie I think you say in English.'

'You've been so helpful; thank you, Herr Rohmer,' said Chloe.

* * * * *

A week after Chloe's first trip to Germany she was sitting at a table in a smart London restaurant with Tom Bradshott and Callum, the director of *Family Matters*.

'Well come on, spill the beans. How did you get on? Let's hear about all Tom's family skeletons.'

'I think that's what I'm eating; there are more bones in this fish than your average graveyard,' said Tom.

'Mine's fine,' chipped in Chloe.

'Well, mineral water, two bread sticks and a rocket salad, Edward Scissorhands could have prepared; it's not what I call a meal,' observed Tom.

'So, Uncle Heinrich, what's he like?' enquired Callum.

'I haven't the foggiest; I was always told he was a bit of a recluse,' Tom replied.

'Chloe, can you enlighten us?' said Callum.

'He was a poppet, poor as a church mouse, so I upped the fee and said we'd pay him fifteen hundred.'

'I hope what you got out of him was worth it,' said Tom.

'Who's for pud?' said Callum.

'No fear,' said Tom looking at the dessert trolley. 'The Pavlova looks too much of a palaver and if that's death by chocolate, I'd rather have death by cancer.'

'Right, the next step is to get old Tom here to meet Uncle Heinrich,' said Callum. 'We'll send you out there again, Chloe, to prepare the ground.'

'Will he agree to see me, do you think?' mused Tom.

'He doesn't seem to have a problem and he's seen you on television,' said Chloe.

'Is he a fan?' asked Tom.

'Sorry, Tom; he was a bit non-committal,' said Chloe. 'But I think he does watch you.'

'Well I'm not so sure it's a good idea,' said Tom looking disparagingly as the waiter brought a selection of cheeses. 'Is that brie, or has someone just sneezed on the cheeseboard?'

'Herr Rohmer is ninety-six and he's not in good health, so if Tom is going to go, he'd better go soon,' advised Chloe.

CHAPTER 8

Tom's restaurant in Pangbourne, The Nosebag, was just about ticking over, but the ratings for his Saturday morning programme, *Let's Do Lunch,* had been on the slide for some time now. The British public seemed finally to have had their appetite sated for evermore, contrived foodie programmes. The premise of Tom's programme was to combine good home cooking with fierce political debate. However, the discourse on each programme was getting more turgid, with the food taking centre place at the expense of conversation. It appeared that none of these parliamentarians got fed properly. The show's last chance was a forthcoming edition involving Dennis Skinner and Nigel Farage tucking into Hungarian goulash and jam roly-poly.

So it was that Tom had agreed to be the subject of an episode of *Family Matters*. It was either that, *The Jungle*, or prancing about in a diaphanous shirt on *Strictly Come Dancing*, such were the last refuges of celebs, whose stars were beginning to wane.

Tom, having completed his book tour, told Bonnie that he was having a 'business meeting' with Kat and his publisher one evening to review how it had gone. In fact, it had not gone very well at all. *Zest of Life*, his book on how to cook with citrus, had left a somewhat bitter taste in the mouth. Sales had not been helped by a less than kind cookbook reviewer who had written:

Turns out, Oranges are the Only Fruit! And Tom Bradshott shows you how un-versatile they can be. The book should be retitled Zest in Peace and then be allowed to crawl away into a handy waste disposal unit and die.

'So how was it for you, Tom Kitten?' said Kat climbing off him reluctantly, rather as if Tom were a fairground ride.

'I tell you what, I nearly had to send on a substitute for the second half; you really are one hell of a woman,' sighed Tom.

Tom's phone rang.

'Hello, Evie... Evie, is that you? What's that? ...Mummy's been crying... well go and give her a cuddle and when you've had one more... yes one more sleep, Daddy will be home... yes Daddy will be on the telly soon, but not tonight. Okay, Evie, be good, night, night...'

'Shit!' shouted Kat from the kitchen.

'Everything okay?' called Tom.

'My sole is burning.'

'Very poetic.'

'No seriously, Tom; the fish, it's on fire!'

Tom grabbed a dressing gown (one of Kat's, a red kimono with yellow dragons on it) and ran into the kitchen where flames were rising from a pan on the hob.

'Christ! You have to use more water when you are steaming. Turn everything off and fetch me a damp tea towel.'

'Oh, I'm sorry, darling. Is it ruined? Never mind. Let's go back to bed; you in that kimono is really turning me on.'

'I am starving. That restaurant at lunchtime was a disgrace; I'd have got more satisfaction in a nunnery during Lent. Get your coat; didn't you say there was a chippy round here?'

'The great Tom Bradshott in a fish and chip shop!' mocked Kat.

'Well it's nice to slum it from time to time. Besides, with any luck I won't get recognised.'

Five minutes from Kat's flat they arrived outside the chip shop.

'*Fry Me to the Moon*; six and a half out of ten for the title! Now let's see what the food's like.'

Tom received a call.

'You go in and choose for me,' he whispered to Kat.

'Hi yes, Bonnie. Look, I'm sorry the meeting went on longer than I thought. It turns out my family is quite complicated, anyway the production company are putting me up in town tonight. I'll get the first train back in the morning though.'

Tom had become such a creative liar in recent months that he was at risk of confusing the excuses for his absences. Now he thought about it, he wasn't sure he'd originally given *Family Matters* as the reason for tonight's absence.

Meanwhile, inside the shop, Kat was not the only customer. There were two overweight, middle-aged men half watching football on a TV installed by the shop owners for customers while they waited.

'Hello, I'll have two cod and chips... twice you know?'

The owner didn't turn round as he replied to Kat.

'Sorry, love.'

'Twice cod and chips and salt and vinegar on only one please.'

'Ain't you got chippies back home, love?' said one of the two other customers.

'Excuse me,' said Kat.

'Polskis' shop's down the road, love. This is Brits only,' said the other man.

'Sorry, my love, you'll have to wait for chips. Is that alright?' said the chippie.

'Course it's alright, like you should wait for jobs and houses and schools,' said the first man.

Tom came into the shop.

'What's going on?'

'It's alright, mate. We was just explaining to our overseas friend here that we could find the ferry times for her to get back to friggin euro land.'

'Now hang on a minute!' interjected Tom.

'Sorry, mate. Didn't know you was hanging round with the polak slag.'

A melee ensued; Tom, younger and fitter than the two men, landed a punch on the nose of the first man and kneed the

34

second in the groin. Meanwhile the chip shop owner jumped into action, but instead of coming to Tom's aid, he started taking photos on his phone.

CHAPTER 9

At the Bradshotts' house the next morning, Bonnie was sitting in her dressing gown reading the paper, when Tom breezed in.

'Hi there. Hey, guess what, the train was actually three minutes early and my coffee had a slight coffee flavour too.'

Evie was helping her mother by doing the washing up. She was up to her elbows in bubbles.

'Hi Evie!'

'You're naughty, Daddy.'

'Why, what have I done?'

Bonnie smiled sweetly and showed him the front of the paper; the headline read:

BRADSHOTT IN STREET BRAWL. BUT WHO'S THE MYSTERY GIRL?

There was a photo of Tom and Kat outside *Fry Me to the Moon*.

'Tom, I think we need to do some stuff. This doesn't really work for me.'

'I don't see what the problem is. The meeting had finished and yes, it is Kat in the picture. She happens to be my agent, in case you'd forgotten.'

'That's the point, Tom. She is 'in' the picture isn't she? The thing is, ever since we met, you have been 'the one' and we southern gals ain't partial to sharing.'

'Look, I feel like I need to explain, when there's nothing really to explain,' said Tom defensively.

'Don't explain, Thomas; just listen awhile. I have Evie to think about and right now this isn't any kind of home for her. Do you know where I was the other day, Tom, when I asked you to mind her? I was with my therapist. Evie will never thrive with her ma and pa at each other's throats. I don't blame you, Tom. Well as a matter of fact I do, but that's by the by. I remember being a 'chef groupie' myself, watching you hot, sweaty men in the kitchen at the Savoy. All of us waitresses used to get off on it, as you tossed your noodles and played with your asparagus tips. The thing is, Tom, you've got to decide, time is not on your side. Soon you could end up a horny, fifty-year-old with a Michelin star and a reputation for fumbling the waitresses in the cold store. The trouble is your sciatica and your cock are beginning to let you down and us girls sure like it served hot. Believe me, honey, I was actually in that cold store... his name was Edvard, married with two kids. He made the best boeuf en croûte I've ever tasted and the worst lover I ever had. I have never felt more dissatisfied until now.'

'What do you mean by that?' said Tom.

'Tom, the fact that you've been playing around hurts like hell. But what hurts almost equally as much, is that you think that I haven't known.'

'Oh God, Bonnie, I don't know what to say.'

'Nothing is fine, Tom. I'm thinking that Evie and I will go to the States and visit my folks for a while.'

'I have to go to Germany in a couple of days, please don't make any rash decisions while I am away,' pleaded Tom.

'I suggest you go and stay with your mother for now, give us both some space,' said Bonnie sipping her coffee.

'You sure know how to turn the screw,' said Tom bitterly.

'So, Evie, are you going to give Daddy a kiss before he goes?'

Evie folded her arms and turned her back on her father.

'Don't worry, Tom, she still loves you – on the TV,' said Bonnie laconically.

* * * * *

Chloe had returned to Germany ahead of Tom and the film crew. She was greeted warmly by Heinrich; he seemed slightly frailer than on her last visit.

'After you left, Miss Whiting, I remembered I had kept hold of various correspondences from those times. I thought this one might interest you; it is to me as an idealistic twenty-one-year-old from Ingrid my sister-in-law.'

'Yes, that would be interesting,' said Chloe.

'You see, despite or perhaps because of the age difference and some other factors, Ingrid and I had an understanding.'

'An understanding?' queried Chloe.

'Not in the way you mean it,' said Heinrich.

'I am not with you.'

'There were no secrets between us.'

'Did Ingrid have secrets then?'

'In Berlin, in those days, everyone had secrets; here, read the letter and you'll understand a little better. On second thoughts your German is good, but perhaps it would be easier if I read it to you.'

My dearest H,

Thank you for your sweet letter, you are the kindest brother-in-law anyone could wish for. It is now three weeks since Gunther's posting. The house seems very quiet, just me and dear little Freddy rattling around like two bluebottles in an enormous jam jar. At the weekend, we received a visit from Dr Albrecht and an SS officer by the name of Von Geysell. Von Geysell was most charming; he said that because of the high regard the Reich had for Gunther, a place had been reserved for Freddy at a special clinic in Berlin, where Freddy will receive only the best treatment.

I do not know what to do, dear H and I need your advice. You are so wise beyond your years. You see, I have good reason to dislike this man Albrecht; he visited the house before on the night Gunther attended a reception given by the High Command.

He is an odious little man who wears a fur-collared overcoat at least three times too big for him and, Heinrich, he is obscenely hairy. It's awful, it's everywhere: in his nose, in his ears and his eyebrows, like one enormous hairy caterpillar.

I have written down an account of the exchange that took place between us then (I have good reason, dear Heinrich, for remembering it almost word for word) in case for any reason things do not go as I hope and Freddy doesn't receive the treatment he needs. This way, someone will know what occurred in my own house! I am sending it ad verbatim to the one man I can trust. Gunther must never know. You know what a temper he has.

I welcomed Dr Albrecht into the house.

'Thank you, Frau Rohmer. Your son sounds a particularly interesting case and just the kind of subject we are looking for.'

'Freddy is my life, Dr Albrecht,' I said.

'So where would you like our little consultation to take place?'

'Oh, I am so sorry! I forgot to mention that my husband has been called away on army business. Can we still proceed?'

'We must proceed, Frau Rohmer; time is of the essence. I have other prospective patients to see,' said Albrecht.

At this point I called Freddy over, but he would not come. He just stood at the top of the stairs, watching the moonlight coming in at the window.

'Come on, Freddy, come and say hello.'

'He has speech then, your little man.'

'No, but we have special signs, don't we, Freddy?'

Poor Freddy; at this point he started to become very agitated, banging his head against the wall.

'Oh, I am so sorry, Dr Albrecht.'

I felt so embarrassed.

'Do not trouble yourself; let us go somewhere where we can be more comfortable. I want to know all about the family

history. Details of birth; when did you first think there was a problem... Oh and a short physical examination.'

'Examination?'

'Yes. We need to look at ethnic traits in the family. The physique of each parent. Treatment is tailored to racial grouping you understand.'

I became annoyed at this point.

'Freddy is German, Dr Albrecht, I can assure you his father fought in the trenches for his country and received an Iron Cross. His grandfather was in the Prussian cavalry and my side of the family have been farmers in Saxony since the thirteen hundreds.'

'The examination is purely routine, Frau Rohmer. But any treatment we might be able to offer will be dependent on getting what might be called a full picture.'

'This is not right – what do you mean by 'ethnic' traits?'

'Frau Rohmer, may I remind you your son requires resources that could be supporting the Fatherland in its glorious war efforts,' said Albrecht.

'I think it might be best if you left this house immediately, Dr Albrecht,' I said as sternly as I could.

'There is really no need for any unpleasantness.'

'My husband is the guest of the High Command tonight and if I tell him...'

'I know where your husband is, Frau Rohmer. I think this consultation is over, for the moment. But I will be in contact within the next few weeks; you may be assured of that, until then I bid you goodnight.'

'I received only one more letter from Ingrid,' said Heinrich. 'Here, something for the cold.' He offered Chloe a small glass of brandy.

'Thank you, how kind. May I see the other letter?'

'Yes of course, but not tonight.'

'I am so sorry; you must be tired.'

'Only a little, my dear.'

'May I bring Tom, your great-nephew, next time I come? He is anxious to meet you.'

'Really? This surprises me; you see, I am known as the black sheep of the family,' said Heinrich.

'Well, you mustn't worry. A little birdy has told me Tom is creating a bit of a reputation himself these days too. I am sure you will find you have a great deal to talk about,' said Chloe getting up to leave. She gave Heinrich a peck on the cheek.

CHAPTER 10

In the days since the incident in *Fry Me to the Moon*, Tom Bradshott had become something of a controversial figure. Many saw him as a standard bearer for a multi-ethnic society; others saw him as a leery-eyed, liberal elite tosser, making something out of nothing. *The Daily Mail* made much over Tom being Sir George Robert's grandson and how privileged he'd been and how Sir George would have disowned him as a wishy-washy liberal. They demanded his instant dismissal. Meanwhile, *The Guardian* suggested he stand as Labour candidate at the next by-election.

The other big news at the time was the death of the American rock legend Prairie Dog. The harvest from the pantheon of the music business in 2016 had been truly extraordinary: Prince, Pete Burns and, as it turned out even the Thin White Duke were mortal. Now Prairie Dog was gone too! Apparently, he had finally succumbed to his many addictions and in recent months had not been outside of his house in the Hollywood Hills. The previous year, his valedictory album *Last Bend in the Creek* had been his best seller since his heyday in the seventies. Not reported in any of the copy of the day was the fact that Prairie Dog's 'muse' while he was putting together *Last Bend in the Creek* was none other than one Kat Kawalski, publicist to Tom Bradshott.

For Tom Bradshott, the news of Prairie Dog's demise was double edged. Kat had been an emotional wreck the last time he saw her. She was booked on a flight to Los Angeles to oversee Prairie Dog's funeral arrangements, as she was the sole executor to his will. His only child was somewhat out of the picture, serving twenty years in a Californian penitentiary for trying to murder his father.

Kat's trip to the States meant that Tom had some head space and no one apart from the press giving him grief. The trip to Germany, if discreetly handled, he concluded, might keep him out of the papers for a while as well.

'So, Uncle Heinrich is a bit of a black sheep by the sound of it. I wonder what his secret is?' said Tom.

Tom, Chloe and the TV crew were being driven from the airport to a meeting with Heinrich Rohmer and Chloe had been filling Tom in on what she'd learnt so far.

'That's what he says, but he's a pussy cat really.'

Sleety rain greeted them as they drove onto the estate. Heinrich could be seen peering from his window and Chloe remembered what the old man had said about the infrequency of visitors. She wondered how he would put up with the crew invading his privacy.

'It's good to meet you,' said Tom proffering a hand to Heinrich.

'Welcome, welcome! You will have to excuse the way I live. Who was it who said living to great old age is like living in a sandcastle in the very top turret, knowing that the tide will still come in.' Heinrich shepherded Tom and Chloe into his living room.

'I am sorry to bother you with this, it's always a bit of a circus, I'm afraid,' said Tom, gesturing at the film crew as they followed him in with various pieces of technical equipment.

'It's not a problem. Miss Whiting here has been a very gentle inquisitor. How is your mother by the way?' Heinrich enquired.

'Oh, she's fighting fit,' Tom replied.

'She was a typical two-year-old when I knew her, prone to tantrums when she'd didn't get her way, but could turn on the charm.'

'No change there then,' quipped Tom.

'She could wind your grandfather round her little finger. Now let me get you some coffee.'

'There are quite a few of us, let me help, Herr Rohmer, please?' said Chloe.

Tom was already feeling the cold, but to divert his attention from this, he allowed himself a long glance at Chloe. She couldn't have been much more than twenty-five, in her little, faux fur wrap, figure-hugging jeans and thigh length boots bought for 'the German cold' she'd said. He couldn't help thinking, life is short and everything at home is a mess, what happens in Germany stays in Germany. Chloe gave him a shy, girlie half smile as she left the room. He felt this trip away might be just what he needed.

'My flat is a little cold, I'm afraid. We've had no heating for two days; German efficiency for you! But I will bring blankets,' said Rohmer.

'Is there someone we could ring for you, Herr Rohmer, about the heating?' said Callum, who seemed to be feeling the cold the most.

'You are very kind, but our janitor says he's on the case; we are on a waiting list apparently.'

'You shouldn't have to put up with this,' said Tom.

Heinrich shuffled off to find some blankets.

'It's bloody freezing in here; it could finish him off!' exclaimed Tom.

'He's lovely, Tom, but he's also quite proud. I don't think he'll take kindly from too much interference from us,' said Chloe.

'Perhaps my mother was right about him being a recluse,' mused Tom.

'That's what she told you, did she?' said Heinrich, coming back into the room.

'I'm so sorry, my mother is a law unto herself.'

'It's not her fault. She probably got that story from Gunther. It would have suited him to say such things about me. It was easier for him than facing reality.'

'It's not just about the programme. I really want to know all about the family. You know all that stuff about grandfather.

Was he a Nazi? I want to know all the family's dirty laundry?' enthused Tom.

'Be careful what you wish for,' cautioned Heinrich.

The cameraman was fretting about the light.

'Can we start filming? The light isn't great in this room,' said the cameraman.

'Yes, good idea,' said Callum.

'We talked about a letter the last time I was here,' said Chloe.

For some reason, Heinrich was becoming agitated, pacing in and out of the kitchen.

'Has this got anything to do with what Mother called the family feud?' Tom asked.

'I want nothing from you, nothing, do you understand?' snapped Heinrich.

'But, I thought we'd agreed a fee?' said Tom.

'Tom, can we leave the details for now,' Chloe interrupted.

'Sorry, I'm just aware of budgets and that kind of stuff, but hey this is not my show, so God knows why I am worrying.'

'Listen to me please. There is no family feud, well, not on my part at least. It was all a long time ago and due to your grandfather's bigotry. Now I must ask you to go. I am exhausted. This was all one big mistake.' Heinrich ushered them to the door.

Outside Heinrich's flat a small crowd had gathered out of curiosity, to watch as the film crew packed their equipment into the hired minibus.

'Must be a slow news day,' observed the cameraman.

'So, what happens now?' queried Chloe.

'Back home with our tails between our legs,' said Tom. 'We could try looking at my father's side of the family. He came from a long line of chartered accountants in Haslemere,' Tom continued, as he squeezed in next to Chloe. 'My, this is cosy.' He gave her a cheeky schoolboy grin.

Tom's mobile rang. He got out of the minibus.

At this point, Heinrich came to the door, with a hand mic the crew had left behind.

Tom took his call

'Hello, Bonnie... What's the problem? ...What do you mean disappeared? ...How long for? ...Okay, okay I'm on my way home.'

'What's happened?' said Chloe.

'It's Evie, she's gone... I'll have to get the next plane.'

'Evie?' queried a concerned Heinrich.

'Tom's daughter,' said Chloe.

'How old?' asked Heinrich.

'Eight,' replied Tom.

'I will come with you,' said Chloe.

'No, it's okay. Stay here; you've got a programme to make,' said Tom.

'Not much of a programme, if you're not here,' observed Chloe.

'I never knew you cared. No, you stay.'

'Is there anything I can do? I feel I have been so rude,' said Heinrich.

'She has no sense of danger really, always sees the best in people. Oh Christ anything could have happened to her.' Tom wiped some moisture from the corner of his eye.

Chloe put her arm around him and he momentarily enjoyed the scent of her Dior perfume.

CHAPTER 11

Kat Kawalski stood in arrivals at Los Angeles airport half expecting Prairie Dog to be there to greet her. The fact that she had come out to oversee his funeral momentarily slipped her mind.

She thought of previous occasions when he had been there, always in disguise to avoid the paparazzi; in a wig and dark glasses and a hoodie looking for all the world like some superannuated hoodlum. But today, no Prairie Dog. She took a compact out and made some repairs to her face. In LA, appearance was everything and tear-stained make-up just wouldn't do. Although saying farewell to one's current lover and an ex-lover in the space of a couple of days, surely meant a little show of emotion could be forgiven.

Kat had two appointments that day, one with D. K. Wormelow, Funeral Director and Mortician to the Stars and the other at California State Prison to see Prairie Dog's son, Jo Jo.

Prairie Dog had stipulated in his will that he wanted a private ceremony. However, fans would be able to pay their respects, by filing past his open casket prior to the day of his funeral. All these arrangements were being overseen by D.K. Wormelow himself, who greeted Kat at the entrance to his funeral parlour; an entrance which would have put the Pearly Gates themselves to shame

'Ms Kawalski, I can't tell you what a privilege it is to be handling Mr Prairie Dog's last journey.' Wormelow spoke like one of the Queen's under butlers. He was a picture in a purple suit, black cummerbund, setting off his complexion which was the colour and texture of a deep-fried, chorizo sausage.

'We've organised security for the "file by", limousines for the cortège and we have the use of a local helipad.'

'We are clear here, aren't we?' said Kat. 'The funeral is private – family and friends only.'

'Yes, the helicopters are for Mr Bono and Mr Alice Cooper; no doubt you are aware both were very close associates. Will you be the leading mourner, Miss Kawalski?'

'No way! Keep me well out of the frame. Prairie Dog and I were close a couple of years back, but I wasn't family.'

'As madam wishes, of course. Now would you like a private viewing of he who has gone before?'

'Excuse me?'

'The departed.'

'If I must, I suppose,' said Kat.

'Step this way and I shall escort you to our Citadel,' said D.K. Wormelow, a man who obviously took great pleasure in his work.

Prairie Dog looked considerably better than the last time Kat had seen him. His walnut skin had a kind of translucent evenness to it. His ancestry was part Mexican, part Cree Indian and frankly, Kat thought he looked magnificent. Of course, self-embalming oneself by means of every narcotic known to man in life meant death was always likely to bring a physical improvement to one's appearance.

Theirs had been a relationship of two restless souls finding each other at different stages in life. Prairie Dog had just come out of his fourth marriage, his seventh period of rehab and a long legal battle with his ex-manager. For Kat, this was her first big assignment for Storky and Co., the exclusive literary agency, which she had joined after eight years with a small publishing press 'Slit Lit' devoted to a certain school of female poets. To be honest, working for Storky and Co. had been a refreshing change; there was only so much a girl could take of other girls' poetry focused exclusively on how all men are bastards or what kind of mood their vagina was in today.

She had gone out to meet Prairie Dog, expecting to dislike the guy on a personal level, having read up on his womanising and other generally scathing remarks around what he referred to as the 'feministas'. After only a few days in his company, she began to fall under his spell. There was a vulnerability about the old scoundrel that in the end she couldn't resist and after a night of star-gazing from his rooftop and drinking far too much Jack Daniels, she fell into his bed.

'We hope to catch our clients as if in some moment of ecstasy,' said D.K. Wormelow.

'Well, he certainly had a few of those along the road,' said Kat.

'Would madam like a few moments alone with the deceased?' enquired Wormelow.

'I don't think so, thank you very much,' said Kat making the sign of the cross as she left; old habits die hard

CHAPTER 12

Phyllis Bradshott was trying to placate her daughter-in-law. She had offered somewhat begrudgingly to come and help look after Evie as Bonnie was in the middle of writing a book. For Bonnie, her mother-in-law was always a last resort but since all her family were back in America there was no one else. It meant having Phyllis to stay, of course, which was never easy, as Phyllis would interfere in practically every part of the running of the household apart that is from paying her granddaughter any real attention.

'Bonnie, I really am sorry, but I did tell you that I found it difficult keeping tabs on Evie. She can be a little monkey you know. She'll turn up, I am sure.'

'Like the bad penny, no doubt. It's two hours, Phyllis! Anything could have happened. Why did you say you would help in the first place if you find it so difficult?' said Bonnie.

'I wanted to give you a break with that son of mine gallivanting all around Europe,' explained Phyllis.

'You wanted to stick your nose in and see what's going on in terms of Tom and me, more like.'

'That's very unkind,' said Phyllis.

'Someone's taken her; I know they have,' said Bonnie.

'Oh no, I wouldn't think so for a moment,' said Phyllis.

'What's that supposed to mean?' Bonnie glared at Phyllis.

'Nothing but...'

'Oh, I get it. You mean not even a child molester would be interested in my daughter.'

'That's a dreadful thing to say. If Tom's father were alive...' said Phyllis.

'Look I haven't got time for this. The police are on their way. I need you to remember exactly where she was when you saw her last.'

'Well I was just taking a bath... my arthritis. The thing is the doctor said warm baths help and so I borrowed your radio. There was a lovely lunchtime concert on Radio 3, Schubert I think.'

'Phyllis! I swear I won't be responsible for my actions if you don't focus and remember. Something your family seem incapable of doing is understanding that life isn't always about you!'

It was at this point that Evie walked in through the door hand in hand with a somewhat dishevelled middle-aged gentleman.

'She came up to me in my garden, told me she was looking for her daddy.'

'Oh God, Evie! Are you okay?' cried Bonnie.

'Evie okay, Mummy, yes,' said the little girl.

'I told her I didn't think I could be her father, although strangely enough, I was a father some time ago.'

Bonnie looked at the undoubtedly eccentric figure before her. For one awful moment she thought back to what she had said to Phyllis. Had this man interfered with her beautiful Evie?

The man looked her straight in the eye.

'You have a beautiful daughter you know.'

'I know,' said Bonnie.

'She's a bringer of joy, like Jupiter.'

'I know that too,' said Bonnie.

'Well, I'll leave you in peace.'

'There you are; all's well that ends well,' said Phyllis. 'Bonnie, will you put the kettle on. You will stay for a nice cup of tea.' Phyllis excused the man's strange appearance, on the basis that he had a modicum of culture about him, besides she needed someone, or something to distract her daughter-in-law, who had got herself in a dreadful state about nothing at all really.

'Are we going to have a party?' said Evie hopefully.

51

CHAPTER 13

In Germany, Chloe had stayed behind with Heinrich, who seemed terribly upset on hearing that Evie was missing.

'I am so sorry, Miss Whiting; I fear I have not behaved well. You see there *was* bad blood between Tom's grandfather and myself, but it was unforgivable of me to take it out on Tom. I do hope the little girl will be alright.'

'I hope so as well. I guess we'll get some news soon,' said Chloe. 'If it's okay, can you tell me what the rift was between you and your brother?'

'Well after the war I asked Gunther for some help over a personal matter. He was still in Germany and had considerable influence with the occupying powers, who saw him as a link to old pre-Hitler times. I think that it may have been the help he gave the Allies immediately after the war that eased his way to a new life in England, though why he didn't stay in Germany and help with the rebuilding of the place, I don't know. Perhaps he found it all too painful.'

'Please go on, you were saying there was a personal matter you wanted Gunther's help with,' said Chloe, kneeling beside the old man.

'Have you ever been in love, Miss Whiting?'

'I suppose so, yes,' said Chloe.

'Well then, you will understand what it's like when you are kept apart as Werner and I were.'

'Werner?'

'My boyfriend, the love of my life.'

'Oh, gosh! I see.'

'We fell for each other at university, but those were very intolerant times. Any hint of impropriety and the punishment would have been severe. Homosexuality and the master race were mutually exclusive and anyone caught in a homosexual relationship was in mortal danger.'

'So, what happened?'

'During the war, I was a non-combatant due to having had polio as a child, but for Werner there was no escape. He saw action in the western desert, France and the Rhineland towards the end of the war.

'He managed to write the occasional letter, unable to give much information, or declare any affection for me. Of course, we did have our little coded messages.

'Once the war was over, we began to hope that we might be able to be together. Werner was in a POW camp in the east near the Polish border and I was living in West Berlin at the time. The country was being divided; there was a real danger Werner and I would be kept apart.

'I went to see Gunther, poured out my heart to him but he refused to help. He said that it was a boyish infatuation and just a phase. I told him that we had been in love since university.

'He said that love wasn't the right word for what was going on, told me I needed to show more self-control.

'I was so incensed, I told him what I thought of him, that he was a narrow-minded prig with fixed ideas and that Ingrid would have taken my side against his, at which point he told me to leave.

'As we feared, Werner and I were trapped on either side of the border. I kept writing to Gunther asking him, pleading with him to help. But then, of course, he moved to England and had a new wife and baby.' Heinrich was exhausted by recounting these events.

'So, what happened with Werner?'

'When the Russians finally released him, he got a job in a tractor factory of all places. He had a fine mind and the monotony of the work drove him crazy. The communist East German authorities of course were very suspicious of this "intellectual" and he was periodically questioned and detained for months at a time.'

'How do you know all this?' asked Chloe.

'We wrote to each other, although getting communication across the border was very problematic and involved a good deal of bribery.'

'Please go on.'

'In April of 1962, it all got too much for him: the drudgery of the factory and the constant harrying of the security forces. One night, he drove all the way to Berlin in the factory manager's old tank of a car with two others, both with family in the West. They parked up and made their way to the wall. One of them made it, but another was shot halfway up the wall. My dearest Werner, according to eye-witnesses, had only got a few paces inside the first perimeter fence when the guards, who could have walked through the gate and arrested him, instead chose to machine-gun him.'

'God, how awful. I am so very sorry,' said Chloe.

'My life ended then you see really; all the rest has been mere existence.'

'I cannot imagine what you've been through.'

'Forgive me; the onset of winter always makes me melancholic. That reminds me though, what is it I can do to help?'

'Last time we talked, you said something about another letter you received from Ingrid.'

'Oh yes, I did,' said Heinrich.

'I was wondering, while we wait for news of little Evie, might I look at it?'

'Yes, it's the least I can do. Here, it's over here. Now, would you like me to translate again for you?' asked Heinrich. Eager to make amends, he began to read.

My dear Heinrich,

It is a long time since we've been in contact and I have so much to tell you. Gunther has been away for three months and he has missed some really exciting progress with dear Freddy.

The other day as we were about to go to the shops, without prompting, Freddy took me by the hand and led me to the back door. He wanted to show me something; it was a poor little dead mouse, but it was the fact that he wanted to include me in his world that was wonderful. It was a real first.

Unfortunately, I also have some sad news. You remember my friend, Hilda and her little crippled daughter Brigitta? Well Hilda called me the other day in a distressed state. She told me how her daughter had been taken to T4 or to give it its full title, 'The Charitable Foundation for Curative and Institutional Care'. A few days later, she received a letter to say Brigitta had passed away in her sleep. The thing is, dearest Heinrich, this is one of the places Dr Albrecht spoke about as a possibility for Freddy's treatment. As I may have mentioned before, I loathe Dr Albrecht. Anyway, I feel so under the spotlight what with Gunther being away and I don't want to do anything that might blot his copybook.

Dear Heinrich, I do hope you find happiness; you really deserve to.

Much love from me,

Ingrid.

'It's a lovely letter. Do we know what happened after this?' asked Chloe.

'I have been able to piece a few bits of the jigsaw together, but you see I was leading something of a secret existence myself at the time, so I was unable to go to her and offer support. If I had, things might have been different.'

Chloe's mobile rang.

'That's good news, Tom. ...I see. Well your great uncle has given me more of the story. It's really intriguing. Okay... I get back tomorrow afternoon. The rest of the crew are on their way to the airport. They managed to wangle an earlier flight. I don't want to put your uncle through more at the moment, so I'm going to head back to the hotel. There are a couple of bits of research I want to do in the morning.'

'Good news? Is the little girl safe?' said Heinrich.

'Yes; all's fine apparently. She's been found safe and sound.'

'Oh good,' said Heinrich.

'So, what more do we know about Ingrid and Freddy?'

Heinrich pulled out a rather grubby handkerchief and wiped away a tear.

'Well I'm afraid that things didn't turn out well. About two months after I received that letter, I received confirmation that both Ingrid and Freddy were dead. According to the communiqué, both had been killed in a raid by your bomber command.'

'Oh, that's so awful. How did you find out?'

'Gunther had received a letter informing him. He sent me the briefest of notes... all very formal. That was Gunther; to show emotion, was a sign of weakness.' Heinrich wiped his eyes again.

'You must have been devastated,' said Chloe.

'Yes, but I had my suspicions even then,' said Heinrich.

'Suspicions?'

'It was all such a long, long time ago... my poor Ingrid. Oh, I'm afraid it's started to snow again and you need to be getting back to your hotel.

'Will you be okay?'

Heinrich shuffled over to the window.

'I like it when it snows; it covers so much ugliness in the world. Would you not agree, Miss Whiting?'

CHAPTER 14

California State Penitentiary stood laid out before Kat, numerous flat-roofed buildings, behind several fences increasing in height. For a moment she almost turned on her heel and beat a hasty retreat. She had made a promise to herself to visit Prairie Dog's son. She knew that Prairie Dog had felt bad about what had happened with Jo Jo. The singer had returned from a European tour to his sprawling mansion in the hills. As he walked through his own front door, Jo Jo shot his father three times with an automatic weapon.

He put up no resistance, nor gave any explanation, when the police arrived. Prairie Dog was in intensive care for three weeks. At one point, they were unsure whether he would live, let alone walk again.

Passing through the clanging gates and doors on her way to the visitors' suite, Kat was still not sure why she had come and what she could do. She knew Jo Jo had no family left. His mother had died of an aggressive colon cancer ten years ago. Jo Jo's mother and Prairie Dog had been together for five or so years, something of a record for the old rocker, but his head had been eventually turned and Jo Jo blamed his father's leaving for his mother's premature and painful death.

Often when Kat and Prairie Dog had been together, he would say, 'If there's one thing I need to do before I die, it's to make peace with that boy of mine.' It was this that had prompted Kat into action.

She had seen photos of Jo Jo, but she was not prepared for how beautiful he was; he had flawless skin and high cheekbones offset by large, languorous, brown eyes. He sat opposite her, strangely composed, almost serene.

'Hello, Jo Jo. Do you know who I am?'

'I guess so,' said Jo Jo, meeting Kat's gaze. 'You were one of my father's chicks, ain't that right?'

'I came because I knew you would have heard about your father's death.'

'What's that to me? Just finished off what I should have done all those years ago, if that damn gun hadn't gone and jammed.'

'Your father cared about you, you know,' said Kat.

'No, ma'am, the only thing that man cared for was himself.'

'He cared for your mother once.'

'You don't know jack shit. Why you come here? He killed my mother when he left her. She'd never had a day's illness till she met him.'

'Jo Jo, I'm sure...' said Kat not knowing what to say.

He stared directly at Kat.

'You seen someone die like that? She was screamin', I tell you, messin' everywhere, no sleep, no life. Why, I should have shot her too. Put her out of her misery.'

'I am so sorry, Jo Jo.'

'That so.'

'You ever thought what you will do on the day you're released? Your father has left generous provision for you in his will,' Kat explained.

'I won't be needing that, ma'am. First thing I'll do when I get out of here is find a nice spot and blow these old brains of mine out. So, I won't need to see any more pictures in my head.'

'Pictures?'

'Pictures of my ma writhing on the floor and pictures of that scumball my pa, smiling down on me from every billboard in town.'

CHAPTER 15

Chloe was surprised to see Tom in the bar of the hotel. She knew all about his reputation as a lady killer and that his soubriquet in some of the gossip magazines was 'Studulike', but he really wasn't her type. She tended to go for the weedy, angry, cerebral type, the kind of man who got out of bed the wrong side every morning and then wrote a poem about it.

'So, if it had turned out badly and there had been a real emergency, you might not have been able to get back anyway,' observed Chloe walking across to where Tom was sitting. 'No flights out of Berlin tonight: ice, fog and snow on the runway,' explained Chloe. 'The four horsemen of the apocalypse are making merry in the duty free; Scylla and Charybdis are interfering with passengers in the car park; you get the picture?'

'Was old Heinrich more forthcoming once I'd gone?' asked Tom.

'Well yes as a matter of fact he was, but the more I find out, the more questions seem to arise,' said Chloe. 'He showed me a beautiful letter from Ingrid, regarding Freddy; she obviously adored him.'

'You have a little icicle on the end of your nose by the way,' said Tom.

'Oh God, do I? Sorry.'

'Don't apologise; it quite suits you. Shall we order now?'

'Yes, what do you suggest?' said Chloe.

'The veal will be good over here, if you like it practically embryonic,' suggested Tom.

'I don't eat veal.'

'Well how about cream of asparagus soup and then the sea bass?'

'That sounds nice.'

'I suggest the Riesling; at that price, it will probably be quite harmless.'

'Tom, I want a bit more for the beginning of *Family Matters.*'

'Okay, so what do you mean?'

'You know a kind of pen picture, facts the public wouldn't necessarily know about Tom Bradshott.'

'Chloe you must have realised, I'm an open book.'

'We all have an interior world, Tom,' said Chloe.

'Not me, I'm afraid. Nothing much going on. You see it wasn't really approved of when I was as boy: too much self-reflection. At school, if they saw you getting too dreamy, you were sent on a run and then when I started chef-ing, there wasn't much time for navel-gazing,' explained Tom. 'How about you?'

'Not much to know really.'

'You strike me as someone who in their demure way knows what she wants from life and I've seen how bloody good you are at your job. Very much the real deal in fact. By the way, do you want schnapps to go with that? Help keep the cold out and to stop any more icicles forming on that delicious little nose of yours.'

'So, tell me a bit more about your childhood?' said Chloe changing the subject.

'Not much to tell really. I was a plug ugly, little boy, overweight, under confident.'

'I find that hard to believe.'

'Which bit? The plug ugly or the under confident and be careful how you answer. Our whole future as an item might depend upon it.'

'Silly boy! So where did you go to school?'

'First a barbarous, little nonentity of a prep school, where little boys like me were taught the ways of the world in no uncertain terms. There was a hierarchy of tyranny. Older boys devised many humiliations, including frequent heads down toilets and being ordered to strip down to one's underpants and run round the headmaster's wife's herbaceous border three times or face the consequences. The teachers had more exquisite tortures involving press-ups in front of the whole school and reading out letters in class, which had been sent to your parents about your bedwetting.'

'Sounds awful. How about secondary school?'

'Yes, for my sins, I actually found I quite enjoyed my time there mainly because I grew, so I proved useful on the rugby field and cricket square. I was thick as two short planks, but for some reason my old English teacher, Ralph Turner, took a real interest in me. He was well over retirement age but would give me extra tuition. No one had paid me much attention before. My mother was at times openly hostile and my father saw me as somewhat of a disappointment, but useful in the sense of being a boy and therefore carrying the Bradshott name into the future. I never understood why old Turner picked on me, until one day he invited me to his rooms for afternoon tea.'

'I'm not sure I like where this is leading,' said Chloe.

'No, it was nothing like that, but it was a bit weird. There on a bookshelf was a picture of someone who looked uncannily like me. I was so flabbergasted I just asked him straight out who the geezer was. For a moment I thought he was going to tell me to get out. But then he took the photo down off the shelf, breathed on it reverentially and wiped it on the sleeve of his old thorn proof jacket.

'This is my brother Edwin,' he said. 'He was killed in the Battle of Britain; he was only a year or two older than you are now. So, Bradshott, dear boy, make sure you make the most of things. There's a good chap.'

* * * * *

Coincidentally, back in Berkshire, Bonnie and Evie were looking through photo albums. It was not Bonnie's idea but

Evie's, who loved looking at pictures of babies and particularly pictures of herself when she was a baby.

'Oh look, Mummy... me!'

'You sure were a keeper,' said Bonnie, remembering the advice of most people (including her mother-in-law) at the time of 'Never mind, there's still time for you to have another.' She had been in a relatively high risk group, but had never considered that her pregnancy would be anything other than normal. So although immediately aware that there was something different about Evie, (she was too good and undemanding for one thing), Bonnie had calmly awaited confirmation from other health professionals, which came in dribs and drabs during the first few years of Evie's life. Tom's reaction to those years had been totally different. He seemed incapable of accepting that Evie would develop at a different rate to other children. He would buy her the latest electronic gizmo, arrange for various therapists to call, both orthodox and unorthodox: an acupuncturist, a physiotherapist and an art therapist all trooped in and out of the house at great expense. Increasingly, he found excuses not to spend much of his leisure time at home. So, Evie saw less and less of her father apart that is from when he was on the telly.

Bonnie was still weighing up whether to take Evie to the States; her large family all adored Evie and Bonnie knew she would be spoilt rotten. She also knew that for Evie not to have that time with her father, however little, would be a terrible deprivation. Bonnie could see that for Tom, time alone with Evie was sometimes difficult. He became frustrated when she appeared not to understand him. For someone who appeared at ease in any situation, Bonnie found it strange that Tom seemed so ill at ease in his own daughter's company. In her less than kind moments, she put it down to him thinking he was not the centre of attention, when of course the reality was that he was the centre of the universe, for Evie.

* * * * *

'Tell me, Tom. Do you think you deserve your reputation as a bit of a silver fox? Because your technique strikes me as a little obvious,' said Chloe.

'I'm sorry; the thing is, once you are stereotyped, it becomes a bit of a duty to play up to it. It's what my average menopausal fan expects.'

'I'm flattered, I think,' said Chloe.

'God, sorry. I'm being an arse, aren't I? You don't want to believe all you read about me.'

'Kitchen Casanova, likes his food hot, with plenty of variety and several different dishes depending on what mood he's in,' said Chloe paraphrasing from one of the trashy 'celeb mags'.

'That might have had a mustard grain of truth in it once upon a time, but the reality is generally now that I'm as boringly middle-aged as could be, that is if...'

'If what?'

'Well, if Berlin didn't look so stunning in the snow and I didn't have such a delightful dining companion. I can't help it. The whole thing is so devilishly romantic, don't you think? We'd be good together, you know. Do you have a Rhine maiden costume by any chance? I could be your Siegfried and we could lock horns and whatever else you cared to lock.'

Chloe looked at Tom. Part of her felt a modicum of sympathy for the poor boy, more than fifteen years her senior. How was he to know that her previous boyfriends devoted themselves to making her as miserable as them and that was strangely how she liked it.

Thankfully, she was of a sunny disposition, which all her beaus had found attractive and repellent at the same time.

'Thank you, Tom, but I'm quite happy as I am,' she said brusquely.

'Well you can't blame a chap for trying,' said Tom.

'No, but I think your wife might,' said Chloe.

'The trouble is, my wife understands me.'

'Oh! That's a new one.'

'Or rather, I should say we have an understanding. You see after Evie was born, she practically shut up shop in the bedroom department.'

'You really should get a Michelin star for effort, I suppose, but in case you've forgotten, we've got a programme to make.'

'Good point. My rescheduled flight doesn't leave until tomorrow evening, so I could put myself at your disposal,' said Tom.

'Well, I thought I would go to the old Rohmer house, get some pictures, see if any of the locals remember the family. There is something you could do.'

'Anything,' said Tom.

'I've made an appointment at Das Bunderarchive with a Professor Schiller. He specialises in German military history, from Bismark to the Second World War. You could go in my stead. He knows it's background for the programme we are after. I think you'll get more out of him, being the actual grandson of General Major Gunther Rohmer.'

* * * * *

Kat Kawalski arrived at D.K. Wormelow's 'Cathedral of Rest' early on the day of Prairie Dog's funeral. She had declined an offer to be among the chief mourners, so she watched from a seat at the back. Those who Prairie Dog had permitted to attend, including several rock legends, slowly trickled in. Outside lining the road were several thousand fans, some holding up pictures of the old scoundrel, others with single red roses ready to throw as the cortège went past. Some people were openly weeping. Also in the congregation were several of Prairie Dog's ex-wives, who seemed to be collectively scrutinising Kat. Prairie Dog had told Kat a little of his history with these women, how for a time they'd all enjoyed an open relationship. Group sex was a regular occurrence and wild pool parties had been the order of the day.

She glanced back at them; they had all had plastic surgery in the nineties. Boobs had been reupholstered, tummies had been tucked and were now as flat as ironing boards and their faces had been so rearranged that they held permanent expressions as though they'd walked in on their own surprise parties. Prairie Dog had not been a fan of the surgeon's knife, describing the results as 'Chicks coming out with a face whittled like an in-season racoon's arse.'

They were perhaps not looking their best and were probably not overjoyed by the news that apart from several animal charities, Kat and Jo Jo were to be the main beneficiaries of the will.

D.K. Wormelow busied himself around the place, making sure his more illustrious guests from the rock pantheon were comfortable with a cushion here, a bottle of mineral water there. For Wormelow, this was about looking after business, as here were several prospective customers for the next few years.

Kat had other things on her mind: her newfound wealth meant she had some choices to make. There was no doubt she was very fond of Tom. In many ways, he was like Prairie Dog; they were both overgrown schoolboys with commitment phobias, who could nevertheless never be on their own for long.

Tom had been the change she needed after being in effect Prairie Dog's therapist, carer, as well as lover, while they were together. Things with Tom had been far less complicated: eagerly anticipated nights in quaint English pubs, meals out in the best London restaurants and al fresco love-making. They would earmark targets for quickies, including the Albert Memorial and in the dark of the reptile house at London Zoo. It was amazing how much fun you could have, while still keeping most of your clothes on.

But she found herself becoming increasingly jealous of Tom's family commitments and the fact he beamed, when given the slightest bit of attention from another female. As someone who considered herself a feminist, she hated the debilitating jealousy that increasingly burnt inside her. Was she looking to break out of this cycle of, let's face it, pretty disastrous relationships? She knew she needed to do something, but she wasn't sure quite what.

The strains of 'Last Bend in the Creek' started up as Prairie Dog's coffin was wheeled in.

> *I find myself at the last bend in the creek*
> *My heart is strong but my body is weak*
> *I've been through the white rapids*
> *And where the river runs slow*
> *I'm at the last bend in the creek and*
> *And it's time for me to go*

Bono wiped a tear from his eye and one of Prairie Dog's ex-wives appeared to topple into one of the celestial palm trees, whether through grief or alcohol was not entirely clear. D.K. Wormelow was there to minister to her with a sick bucket and a stream of tissues.

CHAPTER 16

Tom arrived at the Das Bunderarchive. It was a comparatively modern building with a number of people milling around. It was not obvious who worked there and who were merely visiting researchers. He was shown down a long corridor to Professor Schiller's office, through room after room of shelves reaching to the ceiling full of files.

'Sorry to disturb you, Professor Schiller.'

'You don't look like a Ms Whiting.'

'No. My name's Bradshott, Tom Bradshott. Ms Whiting has been called away,' Tom explained. 'I've come about my grandfather, General Major Rohmer.'

'Ah yes! You're the famous chef in *Let's Have Lunch*,' said the professor.

'It's actually *Let's Do Lunch*,' corrected Tom.

Professor Schiller cut a corpulent figure. He was extravagantly bald, with a pair of darkly tinted glasses perched on his head and veins on his skull that stuck out in an alarming fashion, like ivy tendrils on a dead, barkless tree. Dressed in a loud check suit and with one of the droopiest, green bow ties Tom had ever seen, he looked more like a circus owner than an archivist.

'Yes, yes of course. Come in, Mr Bradshott. You'll have to forgive us; the department is in the process of putting most of our records online, so we are in a state of chaos. May I offer you some tea or coffee?'

'Coffee would be great,' said Tom.

'Ah Monika, can you bring us some coffee?' said the professor.

Tom couldn't help but notice Monika's curves, even under the modest, well-tailored twinset she was wearing and when she returned with the coffee, he gave her one of his winning smiles.

'Oh, gosh, *danke*; you are a life-saver; you really are.'

Monika returned his attention with a wintery smile.

'My pleasure. I'm afraid we've no biscuits to offer you; budget cuts, you know.' Her English was pitch perfect.

'Thanks for agreeing to see us, Professor.'

'Not at all. We are supposed to be quite neutral about such things, but sometimes that can be very hard and your grandfather was a brave soldier and a great patriot.'

'I know very little about him,' said Tom.

'His record in the Great War was extraordinary, but it's really with the coming of the Third Reich that his story becomes more intriguing.'

'Sounds fascinating.'

'I have some documents I wish to show you which will, I think, make things a bit clearer,' said Professor Schiller.

'My German isn't very good,' explained Tom.

'Don't worry; I've had Monika transcribe them into English.'

'Wow thanks, Monika. Obviously a lady of many talents.'

'I did my degree in English at St Andrews.'

'Oh, I see. So you must be used to the cold.'

'And the British; we all used to watch your show, when we didn't have lectures.'

'I'm flattered,' said Tom.

'It always reminded me of my home in Saxony. My mother is your number one fan; she says you remind her of my father.'

'Really,' said a deflated Tom.

'These were papers captured by the Allies when Berlin fell. The Nazis destroyed as much incriminating evidence as they could, but some interesting things miraculously survived,' explained the professor, placing a large dog-eared file on the table in front of him.

'It amazes me that anything survived at all,' commented Tom.

'Here we are then. This is the document concerning your grandfather. It appears he was of particular interest and concern to the SS,' said Professor Schiller, mopping his brow with an enormous silk handkerchief.

'This is a report from a German SS officer named Oberscharfuhrer Von Geysell, attached to the Gestapo. He had responsibility for profiling any possible dissidents and his report concerns events leading up to the night of the 14th May 1941.'

> *Subject of Interest*
>
> *General Major Gunther Rohmer*
>
> *Interview held 3rd April 1941*
>
> *I informed the General Major that he had the opportunity to do a great service for the Reich by helping us in foiling a despicable plot against the life of our beloved Fuhrer.*
>
> *Oberscharfuhrer Pieter Von Geysell.*

'So do we know what happened next?' asked Tom.

'Well, from contemporary reports and some unofficial sources, plus a debriefing account your grandfather gave after the war, we've managed to build up a rough picture of the course of events. Herr Rohmer agreed to help and over the next few weeks he gained the confidence of those plotting an attempt on the Fuhrer's life. He reported in his debriefing with British intelligence services after the war that the plot was intended to distract the SS; he was aware of another plot running simultaneously, which he considered much more likely to be successful. He was also aware of the precarious situation of his wife and son, if he failed to cooperate with the SS. Crucial to his thinking was that the plotters, who included his old friend Conrad Meyer, needed to believe that Gunther was going to help them. A planning meeting was arranged near the estate of Meyer, who lived in an isolated spot in the country. It was agreed on the night in question that your grandfather would lead Von Geysell and the Gestapo to where the conspirators were to meet.'

'He was playing a very dangerous game, then,' said Tom.

'You must not forget your grandfather as a General Major, was an effective military strategist, with a wide network of associates in the regular German army, few of whom would have shed a tear at the Fuhrer's demise.'

'So what did he do then?' said Tom.

'He took a calculated risk,' said the professor.

'How do you mean?'

'It appears that several miles from the proposed rendezvous with the plotters, with Von Geysell's men following him, he staged an accident by driving his car off the road on a tight bend.'

'He could have been killed,' said Tom.

'But as we know, he wasn't; he did, however, break his arm. They questioned him in hospital, but he never gave Von Geysell any real information.'

'So what about Meyer and the others?'

'They escaped on this occasion.'

'So grandfather saved the day?'

'Not exactly! The simultaneous plot was bungled. In fact, the two officers involved managed only to blow themselves up. As for Conrad Meyer, I'm afraid your grandfather leading the SS on a wild goose chase was only a temporary stay of execution. Meyer and ten others were rounded up that summer and Von Geysell personally oversaw their execution. He lined them up and made the first man shoot the next man and so on, until he himself despatched Meyer. We know this because of the testimony of junior SS officers after the war, who testified against Von Geysell in his absence.'

'And what happened to my grandfather?'

'Once he had recovered from the accident, he was sent to the Russian front.'

'At his age!'

'The Gestapo were highly suspicious of your grandfather, but such was his war record and the regular army's high regard for him, they decided not to move against him directly. It was hoped that enemy action or the Russian winter would do this for them.'

'How do we know all this?'

'Your grandfather was interrogated by the Allies after the war.'

'He really had a tough time; he lost his wife and son you know,' said Tom.

'Yes and under somewhat mysterious circumstances by all accounts,' said the professor, searching through another box of files.

CHAPTER 17

Bonnie Bradshott had been brought up believing that if your neighbour did you a good turn, you returned the favour. So it was that the gentleman who had brought Evie back to her was sat at Bonnie's table tucking into a pot roast and all the trimmings. His name was Gerard Casey and he ate as if he hadn't had a square meal in months. Evie had moved her chair so close to him, she was practically sitting on his lap.

'You look like you could use some more,' smiled Bonnie.

'It's delicious, thank you.'

'Tell me, Gerard, how long have you lived in the village?'

'Just a couple of months.'

'Forgive me for being nosey, us Yanks can't help it: do you live alone?

'Yes, my wife died last year.'

'Oh gee! I'm so sorry.'

'Thank you. It was quite sudden. You see, one moment she was there and then I was left alone and everything that was familiar to me now looks new and very, very odd indeed.'

'I'm sure; it's something I can't begin to imagine. I lost my grandpa when I was fifteen, but he was an old snake. The only person who mourned his passing was the guy who owned the liquor store... more potatoes?'

'Please, thanks.'

'Are you retired now, Gerard?' said Bonnie.

'Well I was retired some years ago, by my employers.'

'Who were they?'

'The Catholic Church,' said Gerard. 'You see they disapproved of me.'

'How come?'

Evie, who had finished her meal and was getting a little bored, started to tickle Gerard under the chin.

'Are you Father Christmas?' she asked.

'Well no, but I know him very well and I told him what a good girl you were the other day, when we came back to find you mother.'

'Oh good. Tell him he's a good boy too!' said Evie.

'You were saying, Gerard.'

'Oh yes; I made the mistake of falling in love.'

'Falling in love can't be a mistake can it?' said Bonnie.

'In their eyes it was,' said Gerard.

'Religion, I never did get it,' said Bonnie. 'Sounds like you were well out of it.'

'Oh, I think you misunderstand me. I never lost my vocation,' explained Gerard. 'It's just that I couldn't live without Eileen. She was quite literally my other half and when she died, I felt as if I'd been pulled apart like a wishbone.'

Evie had given up tickling Gerard under the chin and was now busy rearranging what was left of his hair.

'You must have both gone through a lot,' said Bonnie.

'All worth it, I can assure you, although it took me some time convincing Eileen that we were meant to be together. Eventually she came round to my way of thinking.'

'Did you ever have any regrets?'

'Never. On the whole, I believe one should never run away unless you're running towards something. Sorry that sounds very Irish doesn't it.'

'And what's wrong with that; my grandfather was from Kerry,' said Bonnie.

'Never in the world! You were asking about regrets... I loved my time as a priest and then I loved my time as a husband, so no.'

'There you look soooo beautiful,' said Evie tying Gerard's hair back in the tiniest of ponytails.

* * * * *

Meanwhile in the archive in Berlin, Monika had brought fresh tea as Tom and Professor Schiller pored over another set of documents.

'You see, Mr Bradshott, it was almost impossible for Ingrid and Freddy to have been killed in the way the Nazis reported on the night in question. The whole city was fog-bound; no enemy aircraft were reported over Berlin on that date,' explained the professor.

'So where does that take us?'

'You need to look at these papers. They're on work carried out as part of the T4 project.'

'What did that entail exactly?'

'It's all in here; you may take them with you. I have the originals. I've also listed several websites that may be of interest. A word of warning: it does not make pretty reading,' said the professor.

*****

Chloe Whiting was sat sipping a coffee outside the house in Alexanderplatz once owned by Gunther Rohmer, when Tom arrived.

'So how did you get on at the Bundersarchive? Was it riveting?'

'Well he sent me off with a lot of bumph to read. How about you?'

'See that great pile over there?'

'Yep.'

'That was your grandfather's house.'

'Blimey!'

'Gunther was not just a distinguished soldier. He had been rich, but under the Soviet sphere of influence his estates in the country were run by the State as a commune in East Germany. When he came to England in 1948, he had practically nothing, apart from a new wife and a new-born baby, your mother.

'Well yes, but as we know he went on to make a fortune in England. I knew a bit of this, but you are ahead of me with some of this stuff. My mother hardly talks about her German background,' said Tom.

'I was talking to an old girl across the way,' explained Chloe. 'She's in her late eighties, but she remembers your grandfather and your mother as a baby. She also remembers someone she referred to as the Herr General's Dumkopf, which I'm afraid might refer to your uncle Freddy.'

'Where is she? Can I talk to her?'

'I don't think so; she got very upset when I told her we were making a film about your past.'

'Oh God, not another grouchy old German,' said Tom.

'She said the British are always in Germany, dragging up the past and how were they ever to get on with their lives. She went on about every country having their fascist dictator; Italy had Mussolini; Spain had Franco and we, apparently, had Mosley and 'that King' who ran off with an American harlot.' Chloe giggled at her own attempt at a German accent.

'Well she sounds a barrel of laughs.'

'Tell me more about what Professor Schiller had to say.'

'Let's go and get some lunch.'

CHAPTER 18

On the plane home, Tom began to read about the killing of infants and toddlers deemed in some way to be genetically deficient. Professor Schiller had provided copious notes

Long before the atrocities of the 'Final Solution', children were bussed out to what had been old psychiatric hospitals and marked with a red cross for death, a blue line if to be spared or a question mark for further assessment. Tom found it difficult to take it all in. It certainly made the murderous fundamentalist Daesh the world was confronting in 2016 look like amateurs.

Tom knocked his whisky back. He knew the Nazis were responsible for the deaths of over six million Jews, but he hadn't realised their ambitions for a master race had stretched to killing many thousands of children. He read further, finding himself nearer and nearer to tears

He started fidgeting in his seat. What had Bonnie said to him? 'I need to think about Evie...' He ordered another double whisky and glanced to the next page in Professor file.

Schiller's words echoed in his head: '...it was almost impossible for Ingrid and Freddy to have been killed in the way the Nazis reported.'

He slammed the file shut and glanced up the aisle to see if the steward was bringing his whisky. If he didn't bring it soon, they'd be landing and it would be too late.

CHAPTER 19

Kat had arrived back in London and was sitting in the office of Storky and Co. A letter had arrived from the company responsible for *Let's Do Lunch* to say that after due consideration, the BBC had decided not to recommission the series. While expressing their enormous thanks to Tom Bradshott and all the team, the BBC felt that a fresh, more youth-centric approach was required. For too long, this constituent of the viewing public had received a raw deal in weekend scheduling.

These people seemed to change their mind like the wind. A few months ago, *Let's Do Lunch* was described by the BBC as a flagship show.

Poor Tom. She wondered how he would take the news. He was not used to taking knock backs and now he was going to receive two together: the cutting of his show and her decision to end both their professional and personal relationships.

* * * * *

Phyllis Bradshott hated it when she was really ill. There had been plenty of occasions when it had been very useful to appear unwell, but the real thing was not for her. When Roger, her husband, had been alive, at the slightest hint of a migraine or the mere suggestion of a head cold, flowers and chocolates would arrive and when she'd had cause to have her appendix out, a silver bracelet from Asprey's had appeared miraculously on her bedside cabinet. Now the doctors were talking about congestive heart failure, so Tom had been summoned to The Pink Cottage.

'Mother, you will live to be a hundred.'

'No, Tom, about eighteen months is the best estimate from the doctors.' Phyllis was propped up on a day bed, like some latter-day Elizabeth Barrett Browning.

'I asked you to come to tell you firstly about my funeral arrangements and also about the will. You see, I'm afraid the house is re-mortgaged and seeing you make something of yourself on TV at least, I have spent what money there was. Unfortunately, most of my father's fortune went in death duties.

'I knew you'd understand. Now I'd like the service at St Joseph's and on no account at All Souls, do you understand? They have a woman there, who calls herself a priest, thank God your father's not alive. Personally, I blame that Archbishop of Canterbury we had, you know, Welsh, with wandering eyebrows and a way of making the Gospel entirely indecipherable in his sermons. I would have left Evie a little something, but really it's pretty meaningless for someone in her position and you and Bonnie are getting a bit old to produce any more grandchildren.'

'Right you are,' said Tom. 'Is there any other little bombshell, you wanted to leave with me?'

'Only this, Tom. Your father and I lavished a good education on you, paid for you to go travelling, had your teeth privately realigned and arranged for you to spend your summers in Cornwall at Rick Stein's prestigious restaurants on work experience.'

'That was only because you didn't want me cluttering up your love nest in the summer holidays,' muttered Tom under his breath. 'Anyway, I've brought you something,' said Tom.

'Oh, where is it then?' said Phyllis.

'Here, it's a diary your father kept during the war.'

'The war, the war, always the war! Why would I want to look at that?'

'I thought you loved your father.'

'I did, but this will be about his life before he and Mama got together; about his first family and all that tragedy! Why do you purposefully try to upset me, when I have so little time?' said Phyllis theatrically.

'Okay, I'm sorry. I will take it away again.'

'Why will you not just accept that he was a marvellous man, Tom?'

'So you've told me, Mother.'

'What's that supposed to mean?'

'Well, it's just that I never knew him and we've got a slightly different story than yours from his brother.'

'Oh, that embittered old queen!' said Phyllis. 'What's he been saying?'

'He says Grandfather could have saved him great heartbreak after the war.'

'What rubbish!' said Phyllis. 'I happen to know that when he started making money, my father sent his brother a generous cheque every Christmas.'

'It wasn't about money; it was a personal matter.'

'I really don't want to know, if it's something sordid,' said Phyllis, plumping up the cushions behind her.

'No, Mother, nothing must tarnish the hero's reputation, must it?'

'He had more courage in his little toe than most men.'

'I know, Mother. I've discovered a lot to admire about Grandfather, but it seems to me he had his blind spots.'

'He had standards, if that's what you mean.'

'Did you know what happened to Heinrich's partner, Werner?'

'Why would I?'

'He was killed trying to cross the Berlin Wall.'

'So? What has that to do with my father?'

'He did nothing to help Heinrich and Werner be together after the war, when he might have been in a position to help.'

'Tom, this is the wittering of a lonely old man. What you need to understand is Father had standards of behaviour. He believed in self-control, he believed that men should not lie down with other men.'

'So, he would have approved of how the Nazis – who he supposedly hated – treated the gay community and presumably count it as no loss when Werner was killed trying to get to Heinrich.'

'Don't be ridiculous, Tom. How was he to know this man Werner was going to attempt to do something as foolhardy as try and climb over the wall?'

'He did it for love, Mother.'

'Don't be disgusting, Tom. Now don't forget, my funeral is to be at St Joseph's.'

'Can we set the date now?' said Tom under his breath.

CHAPTER 20

August 1941

It had been three months since Freddy had been admitted to the clinic. Ingrid had been allowed to visit on two occasions. The staff were polite and business like and there was a strong smell of disinfectant throughout the clinic, which Ingrid took as a good sign.

A lot of building work was going on, including new shower rooms. She thought she saw Oberscharfuhrer Von Geysell, who appeared to be supervising their installation.

She passed Dr Albrecht in one of the corridors, but on this occasion he studiously ignored her. A young nurse explained that numbers of in-patients had increased over the last few months. Despite this influx, Freddy had seemed in reasonably good health and appeared to have adapted to his circumstances quite well. Ingrid noticed, however, how tired he looked and how dull his dark, jewel-like eyes had become. She had received one letter from Gunther since his posting. It was full of Gunther-like observations about the weather and barbed comments with regard to the quality of weapons with which his men had to fight.

After Ingrid's visits to see Freddy, Dr Albrecht had called at the house on one further occasion, ostensibly to give a progress report on her son. But again, he had made it clear what he expected for having admitted Freddy to the clinic. She had resisted him, despite the veiled threats he made between his breathless fumbling. He talked about moving Freddy to another programme at the clinic, which in the long run would be the best solution, if she didn't become more amenable.

Thankfully, one of the maids walked in just as he was making his final move and Albrecht retreated in a hot, loathsome little bundle of lust. For several days after his visit, Ingrid could smell Albrecht's fetid breath on her clothes and feel where he

81

had placed his stubby, little fingers. She decided that she must tell someone in authority of his behaviour.

So, although she knew Gunther would disapprove, she had spoken with Oberscharfuhrer Pieter Von Geysell by telephone. He had said that he was sorry to hear of her distress, but there must be some mistake. Dr Albrecht, he told her, was a man of impeccable moral standing and he was doing vital medical research for the Reich. She thought if only Gunther were here, he would know what to do.

It was the day before her third planned visit to the clinic when she received the call. The nurse said she had bad news.

Freddy had unfortunately contracted a virulent infection and had a high fever and despite medication, he had not survived the night; she said the family would be receiving a full report in due course.

Ingrid walked out of the sitting room and up to the top of the stairs to where Freddy used to stand and looked out at the stars; she eased open one of the large landing windows on the third floor and stepped out into the Berlin night.

CHAPTER 21

Bonnie sat in her kitchen with a mid-morning cup of coffee; tears were rolling down her cheeks. On the news channel, a young Syrian mother was sitting crossed legs on the floor of her tent, one of five thousand identical emergency shelters. Her English was good as she recounted calmly what her family had been through. When Islamist fighters had come to their home in a village just outside Mosul, her husband Salem had been recruited forcibly into Daesh and she had no idea where he was. Her fifteen-year-old daughter lay on a mattress behind her, her face obscured to the television cameras. Her mother explained that when they came for her husband, two of the insurgents had stayed behind and taken turns to rape the young girl. The woman explained that she had offered herself in her daughter's stead, but the two young men looked at her with disdain and continued their assault on her daughter.

Bonnie was not sure who she was weeping for: was it for the mother, for the girl on the mattress, or were the tears for herself?

Evie came into the kitchen.

'Come on, Mummy! You promised we could go swimming this morning.'

'Give me a few minutes to finish my coffee, honey,' said Bonnie, trying to hide her tears from her daughter.

The piece on Syria had finished and the news presenter was now talking to a man, who claimed his dog could predict the Premiership football results that coming weekend.

'Come on, Mummy, please!' called Evie from the back door.

'Two minutes and I'll be there.'

To return to America, for Bonnie, seemed like admitting defeat, but she was exhausted by everything. She felt angry with Tom for taking her for a fool. She had attended an Ivy League university for Christ's sake and had a Master's degree in psychology. She felt angry with herself for allowing things to get to this stage.

There had been men before, even suitable men. When she'd lived in London, there was Gav, a kindly Australian footie player, who treated her like a princess and wanted to take her back to Perth and the family meat processing business, which he would in due course inherit. Gav was not big on intellectual discourse, but he was big in other areas. She had been tempted to take him up on his offer. He was a genuinely lovely man and sex was more than satisfactory. But Bonnie knew, although she liked him very much, she didn't love him.

She knew this because unlike how it was with Tom, she felt no physical pain when Gav was not around. The feelings she had for Gav were more like how she felt about her pet rabbit when a child back in Texas: he was great to cuddle but easy to forget when the rodeo came to town and for her, it was only Tom who could take her to the rodeo.

There was a sudden loud bang outside the house which almost made Bonnie drop her coffee.

* * * * *

It had been a month since Tom had been over to meet Heinrich Rohmer and against his better judgement, he had invited himself to his mother's to stay.

It had been a month to forget in many ways. *Let's Do Lunch* had been dropped by the BBC and Kat had been avoiding him. He was feeling horny as hell and started fantasising about Mrs Tomley-Phelps, the village postmistress, who was eighty-two, almost totally blind and had lost a leg after a bad fall at The Trotfield St Giles Gymkhana of 1958 (which in Tom's overheated imagination would make her easier to chase). He was going stir crazy. Bonnie had barred him from the family home and so there he was tied to his mother's bedside by some odd sense of filial duty, which he knew would not be appreciated.

He was ecstatic then when Chloe phoned, to say that the makers of *Family Matters* were going to make one more trip out to Heinrich Rohmer's to tie up a few loose ends and they wanted him to go with them. They planned to fly out in a couple of days.

Tom knew it was not going to be easy getting his mother to agree to his absence. She had become truculently dependent on him, but he managed to sell it to her on the basis that the programme would never get shown, if he didn't make the visit. He also reminded her how photogenic Callum had said she was and what a cracking start to the programme her input was going to make. Tom arranged and paid for Phyllis's team of visiting domestics from Downstairs Downstairs to double their hours and reluctantly Phyllis agreed to his going, but not without a passing shot.

'Well, Tom! You may kiss me, as this may be the last time you see me.'

Tom got in the car already putting to the back of his mind his mother's theatrics.

CHAPTER 22

Bonnie rushed to the kitchen window. At the bottom of their drive, her old Citroen was right across the road and a white van with one of its wings badly dented was up against her garden wall. She rushed down and found Evie bending over head in hands.

'Honey, are you okay? What happened?'

Evie looked up; she was laughing her head off.

'Phew! That was a close one, wasn't it, Mummy?'

'What the bloody hell?' It was the driver of the van dressed in a white boiler suit and a furry Russian hat; he stomped towards Bonnie and Evie.

'Look, Mummy, a Womble!' said Evie cheerfully.

'Lady, is this your kid?' said the man. 'She looks simple to me, so what kind of mother do you call yourself, letting a retard get control of your car.'

'Now look, you son of a bitch,' said Bonnie who was still in a state of shock.

It was then that she noticed Pamela Richards (the woman from the playground), walking her dog.

'Hi there,' Bonnie called out. 'How's your daughter?'

The woman walked studiously past her.

'So, lady, what you going to do about my van? Or do I call the old bill?'

'Call who you like, sunshine. Just now, I need to check my daughter is okay.'

'A ton would do it and we'll keep the cops out of it. Can't say fairer than that,' said the van driver, rubbing his hands in expectation rather than the cold.

'Not that keen on the men in blue, then are we?' said Bonnie.

'Look you scrub my back and I'll scratch yours.'

'I'll scratch my own, if you don't mind. Here's eighty quid; now if I were you, I'd beat it.'

* * * * *

Tom was suddenly in demand; halfway up to London he'd received a call from Kat asking for a meeting before his next trip to Germany.

'Would that be business or pleasure?' asked Tom hopefully.

'Tom, I just don't want to leave things up in the air.'

'Oh, I see. Want to make sure you're not on the good ship Tom Birdshot when it goes down with all hands.'

'A trifle melodramatic don't you think? Tom shall we say seven-thirty tonight. You chose the restaurant and text me.'

His thoughts returned to the Tiergarten Project and Professor Schiller's comments about the mysterious circumstances surrounding Ingrid and Freddy's death; he smelt a very, smelly rat. For one of the very few times in his life, Tom felt a burning rage rising from the pit of his stomach. Could it be that Freddy's death was unrelated to any Allied bombing? Might it have been another example of the cruelty of the T4 project? Did Gunther just accept what he had been told? Were the SS carrying out some threat for a perceived disloyalty? The past could be such a slippery place at times, like separating the yolk from egg white; often the vital bit got left behind.

He gunned the car up and drove to London like a man possessed.

When he got to the restaurant, Kat was already there, dressed far too sensibly for his liking.

She kissed Tom on both cheeks, in an annoyingly chaste way.

'Thank you for coming, Tom.'

'Well it sounded important.'

'Listen: I'm really sorry I haven't been in touch.'

'I assumed as my agent, you were busy on my behalf trying to get me 'celeb' type work.'

'Tom, I've made a decision.'

'Sounds a bit ominous.'

'I'm relocating to the States. You see Prairie Dog has left me quite a bit of money, in fact enough so that I don't have to work. I'm going over to be near to Jo Jo.'

'Hang on, that's the lunatic son who tried to kill your ex... his father.'

'He has no one.'

'Well that's the strangest bit of cradle snatching I've ever heard of.'

'That's a cheap thing to say, Tom.'

'I'm sorry, but I don't get it.'

'Prairie Dog loved that boy despite everything and if there's a chance he can be rehabilitated, I feel I need to be there.'

'But the papers at the time said that he was out of his head on drink and drugs and shot his father while in an hallucinatory state.'

'None of which is true. Jo Jo had his reasons for what he did. I know that now and he's agreed to me visiting in the run-up to his parole board meeting.'

'So where does that leave us, Ms Kawalski?' said Tom, who feared he knew the answer already.

'Hey, we were great weren't we? But we both know how it is.'

'I'm not with you,' said Tom.

'You were never going to be completely mine. I knew that when I took you on and that's fine, but it's not really what I want. Guess I'm not much of a feminist after all. Free love among free agents, equal in the sight of each other with their kit off. It's for the birds, as far as I'm concerned now. I only had to look at the wreckage Prairie Dog has left behind, all those open affairs and marriages, all that internalised guilt; that's what killed him, Tom. Maybe it's yet a further reaction to my Catholic upbringing, but I'm done with it all.'

'So, will I ever see you again?' said Tom.

'You can count on seeing me again, Tom. You are my hero. I'll never forget you sorting out those pigs in the chip shop.'

Tom and Kat finished their meal in a kind of nervous, awkward silence, as if they were on their first, rather than their last date.

After a night on his own in one of London's more anonymous hotels, Tom set off to an early-lunch rendezvous with Chloe and the *Family Matters* film crew. He had tried ringing Bonnie, but it went straight to ansaphone. He knew, however, that she and Evie were still in England. He'd seen Bonnie's battered old Citroen in Pangbourne one day, when he was there for a meeting with the restaurant manager at the The Nosebag. Tom was very much the sleeping partner of the restaurant. In the early days, he had worked every hour God sent; establishing the place as one of the foremost eateries in the Home Counties. He was not one of what he called 'alphabetti spaghetti for grown -up' chefs. He liked his food to look – well, like food. Having worked under Rick Stein, seafood was one of his specialities. He also did a mean line in English traditional steamed puddings like jam roly-poly and spotted dick. These days, he was more interested in the bottom line on the spreadsheet at the end of every month and apart from the occasional suggestion of menu changes or the odd impromptu shift in the kitchen, his involvement in the business was minimal.

Chloe and Callum greeted Tom warmly and asked how his mother was.

'Well according to her, she's not long for this world.'

'Oh! I'm sorry,' said Chloe.

'Thanks, but I don't think the next world is quite ready for Mother.'

'Speaking of which, we've tracked down your grandfather's obituary from *The Times,*' said Callum. 'Oh God sorry that's a bit insensitive of me.'

'Don't give it another thought; remember, I never knew him!'

'Well here it is anyway,' said Callum.

September 6th 1971

Sir George Roberts, who has died at the age of 76 was at the forefront of Britain's motorway construction during the 1950s and 60s. As founder of Roberts Road Builders, he spearheaded the drive under successive governments of the time in establishing a motorway network to rival any in post-war Europe. Sir George, having been born in Germany, became a naturalised citizen of the United Kingdom in 1950. A man of wide interests he was a keen chess player and art collector who also served for many years as chairman of his local Conservative Party, married to Lady Elspeth Tweedside and with one daughter. Little is known of his early life in Germany, which was spent for the most part in the German army. He did, it is believed, win the Iron Cross during the Battle of the Somme.

Friends and colleagues remember him as a very private man of considerable personal courage both in supporting his wife through her final illness and surviving a fatal air crash when piloting his own plane on a flight to the Scottish borders. He is survived by his daughter Phyllis.

'Well, Mother never told me the bit about the plane crash,' said Tom.

'And there is no mention of your grandfather's first wife Ingrid, or their son Freddy.'

'I tell you what: my family appears to have more skeletons in it than the Roman catacombs. I'm mixing my metaphors but hopefully this last trip to Heidelberg will put some of them to bed; otherwise this episode of *Family Matters* is going to be about three hours long,' said Callum. 'Don't forget we've hardly touched Gunther's life, when he became George Roberts.'

'Most people have heard the rags to riches story; tragic wife; sponsor of the Tory Party; ya de ya de ya.'

'We will have to be careful not to exhaust your great uncle, I think us being there the last time took a great deal out of him.'

'I want to call on Professor Schiller again at the Bundersarchive, I need to check something with him,' said Tom.

'Well how about if Callum and I go and see Heinrich, while you go to Professor Schiller?'

'That sounds good. I think I made him uncomfortable anyway,' said Tom.

'Meanwhile, I will go through the info on Gunther as George and see if there's an angle we've missed there,' said Callum.

'Pillar of the establishment by the sound of it. I doubt you'll turn up anything as intriguing as his life in Germany,' said Tom.

'Oh well; we'll give it a go.'

'There's an ancient PA of his still alive,' said Tom. 'I think Olive Finch was her name, retired to Eastbourne apparently. My mother's probably got an address. I remember her getting Christmas cards up until very recently, I think.'

CHAPTER 23

Bonnie was waiting outside the school gates, watching the 4x4s pull up outside the school. It was a modern building, which appeared to be made mostly from glass and steel. It had a temporary quality about it as if, like the art equipment in the classes, it could be packed away at the end of each school day.

Evie had always loved school from her first day there. She was a very sociable girl, who her classmates loved, in part because she was always the same, always smiling (often this would erupt into helpless giggles), but also because she could make them laugh. She was a great mimic and her impersonations of various teachers and teaching assistants went down very well, with the children at least. Bonnie had been aware of the pained expressions on the faces of some of the staff, when her daughter arrived at school and guessed that they found her difficult. So, she was on her guard when noiselessly, the headmaster, Mr Parks, sidled up beside her.

Keith Parks was always on the lookout for the next big thing, or even the next little thing to get anxious about. Ever since qualifying, he'd dreamt of finding a post in a small, boy's preparatory school, somewhere where ill-discipline was tempered by the fact that Mummy and Daddy were footing the bill and therefore were your allies in rooting out disruptive characteristics in their offspring. Instead, here he was in a dilapidated primary school, teaching those who he considered uneducable, one of whom was Evie. Evie, on the other hand, found Mr Parks extremely funny most of the time.

She was particularly delighted by his bushy eyebrows, which always reminded her of hairy caterpillars, one of the many types of small creatures, of which Evie was inordinately fond.

'It's Mrs Bradshott, isn't it?' said Parks.

'That's me,' said Bonnie.

'Well, I am glad I caught you.'

'And why's that?'

'It's nothing to worry about really.'

Bonnie was immediately worried.

'It's little Evie.'

'What about her?'

'Just a few concerns really.'

'Oh, yes? What about?'

'Behavioural issues.'

'Good or bad? She has both you know,' said Bonnie.

'I, along with colleagues in social services, have decided a network meeting might be appropriate.'

'May I ask what for?'

'To discuss the future.'

'Well, my oh my: that is a big topic,' said Bonnie.

'We'll be in contact re a date for the meeting; must fly, good to touch base with you, Mrs Bradshott.'

* * * * *

An ambulance was parked outside Heinrich Rohmer's block of flats when Callum and Chloe arrived. The old man was being stretchered out of the building, swaddled in blankets with an oxygen mask over his mouth.

'Oh God! I feared something like this might happen,' said Chloe.

'Is there anyone going with him?' said Callum.

'I don't think he had a great deal to do with his neighbours.'

'I really hate hospitals,' said Chloe.

'I'll go,' said Callum. 'If they'll let me.'

'Okay. I'll phone Tom, let him know what's happened,' said Chloe.

Heinrich beckoned to them.

'I'm frightened,' he said.

'It's okay, Herr Rohmer, I'm coming with you,' said Callum.

Heinrich told the paramedic that Callum was his British stepson.

'You need to keep him awake,' said the paramedic, who didn't sound very German himself.

'Talk to him. It doesn't matter what you say,' he continued.

'Yes, talk to me,' said the old man. Heinrich was having difficulty in breathing. 'Tell me what your life is like as a gay man in London.'

The paramedic pretended to busy himself with the spare oxygen cylinder.

'How did you know?' said Callum.

'Gaydar. Isn't that what you call it?'

'Come on! You heard what my friend the paramedic here said... You need to keep me talking.'

'Okay. My partner's Oli and we've been together eleven years.'

'What does he do?'

'He's in the rag trade.'

'Excuse me?'

'Fashion... We had a civil partnership ceremony.'

'Nothing like that in my day. Werner and I had to make do with a couple of years before that bloody war.'

'Keep taking the oxygen, deep breaths,' instructed the paramedic.

'*Danke*,' said Heinrich.

The ambulance careered round a bend in the road.

'I don't think we will make the hospital at this rate,' said Heinrich. 'Go on tell me more... about Oliver and you. How did your families take the news of this civil partnership?'

'Oliver's were fine, but my parents took a couple of months to come round. I think it was when Oliver paid for them to fly out to San Francisco with us that they began to see the light.'

'So, you are happy now, yes?'

'Oh yes. I have a silly smile on my face almost all the time. I have no idea why Oliver picked me, but he did and my life before I met him seems like it was someone else's, who I can't help feeling sorry for.'

'Heinrich! Heinrich! Can you hear me?' the paramedic stopped shouting and began frantically working on the old man as he drifted into unconsciousness.

CHAPTER 24

Tom arrived at the Bundersarchive in a ferocious hailstorm. Hailstones as big as marbles were bouncing off car roofs, while incongruously the sun shone.

Across the street, an old couple sheltered under a shared raincoat, while the traffic slowed to manoeuvre through the thick, white carpet that covered the road.

'Ah! Mr Bradshott! Welcome once again! You will, I hope, find us a little bit more organised today. More like the efficient Germans you British love to make fun of, yah. Monika, tea for Mr Bradshott, if you please!'

The professor was again interestingly attired in a 'Denis the Menace' red and black striped jumper and a pair of yellow corduroy trousers. You wouldn't get such frippery in the British Library, more's the pity, thought Tom.

'Hello again, Monika,' said Tom chirpily.

'Good morning, Mr Bradshott,' Monika replied. 'How are you today?' She was dressed in a dark, grey two-piece and her hair had been cut somewhat severely short, which only served to accentuate the doe-like beauty of her large, brown eyes.

'Very well. So how's life treating you? Is the professor keeping you out of mischief?'

'You will be pleased to know we have biscuits this morning, Mr Bradshott. A little bit and often isn't that what they say about food for people of your age.'

'Now, now, Monika: don't embarrass our guest! What will he think of us!'

'I'm sorry to keep bothering you like this, Professor, but there is something that keeps playing on my mind with regard to my great uncle Freddy's death. It began when you talked about "mysterious circumstances."'

'I see,' said the professor. 'Not sure how I can help though.'

'I've got a bit of a hypothetical question, really. But if, say, the disabled son of a well-connected German family were taken into one of the T4 projects, would any enforced euthanasia be covered up to avoid a fuss?'

'Well, that is a very interesting question, Mr Bradshott. You see, for whatever reason, Herr Hitler officially suspended the euthanasia project at T4 in August 1941 bowing, it is said, to protests from the Church among others. However, what evidence there is suggests the programme continued in a covert way after that date.'

'So, Freddy may well have been murdered by these so-called doctors,' said Tom.

'Yes, it is certainly a possibility.'

'But then, what about Ingrid. Given Gunther's high profile, would they have dared harm her?'

'One can only surmise. We have no death certificate, so no cause of death. We do, however, have this brief newspaper report from 9th September 1941, recording that a body of a female was found near Alexanderplatz. The woman was thought to have been in her early thirties and the cause of death unknown.'

'But that's two days after they were both reported killed in enemy bombing raids.'

'It is possible, of course, that this is a coincidence?'

'She was killed, wasn't she?'

'We may never know, but from what you tell me about Ingrid's character, if her beloved Freddy were dead, would she really have wanted to go on living?'

'Poor woman, whatever the truth was,' said Tom.

'Yes. Dreadful business, really,' said the professor.

'Thank you so much for your help, Professor,' said Tom.

'Oh, there is just one more thing, before you go. It concerns Dr Albrecht.'

'Odious little man by the sound of it.'

'Well, it appears he escaped any form of justice after the war.'

'How?'

'It seems he too went to England in the late forties, to start a new life.'

* * * * *

Heinrich Rohmer was the first dead person Callum had ever seen; for despite the paramedic's best efforts, dead, Heinrich, certainly was.

'Oh God, I feel so responsible,' said Callum.

'You must not think that way. We asked you to keep him talking and you did,' said the paramedic.

'But he was talking ten to the dozen asking all those questions, almost manic.'

'People often rally in that way, just before they die.'

'God, this is so sad. I think he had been unhappy for a very long time.'

'Well, perhaps the way to think of it is that he is not unhappy now,' said the kindly paramedic.

'You are not German, are you?' said Callum.

'No. I'm from Bolton, actually, but I've been here ten years. Better money than in England and not so many bricks thrown at you as in England.'

'What do you mean?'

'Well, I've been on several shouts back home, where we were verbally abused and on one occasion I was hit on the head by a brick, while trying to restart someone's heart. It's the uniform you see, red rag to a bull for some it seems. Anyway, by comparison, Germans are as good as gold.'

* * * * *

Tom stayed in Heidelberg to organise and pay for Heinrich's funeral. There were four mourners including Tom and the young paramedic who'd tried to save his great uncle's life. There was an elderly lady, who apparently attended most funerals at that particular crematorium and someone from the housing department, who had the job of disposing of Heinrich's possessions. Apparently, he had not made a will, so the official wanted to find if there were any relatives who may have a claim.

It was a simple non-religious service. Tom had not known what Heinrich would have wanted, so one of Mozart's Nocturnes was played and Tom read from a translation of Thomas Mann's *Death in Venice*. It was the best he could come up with.

After the service, Tom flew back to England. When he got to his mother's, she seemed to have made a miraculous recovery and showed an unexpected interest in Heinrich's passing.

'So, do they know the cause of death? Was it Aids? It wouldn't surprise me.'

'Mother, he was ninety-six years old and had in all probability been celibate for the last fifty years.'

'Were there many at the funeral?'

'The place was packed out,' lied Tom. 'A drag queen sang *Ava Maria* and then we all went off to The Fabulous Flamingo club in Heidelberg's gay quarter and danced the night away.'

'You may mock, Tom, but I'm only showing an interest. After all, whatever he was, he was my uncle, you know.'

'True, so why shouldn't he suffer a tongue lashing like the rest of your family do.'

'Well, if you're going to be like that, I am going to bed. You can bring me up some cocoa in half an hour's time and remember the milk needs to be hot, not boiling.'

'I do know, Mother. I am a trained chef remember.'

'Yes, I know, more's the pity. Fabulous Flamingo club indeed,' Phyllis muttered.

'By the way, have you got an address for your father's old PA? Olive Finch?'

'Now there was another strange bird, Miss Finch. Yes, I've got an address for her, but she's probably ga ga by now.'

He had known old people gaining a sense of schadenfreude from other people's misfortunes, but Heinrich's death seemed to have done the impossible, thought Tom; it seemed to have given his mother a sense of humour.

The next morning, an email arrived from Kat in Los Angeles.

Thank you for making it easy for me to leave. So here I am in LA LA land. Christmas decorations are going up, understated of course. I have had confirmation that Jo Jo will be eligible for release in December, but as yet no confirmation from him that he will let me help with his rehabilitation. But a photo of him and his mother came from him in the post, very obviously with old Prairie Dog's face cut out of the picture. He'd scrawled Happy Families on it, the poor boy.

Remember me to little Evie.

Fondest Love,

Kat.

CHAPTER 25

Bonnie Bradshott had not been in full-time work since before Evie was born, but she had been working on a self-help book for parents, which had the working title *Parenting: It's Child's Play*. Her editor had given her numerous deadlines and Bonnie had reluctantly agreed to get the book in draft form to them by the end of the week. Her ancient laptop was on its last legs and she was on the point of throwing it into the pool, which she'd just swum a few lengths in to calm herself down. The phone rang and it was the school: there had been some kind of incident involving Evie.

'What kind of incident?' asked Bonnie.

'I think it would be best if you came down to the school so we can have a one on one and I can put you in the picture,' said Mr Parks.

'Well okay, but I've got a bit of a rush job on. Evie's okay isn't she?'

'Oh, Evie is fine,' said Parks.

'Shall we say 3pm my office?'

'I guess so. You're not going to give me detention though are you, Mr Parks?'

'School rules have been broken Mrs Bradshott. I'm a little concerned at your casual attitude,' said Parks.

'Well that's us Yanks for you. We like to keep things informal.'

'Three pm then. Good afternoon, Mrs Bradshott.'

* * * * *

Bonnie arrived at the school at 3.10pm.

'Ah, Mrs Bradshott. We were beginning to give up hope,' said Mr Parks.

'Yes, sorry about that, but as I said, I've got a deadline to meet. So, what's the problem?'

'Well, Mrs Wilkes, one of our longest-serving dinner ladies, has unfortunately made a complaint concerning your daughter.'

'What kind of complaint?'

'She says your daughter made a very derogatory comment at lunchtime concerning the tagliatelle.'

'I see,' said Bonnie, who couldn't help smirking.

'Apparently, she referred to it as monkey brains.'

'That's kids for you,' said Bonnie.

'The thing is, Evie refused to retract her statement.'

'Well, she's a gal of strong opinions, like her ma, I'm afraid,' said Bonnie.

'The point being, Mrs Bradshott, we have what we call our 'Dining Room Manners Policy' of which this was a very serious infringement,' explained Mr Parks. 'We've had to send Mrs Wilkes home on stress leave.'

'I could use some of that.'

'Once again, Mrs Bradshott, you seem to have failed to grasp the gravity of the situation.'

'Tell me, Mr Parks, are you for real?'

'I'm afraid you leave us little alternative but to temporarily exclude Evie from school.'

'You're kidding me, right.'

'She's waiting for you in my secretary's office,' said Mr Parks.

'All down to monkey brains!' said Bonnie incredulously.

'I'm sure our forthcoming multi-agency network meeting will map us a pathway that we can all sign up to.'

'If you say so, Mr Parks,' said Bonnie.

CHAPTER 26

Olive Finch lived in a large flat in one of the four-storey Victorian villas just off the seafront in Eastbourne. She had lived alone for the last fifteen years after her mother had died, just shy of her hundredth birthday. Miss Finch, at eighty-eight, was still remarkably sprightly, thought Tom, as she showed him into her tastefully decorated, well-proportioned sitting room, in one corner of which was a baby grand piano festooned with photographs. From one of the windows, it was possible to glimpse the sea, which on that mid-November morning was as calm as a mill pond and hardly discernible from the slate grey sky.

'Welcome, welcome! Do come through and make yourself comfortable.'

'Thank you very much. It's very good of you to see me.'

'Not at all! It's so lovely to have a member of Sir George's family here. Do you know, I could see a resemblance the moment you walked in through the door.'

'Gosh, really,' said Tom.

'How is your dear mother, by the way?'

'Oh well, she's a little poorly, but picking up now, I think.'

'Sir George was awfully fond of her, you know.'

'Yes, so I believe. Of course, I didn't know my grandfather. He died several years before I was born.'

'What a loss to our country that was,' said Miss Finch.

'The thing is, Miss Finch, as I think I said on the phone, we are making a programme at the moment and for some reason best known to themselves, the producers have decided to make it about me.'

'Will you have shortbread or perhaps a piece of Victoria sponge? I'd like to say I made it myself, but I understand you're a TV chef, so I think I would be rumbled fairly quickly. I'm afraid I am a bit of a Radio 4 addict, so I haven't actually seen your programme. I'm sure it's very good though.'

At this point, a small grey cat slunk into the room.

'Ah! This is Augustus. Augustus, say hello to Mr Bradshott.'

'Hello Augustus,' said Tom.

The cat looked at Tom with utter disdain and continued on its path to the windowsill.

'Augustus is something of an indoor ornithologist. He has a keen interest in the different varieties of gull we have here in Eastbourne,' Miss Finch explained.

'He's very handsome,' said Tom. 'Miss Finch, you knew my grandfather for many years. What was he like to work for?'

'Sir George was a real, old school gentleman, polite, courteous at all times, even when he would have had such a lot on his mind.'

'Forgive me, but I've heard it said he could be quite taciturn. Was that your experience?' asked Tom.

'Oh no, I wouldn't say that. He was never overly effusive. But his actions spoke far louder than words.'

'In what way,' asked Tom.

'Well, for example, when Mother lost Father and came to live with me, Sir George gave – not loaned me – the deposit to buy this flat.'

'You were obviously important to him.'

'If you are inferring what I think you are, Mr Bradshott, I need to make it quite clear that there was nothing improper in my relationship with your grandfather whatsoever.'

'Oh! I'm so sorry. I didn't mean to suggest...'

'No! I'm sorry. I didn't mean to embarrass you. It's not... you see there wasn't a time, when I wouldn't have come running to be with him, should Sir George have snapped his fingers. But he just wasn't that kind of man, more's the pity. Now, I've quite forgotten; was it the shortbread or the Victoria sponge? Or perhaps a piece of each?'

CHAPTER 27

Bonnie felt the anger bubbling a way at the pit of her stomach as she and Evie returned home. Evie, on the other hand, was very upbeat.

'Never mind, Mummy. I can help you with your book now.'

'Sure can, honey,' said Bonnie, still envisaging what kind of misfortune she would like to befall that pompous prick Parks.

'It was so nice of Mr Parks to give me some time off, wasn't it, Mummy?'

'Well yes, honey, it was, but do you think you really should have called your lunch monkey brains?'

'Of course, Mummy. It was just how I imagined monkey brains would look.

'Why were you thinking of monkey brains, Evie?'

'Weeell, that's what Mary Bishop in my class calls me,' said Evie.

Bonnie redoubled her thoughts about exactly what she would like to befall Mr Parks.

Shortly after reaching home, there was a knock at the door: it was Gerard.

'Hi Gerard, come away on in,' said Bonnie.

'I just wanted to make sure you were all alright. I heard there had been an accident outside the house.'

'Gee, don't folk have anything else to talk about it? Is it not enough that our dirty laundry gets spread over the front pages of those excuses for newspapers you have over here, but the village as well?'

'Forgive me, but are you having a bad day,' said Gerard.

'Kind of I guess, but hey you can help me. What do you know about methods of torture? We Americans can't have all the answers.'

They both chuckled and Bonnie put the kettle on. She proceeded to tell Gerard about Evie taking off the handbrake of the car and how she'd been excluded from school.

'And the worst of it all is that I can't get hold of Tom,' said Bonnie.

'Oh, that's awful: no one to share it with. Well I'm sure he'll be back soon.'

'No, you don't understand me. We're on a break.'

'I'm not with you,' said Gerard.

'A trial separation,' said Bonnie.

'Oh; how's that going?' asked Gerard.

'It's going,' said Bonnie.

'Are you managing to keep busy? That might help.'

'Busy! Gerard, my publisher has given me a deadline of this Friday to get the first draft to them and now I've got Evie at home all day.'

At this point, Evie came into the room.

'Mummy, Mummy, I've got this great idea of how your book could start. It goes like this: "Once upon a time there was a beautiful lady, who was very sad and very, very, cross!"'

'I tell you what, Evie, why don't you and I go down to the village pond and feed those old ducks?' suggested Gerard.

'Oh yes, but can we feed the young ones too?' said Evie.

'Is that okay with your mummy?' said Gerard.

'More than okay,' said Bonnie. 'Gerard, you're an angel.'

'A somewhat fallen one these days, I'm afraid,' said Gerard.

* * * * *

Back on the south coast, Tom and Miss Finch were taking tea.

'I've never been to Eastbourne, it's a lovely town,' observed Tom.

'As you will be aware, the south coast has several similar towns. The cynic would say that they serve as play pens for the middle classes' cast-off, elderly folk,' chuckled Miss Finch. 'Can I get you more tea, Mr Bradshott?'

'Tom, please.'

'Very well, Tom.'

'My grandmother, of course, died before I was born. No one talks very much about her at all in the family.'

'Poor dear Lady Elspeth,' said Miss Finch, topping up the teapot with boiling water.

'She was some kind of invalid for a considerable time, as I understand.'

'Well, I would not choose the word invalid: in those times, we would have said she suffered with her nerves.'

'How did her illness manifest itself?'

'In the beginning, she was, so they say, very highly strung. Others say she was a vivacious young bride. Sadly, when I knew her, she had retreated into herself so far that she rarely spoke and it was decided that the London house was all too much for her. So, she returned to her family at the Tweedside estate on the Scottish borders. By a strange twist of fate, your grandfather only outlived her by a couple of years.'

'Gosh, that's very grim,' said Tom.

'As you would expect of a man like Sir George, he visited her regularly, hoping for some kind of recovery, but it never came.'

'His life wasn't short on tragedy was it?'

'No! He had more than his share, I think. Excuse me, Tom: it's time for Augustus' exercise. Will you walk with us? He will enjoy the company, won't you Augustus?'

Miss Finch, a very soberly dressed person herself, went out into the hall and returned with diamante encrusted lead and harness for Augustus.

They walked down to the sea front. A bank of fog was rolling in and Tom shivered with the cold. Miss Finch, however, bore all of her eighty-eight years lightly as she led a somewhat bemused Augustus past the boarded-up ice cream vendors and brightly-lit souvenir shops, wearing only the thinnest of cardigans and no hat.

'Augustus needs the walk to keep his figure and I find it beneficial in terms of my circulation.'

'Did you know George's brother?' asked Tom.

'Brother? I wasn't unaware he had a brother.'

'Back in Germany.'

'Oh! He never really talked about that, of course. A few of us knew the truth about his early life from the beginning, but he didn't want it generally known. He said the business might suffer,' explained Miss Finch.

'I'm sad to say his brother died a few days ago in Heidelberg.'

'Oh dear! I am sorry.'

'He was ninety-six.'

'Of course, Sir George lived to a reasonable age. Mind you, he had a few alarms and excursions and not just in wartime. He was nearly killed when the business was just starting up, you know. A road tunnel collapsed.'

'Gosh and wasn't there some kind of plane crash as well?'

'Yes, but that was much later on. He was flying his little plane up to Scotland on an errand of mercy.'

'Was he visiting Grandma?'

'Yes and he was taking a doctor, some kind of nerve specialist,' said Miss Finch. 'They both should have been killed, but Sir George miraculously survived: his companion did not. Funnily enough, he was also originally from Germany, I seem to remember.'

CHAPTER 28

Barry Goldwing, the producer of *Family Matters,* had some good news and some bad news for Tom. They had arranged to meet at Goldwing's golf club for lunch. Tom was preoccupied as he drove through the ornate gates leading to The Bowery Golf and Country Club. He had responded to numerous texts from Bonnie regarding Evie's exclusion from school. He had offered to take Evie for a couple of days but when Bonnie heard he was staying with his mother, she said it was okay and that she would sort something out.

He asked her if she'd decided on whether she was going to the States, but she still hadn't made her mind up and wouldn't be doing anything until she'd met her publisher's deadline.

Tom was considering whether to play hardball with Bonnie and get his lawyers involved to stop them leaving the country, but he was frightened by the idea as it seemed somehow irrevocable.

'Tom, great to see you,' said Goldwing. 'I've got us a room.'

'I didn't know it was going to be that kind of a meeting,' said Tom flippantly.

'Tell me, Tom, do you play golf?'

'Not quite ready for it. Perhaps in ten years' time.'

'I have a single figure handicap and try to play three times a week. Clears the head and heals the soul, so they reckon.'

'My father used to play, his club was at Hindhead and he knew Peter Alliss quite well, I believe.'

The room they had been allotted for their meeting was small and oak panelled with a large picture of the Queen on one wall and the iconic photo of Margaret Thatcher in a flowing scarf with her head poking out of what might have been a Chieftain tank.

It was an appropriate setting given the bad news Goldwing had for Tom.

'So, Tom. Looks like we may have a problem with our episode of *Family Matters*.

'Oh, I see! Why's that exactly?' asked Tom.

'There is a perception disconnect, Tom. It's felt ratings would be affected by your... shall we say, off-piste activities.'

'My what?'

'All that business at the chip shop.'

'But this was a nothing story, which the press decided to blow up out of all proportion.'

'Nevertheless, if you'll excuse the pun in this country, you're seen now as something of a hot potato.'

'So, what you're saying is I'm finished on TV.'

'Here in England, maybe, but I'm here to tell you that every cloud has a silver lining. We think we've come up with another great format for you. Give you a chance to spread your wings in more ways than one.'

'Sounds interesting,' said Tom.

'We want you to do a series of shows taking a sidelong view on what it is to be British, looking at uniquely British institutions.'

'For example?' queried Tom.

'Queuing, the monarchy, Morris dancing, cricket, the village fete, polo, swan upping, you get the idea?'

'Hasn't this all been done before?'

'We're going to set up a number of classic British occasions and then you would guide invited celebrity guests to get involved and explain the intricacies of it all. It's kind of Louis Theroux meets *Britain's Got Talent*,'

'Still not getting it really,' said Tom.

'The twist being, it's all set up and filmed in the good old US of A.'

'Oh right, but won't I be persona non grata over there as well?'

'Tom, no one's even heard of you over there. We are going to sell you as an insider of British aristocracy, you being a scion of the Tweedside family. Believe me, the Americans will lap you up like butter off corn on the cob.'

This was not an image Tom wanted to dwell on, but it seemed Goldwing was offering him a professional lifeline that he would be a fool not to consider.

'A final decision on whether we scrap the *Family Matters* show will be taken in a week or so's time. By then, perhaps the red top press will have lost interest and moved on to someone else.'

'Well thanks very much, Barry, a lot to think of,' said Tom.

'No worries and, Tom, a piece of advice: never intimate to a golfer that it's an old man's game. Now let's eat.'

The smile on Goldwing's face left Tom in little doubt that the man was a force to be reckoned with and it would be best to stay on the right side of him.

'Oh, by the way, the rest of the team of *Family Matters* have no idea we are considering scrapping the show and I'd like it kept that way.'

* * * * *

As he drove back to Pink Cottage and no doubt his mother's continued disapprobation, the thought of putting the Atlantic Ocean between him and her had considerable appeal. Particularly after he'd received the figures on the quarterly takings at his restaurant, The Nosebag. They didn't make pretty reading. It appeared that Brexit had not revitalised his fellow countrymen's taste for good old British fare; well not at the prices he was having to charge at any rate. Half his foreign staff had taken fright and gone home and he was having to up his pay rates to recruit the most poorly qualified and unmotivated of home grown talent.

There was also the small matter of the women in or in most cases out of his life, who all seemed intent on flocking to America too. Things could get very interesting, if Goldwing's project were to take off. Perhaps instead he could go and lodge with Miss Finch and he and Augustus could sit on that windowsill and watch the world go by.

There was something playing on Tom's mind concerning his grandfather, bits of his character which weren't quite adding up.

One thing Miss Finch had said made Tom smile as it totally undermined his mother saying what a fortune they'd spent on his education. Apparently, when Tom was born, Sir George had set aside considerable funds for his education.

* * * * *

Chloe Whiting was wearing those boots again, as she walked into the studio. Callum had called a meeting to see where they were with the programme and Tom had been invited along, although it was not usual practice to have the subject of the programme in what was essentially an editorial meeting.

But Callum wanted Tom's expertise as a front of camera TV programme maker. Callum was also aware that this programme came with particular political and other sensitivities, given the recent newspaper stories regarding Tom and with Sir George being something of an establishment figure. There was also the question of whether Ingrid and Freddy Rohmer's tragic story was just a bit too bleak for Sunday evening viewing.

'Well thanks all for coming,' said Callum. 'In particular, Tom. I just thought we needed to get together to see where we are in terms of what we have on tape. Chloe, would you like to give us an update.'

'At the moment, we have interviews with Heinrich, Tom and Bonnie and Tom's mother. For the intro, we have some filler information regarding Nazi treatment of people with a disability.'

'I wouldn't call it filler material exactly,' said Tom.

'No. Sorry that was clumsily put,' said Chloe.

'How about the archivist bloke Schiller?'

'Well, we haven't got film of you at the Bundersarchive.'

'That's very much the missing part of the jigsaw. We need Tom and the prof on film,' said Callum.

'Well that means the whole crew flying out to Germany again. Can the budget stand it?' asked Chloe.

'I'll tell you what. We'll fly the old boy over here. He'd probably enjoy a bit of a jolly.'

'Excellent idea. I don't think I fancy freezing my bollocks off on another trip to Germany,' said Tom.

'How did the meeting with your grandfather's old PA go, Tom?' asked Chloe.

'She was a scream,' said Tom. 'A sort of Miss Marple with attitude. Immensely loyal to the family and yet I couldn't help thinking she was taking the mickey.'

'Did she tell you anything you didn't already know?' asked Callum.

'Well a couple of snippets I'll use as ammunition with Mother and a bit more stuff on his near-death experiences.'

'Well we know about the First World War heroics and the car crash in the war. Then there was a tunnel collapse in which he could have died, just when the civil engineering business was taking off and then of course there was that plane crash, which he survived, but his passenger didn't.'

'Chloe, could you see what more you can find out about that from official records, the coroner's report, that kind of stuff?' asked Callum.

'Will do, boss,' said Chloe.

'Tom, you've got the old leather suitcase of Heinreich's now haven't you?' said Callum.

'Yes. It's under my bed at Mother's.'

'Can I ask you just to check through it that there's nothing we've missed to confirm what went on in the war?'

'No prob.'

'Okay, people: let's rock and roll,' said Callum and then wished he hadn't.

'Have you been watching too many crime dramas on TV, Callum?' said Chloe.

CHAPTER 29

Gerard and Evie's walk to feed the ducks had become almost a daily occurrence while Bonnie frantically attempted to finish the draft of *Parenting: It's Child's Play*. Her final chapter entitled 'You know best,' was meant to summarise her general hypothesis within the book, that in the final analysis, maternal and to some degree female, instinctual parenting has been unlearnt through professional interference, often with the best intentions. This risk averse yet intense style of child rearing was breeding a generation of high achieving, highly anxious and socially underconfident children.

'Geez what now?' cried an exasperated Bonnie.

Someone was persistently knocking at her front door.

It was Seren's mother, Pamela Richards.

'You do know he is a defrocked priest, don't you?'

'Excuse me?'

'That's the third time, this week. I honestly don't know why some people bother having children, if they're going to leave them with every Tom, Dick, or Harry.'

'I tell you something! You'd make a great case study for my book,' said Bonnie, her hackles rising.

'You know he was openly crying in the village shop on Monday.'

'Well, I happen to know he's had quite a bit to cry about in his life.'

'In men, it usually signals a guilty conscience.'

'Is that right?' said Bonnie. 'By the way how's Seren?'

'Don't change the subject!'

'Okay, but the poor girl is usually your only subject. Now unless there's a point to this conversation, I think I'll take a rain check. Books don't write themselves you know.'

'But I haven't finished,' said the woman.

'Well, lady, I have, so I suggest you go suck a lemon,' shouted an exasperated Bonnie. 'Oh! Wait a minute. I see you already have!'

* * * * *

Professor Schiller had never been to England and had dug out from his wardrobe a rather loud dog tooth three-piece suit specially for the occasion. He was laden down with suitcases and a large rucksack on arrival at Heathrow and was not difficult for Tom to spot.

'*Guten tag*, Professor!' said Tom, in his best schoolboy German.

'Hello, Mr Bradshott! Well here we are again,' said the professor.

'Did you have a good flight?'

'Exceedingly smooth, thank you.'

'Well, thank you for coming.'

'Not at all. I am honoured that you want me in your programme. I have a few new pieces of information with regard to your family, which I think you might find of interest.'

'Oh, that sounds intriguing. I'm afraid we are going to cheat a little. The production company have made a mock-up of your office in Berlin.'

'Nothing wrong with a little subterfuge, Mr Bradshott.'

'Forgive me, Professor, but how do you manage to have such a perfect grasp of English?'

'Ah I have a secret weapon; I have recently married and my bride is English. Lorraine, may I introduce you to Mr Bradshott.'

When a startled Tom had recovered his composure, he greeted the new Mrs Schiller.

'Pleasure to meet you.'

'Hiya! You're thinner than you are on the television. Mind you, they say it puts pounds on you. Just look at that Theresa May. I bet she's like an anorexic stick insect in real life. So, you're going to make my Otto a star, is that right.'

'Well I think he'll suit the screen very well,' said Tom taking in Lorraine Schiller.

She was in her early forties and what Tom's mother would call a 'bottle blond'. Fulsome of figure, she wore a body-hugging, sparkly green dress and short white faux fur jacket; round her neck and dangling down over her ample bosom was an enormous rock crystal.

'You need not worry; I have, of course, paid my wife's airfare from my own pocket.'

'So, you're here to see the sights then Mrs Schiller?'

'Bit of business, bit of pleasure.'

'May I ask what's your line.'

'Like me, Mr Bradshott, she's interested in past lives.'

'Oh, a historian,' said Tom.

'No. Actually, I'm a spiritualist medium,' explained Mrs Schiller. 'I'm thinking of doing a tour over here. I could do a reading for you, if you like, Tom. You look like the receptive type.'

CHAPTER 30

A letter arrived from the Social Services Children's Disability team inviting Bonnie and Tom to a multi-agency network meeting to discuss, in light of a number of recent concerns, an ongoing person-centred plan for Evie. Bonnie had skewered it on the pin board in the kitchen with one of Tom's sharpest chef's knives. The meeting was to be on Tuesday of next week. Pretty, damn, short notice Bonnie thought. She had relented and sent Tom an email suggesting he come and stay the Monday night, so that they could talk and make sure they put up a united front with those Bozos from the school and social services. She would make up a bed in one of the spare rooms for him. She ended the email by saying that all this crap was making her think very seriously about going back to the States with Evie on a more permanent basis.

* * * * *

Tom had agreed to drop the old leather suitcase of Gunther's off at Chloe's flat. Having dropped the professor and Mrs Schiller off at their hotel, he drove like a bat out of hell down to his mother's to retrieve the case. His mother greeted him.

'Oh hello! Now let me think, do we know each other? Your face is vaguely familiar.'

'Sorry, Mother. I haven't got time for this. I need to be back in London by seven.'

'Ah yes, you used to be my son, once upon a time.'

'Okay sorry. How are you?'

'I told you, Tom. I'm dying. Not that you give a damn.'

'Oh, by the way, I know about Granddad.'

'What do you know about my father?'

'That he left money to pay for all of my education, so you and Father never paid a penny,' said Tom slipping out of the back door before his mother could retaliate.

* * * * *

When he arrived at Chloe's basement flat in Islington, it was obvious to Tom that she'd been crying.

'Hi Chloe, sorry I'm a bit late.'

'That's okay,' said Chloe flatly.

'So, here's the case, where do you want it?'

'Oh, just put it anywhere and come and have a drink,' said Chloe.

She showed him through into her living room. There was an empty bottle of merlot on the coffee table next to a box of tissues and three chocolate bar wrappers.

'Shorry, the place is a bit of a shite hole,' slurred Chloe.

'No probs.'

'I'll jus... go and... ger another class. Oh and another bottle,' said a clearly very drunk Chloe.

She made her way unsteadily towards the kitchen. She appeared to be wearing little else but a sloppy joe jumper from which Tom noticed her legs flowed in a thoroughly disconcerting fashion.

Once she'd topped up her drink to the brim and given Tom his, Tom decided a direct approach was required.

'So Ms Whiting. Do you usually get in such a state every Friday night? I don't know; you young people!' Tom said in mock disapproval.

'I have no idea what you're talking about,' said Chloe. 'But you have got the cutest eyes you know.'

'Whoever he is, he ain't worth it, Chloe. You do know that don't you?'

'Lessons in love from a serial adulterer. Why thank you, Mr Bradshott.'

'A trifle harsh perhaps, but let's get back to you and this arse, who let you slip through his fingers.'

'Oh well, he's certainly slipped his fingers through me a few times,' said Chloe colliding with a lava lamp that was doing its best to avoid her.

'So, are you going to tell me about it or what?'

She plonked herself on the sofa next to him resting her legs across his lap.

'Absolutely. Just fill up my glass will you and I'll tell all.'

Tom did as he was told.

'Once upon a time there was a beautiful princess, or so her daddy told her, who fell in and out of love with every musician, troubadour and poet she came across. She found a well-played riff or a passionately delivered stanza irresistible. They came and went and she continued serenely on her happy, carefree way. Then he came along, neither a poet nor a musician, but her landlord. Yes! It was Mr Upstairs.'

'What do you mean? This is his house?' queried Tom.

'It is.'

'What does he do, this Lothario?' asked Tom.

'He's an undersecretary at the treasury, or perhaps, he's under his secretary at the treasury and that's why he's dumped me. My glass is empty by the way,' said Chloe. Her jumper was riding up revealing more of what Tom couldn't have failed to notice were exemplary thighs.

'Married?'

'No. I'm an old spinster.'

'Not you, you idiot, this boyfriend of yours.'

'Ex-boyfriend; haven't you been listening? Yes, as a matter of fact he's very married.'

'Oh, you poor girl. You don't have much luck and you really are such a sweetie.'

'You're not such a bad sort yourself,' said Chloe.

At this point, Tom became very aware that Chloe's left foot was making playful progress up his right leg towards his groin.

CHAPTER 31

Professor Schiller looked around the breakfast area of the hotel to gauge the reaction of other hotel guests to his new wife's arrival. She once again was not dressed for November in England, wearing a thin somewhat see-through silky low halter top over a brown leather mini skirt.

He had already tucked into his muesli, while she was eyeing up most of the items available, to make up one's own full English.

As she bent seductively over the poached eggs, several of the women did little to disguise their disapproval, looking up and down from their fat free yoghurts, shaking their heads and pursing their lips. Some of their husbands, however, could not avoid an admiring glance, wondering why breakfasts could not always be like this.

The professor, in his mischievous way, enjoyed both reactions as he stood to help his wife into her chair.

'I'm famished,' said his wife.

'So, I can see, my dear,' said the professor.

'Still, I never seem to put the weight on. Must be my metabolism,' she said, wiping the best part of a sausage from her lip.

'We have plenty of time, *liebling*, but I was just wondering how you planned to spend your day.'

'Well, I thought I might go up west this morning, have a bite and then take in a matinee this afternoon.'

'Excellent. Then we can meet, when I've finished the film shoot.'

'There's just something I must do this morning.'

'And what is that, my dearest?'

'Have a word with that Tom Bradshott.'

'Oh, what would that be about, my love?'

'Well, I had one of my dreams last night.'

As Tom tried to get some feeling back in his legs, after a night with very little sleep, he began to examine his decisions of the previous evening that led him to spend such an uncomfortable six hours, alone, under a car rug, in the back seat of his car. Chloe, who he'd lusted over for the last few weeks, seemed more than amenable, in an admittedly drunken way, to a night of unbridled 'getting over the ex' passion, which – damn it – he'd forgone.

His reasons for this were not, he knew, due regard for Chloe's inebriated state or failure of arousal. He was certainly physically up for it. Nor was it from fear of her ex arriving from upstairs and running Tom through with one of Her Majesty's government paper knives. It was something else, a kind of loneliness that he knew no amount of cavorting with the luscious Chloe would cure. In fact, it would only make it worse; for the first time in his adult life, Tom was genuinely afraid. For some reason he could not get Ingrid and Freddy out of his mind. It was haunting him in a way he could not get his head round. They were, after all, only distantly related to him and their story was only one of thousands of Nazi persecutions.

* * * * *

Tom pulled up outside Professor and Mrs Schiller's hotel and having shoe-horned the professor into the back of the Jensen, offered to drop Lorraine Schiller of in Oxford Street.

'Thanks, Tom. Actually, I wonder whether you could spare me half an hour this evening.'

Tom felt foolish, but he turned to the professor to seek his approval.

'Don't worry, it's fine by me,' said Schiller. You mustn't be over alarmed by anything she says, Tom, but nor must you totally dismiss it either.'

'Okay it's a date then,' said Tom.

'Shouldn't I be in make-up by now?' chuckled the professor.

At the studios, Callum was busy making teas and coffees for all. He was feeling pretty chipper; his partner, Oliver, had been offered a job as a buyer for one of the top fashion houses in London. This would mean their dream of having a place in the country, as well as their flat in town, might become a reality and it also meant that his ambition to become an independent film maker in the mould of his heroes, Michael Moore and Ken Loach, might be moving a little closer. Chloe had arrived looking a little pale and had retired to the ladies to 'do' her face. Tom and Professor Schiller had just arrived. Tom was swinging his arms to and thro to keep warm; the frost had been so severe that it had even whitened the pavements of the busy London street outside.

'Callum, can I introduce you to Professor Schiller.'

'Hello, Professor! Thanks so much for coming over to help us out.'

'Not at all; I have found Tom's family's story quite fascinating.'

'Well I suggest you and Tom relax while we do a few sound checks etcetera.'

The two men took Callum up on his suggestion and settled into two cavernous, leather armchairs.

'So, Professor, you said you had some new information for me. Sounds intriguing,' said Tom.

'Well, it may be something and nothing, but I found a further file concerning the activities of the SS and medical staff from the T4 project.'

'Does it confirm our fears about Ingrid and Freddy?' asked Tom.

'No, but it concerns Oberscharfuhrer Von Geysell and Dr Albrecht.'

'So, it may still have a bearing?'

'The document I found was from after the war; compiled by the newly formed War Crimes Commission.'

'Please go on.'

'Prior to the outbreak of war, Von Geysell appears to have been linked with many of the excesses of the Reich in Berlin, including the rounding up of those suspected of having any mixed Jewish heritage. A little ironic as things turned out, but I digress. Pieter Von Geysell also worked alongside members of the Gestapo investigating anyone suspected of homosexual activity. If proven, or just suspected, they were sent to labour camps or worse. Gay men were seen as indicating weakness in the gene pool and useless in terms of increasing the Aryan "master race."'

'Von Geysell was the man to sort out the logistics of transporting the hapless victims to their fate, whether that be a special clinic or a concentration camp.'

'Bastard,' said Tom.

'Yes, but the War Crimes Commission, given the bigger fish they were after, saw Von Geysell as a comparatively low-level bastard. They went about interviewing various personnel from the clinic, including Dr Albrecht, according to the report. Albrecht appeared very anxious and evasive while generally protesting that no programme of killing went on in any of the clinics where he worked; he claimed they were purely centres for therapy and research. The Commission was unconvinced, but at this stage decided not to hold Albrecht. However, as their investigations progressed, it became clear that Albrecht was implicated in the killings.'

'So, presumably they took him into custody?'

'Well here's the curious thing. When eventually they went to his apartment to arrest him, Albrecht had vanished.'

Callum skipped over unable to keep the smile off his face; today was a good day.

'Okay, Professor, we are ready for you now.'

CHAPTER 32

The first draft of *Parenting: It's Child's Play* was finally finished and Bonnie had poured herself a large glass of sauvignon blanc. Evie sat at the kitchen table, busy with a colouring book.

'Mummy.'

'Yes, honey.'

'You know when I get married?'

'Er, yes honey.'

'If Daddy is away, you can borrow my husband.'

'Gee thanks, Evie.'

'That's okay.'

Bonnie was mulling over a call she had received from her mother-in-law, Phyllis. Their relationship had never been easy; Phyllis's disappointment with her son was completed by his choice for a wife. Tom had been practically engaged to a lovely girl, Pippa Hobson-Hicks, whose father was a banker and whose mother was from an eminently acceptable Hampshire family with connections to Highclere Castle. Pippa had been educated at Westonbirt and in Switzerland, spoke fluent French, Italian and Spanish and had, very sensibly, chosen not to go to university, instead landing a plum job as a nanny, for one of the – admittedly minor – royals. Then what does her idiot son do? Goes off with some trashy American girl. Phyllis conceded that Bonnie had looks on her side but she was of the opinion that looks fade in a way that breeding never does.

Phyllis had rung Bonnie with a proposal. Tom had told her of the possibility that Bonnie and Evie were going to the States. Phyllis felt this to be an excellent solution to a marriage that had always been heading for the rocks.

In order to facilitate this arrangement, Phyllis was prepared to offer financial assistance in the form of a one off payment into Bonnie's account of ten thousand pounds in two years' time, on condition that Bonnie and Evie continued to reside in the States.

The two women's telephone conversation had not ended well.

Bonnie had declined the offer by saying that her book was about to be published and Phyllis should read it sometime. She therefore had no need of Phyllis's money and even if she had, she would prefer to go whoring around Waterloo station than take money from a twisted, embittered, old woman, who had raised a feckless, philanderer, always searching for the affection Phyllis never deigned to provide.

* * * * *

During a break in the filming, in the time-honoured way, Chloe and Tom gravitated to the water cooler. Neither knew quite what to say; there were a few half-hearted exchanges about the harshness of the frost last night and then Tom cut to the chase.

'So, are you okay?'

'I'm knackered. Listen, I'm sorry about last night. I think I may have got my 'sad' and my 'horny' mixed up. After you buggered off, I made myself a cafetière of coffee and started itemising carefully everything in that suitcase of your grandfather's.'

'Anything interesting turn up that we hadn't seen?'

'I would have thought you'd have had a good rummage yourself.'

'No; it kind of felt odd. So, no I didn't.'

'Well no, there were no surprises really.'

'I'm glad you're okay. You are better off without him, you know.'

'Well funny you should say that; the mister was on my doorstep at seven forty-five this morning, with a huge bouquet and chocolates, saying what a fool he'd been.'

'Don't tell me he'd come to borrow some paper clips for his office in the treasury.'

'We women are generally better at this forgiveness thing than you men are.'

'Oh, is that right and how do you make that out?'

'Well you see, we have more practice than you lot do,' said Chloe smiling sweetly.

* * * * *

'Professor Schiller, you were brill! A natural, thank you so much,' said Callum.

'It was nothing and do you know, I quite enjoyed it,' the professor replied.

Callum was lying. It was one of the rules of making documentaries and the like, that the most extrovert, verbally dextrous member of 'Joe public' placed in front of a camera at once assumes the personae of a jelly fish and has difficulty in getting past 'er' and 'um' in their range of vocabulary; so it was with the good professor. When Schiller had popped to the gents, Callum confessed.

'There's about ninety seconds of usable material and that's if we have an editor with the skill of a neurosurgeon and the eye of David Bailey.'

'Oh dear, he must never know; he would be devastated,' said Chloe.

'Oh, I wouldn't worry. They won't show this in Germany. If we ever get the bloody thing finished,' explained Callum.

'That popular, am I?' said Tom. 'Right, Professor, let's reunite you with your beautiful wife.'

'Well, goodbye, all, if ever you are in Berlin, do look up me,' said the professor in a rare blemish of his colloquial English.

Tom tried not to giggle as he ushered Schiller out of the studios

'Okay, let's knock it on the head for the day,' said Callum.

'Oh, there's one other thing,' chipped in Chloe. 'I managed to get the coroner's report from that fatal plane crash Tom's grandfather was involved in. What with one thing and another, I haven't had a chance to look at it myself yet.'

CHAPTER 33

After the discomfort of the previous night, Tom had treated himself to one of London's top hotels. The manager was an old friend and had given him a good deal at very short notice. Apart from the leather suitcase, the other thing Tom had picked up from his mother's yesterday was a packet that had arrived for him from America. While he regrouped in his room, before his rendezvous with Lorraine Schiller, he opened the package. It contained a CD and a note from Kat.

Dearest Tom,

I still think of you a lot, but not now in terms of us, but in terms of you. I feel a terrible sense of guilt that I have caused your marriage to Bonnie irreparable harm. It was cruel and selfish of me. I am afraid I have always been drawn to those ripe for corruption, although with old Prairie Dog, I was about forty years too late, but you I had to pluck (no pun intended). The strange thing with Prairie Dog is although he never heeded his own advice, he was a wise old critter. That's why I've sent you his final CD. Please listen to the last verse. I've copied it out for you because I know what you're like about what you call Country and Western.

I find myself at the last bend in the creek
My eyes are weak and my voice is hoarse
I've been through the white rapids
And where the river flows slow.
I must return to the first bend
And seek my love at her source.

This was all too elliptical for Tom. He tossed Kat's note on the dressing table and then remembered that he hadn't eaten anything all day. The hotel had a reputation for fine food but there was no time to eat before his date with Mrs Schiller. What on earth that was going to be about, he had no idea. They had arranged to meet at Hannigan's bar in Soho; it had been her suggestion. Though God alone knew why; it had been the haunt of many of London's underworld and was reputed to be where Reggie Kray had once threatened to use a member of the Richardson's gang's head as a dartboard for the evening. Whatever it was that Lorraine wanted to impart was intriguing him. Tom wanted to get an early night as the meeting regarding Evie was at 2pm the following day at the social services offices in Berkshire. There was also the question of what kind of reception he was going to get from Bonnie. Perhaps he should have accepted her invitation to go down tonight; he was certainly tempted, but he'd felt a distinct chill from her email and had responded equally formally.

Right on cue, a Dickensian fog had descended on London as Tom made his way to Hannigan's bar. His step quickened because he had the vaguest impression that he was being followed. Could it be that the professor, consumed with jealousy, was on his tail? Perhaps he had got wind of Tom's reputation. Or perhaps Bonnie had stooped to employing a detective agency to track her errant husband? The thought that he was being 'papped' by a freelance photographer failed to occur to him.

As he hurried down streets that he had been familiar with twenty years ago when working in various restaurants around Leicester Square, Tom became aware that Soho had changed quite considerably. It was no longer dirty mac territory, inhabited mainly by male punters. Now, young couples walked up and down the street popping in and out of the 'Private' shops as if they were buying their weekly groceries. While gentlemen's clubs were offering 'Playfulness' and Very Strictly Come Dancing classes. Posters advertised Tantric Experiences, full of Eastern Promise. Such experiences were more likely to involve a Crouch End maisonette rather than an aromatic Bazaar in Samarkand.

The establishments were still guarded by enormous men, but there were changes here too. These giants were not as they were when Tom had known the place in the early nineties, all brawn with slow eyes and quick tempers. Now, they seemed another species; not flesh and blood, but pressurised balloon people, so full of steroids, they looked as if at any moment they might explode, filling the night sky with tattooed detritus and expensive hair gel.

Hannigan's bar was somewhere that remained much as it always had over the last century or so with blackened, wood panelling, boxing memorabilia on the walls and tall dark stained settles near the door, which all gave the place a sense of age. The establishment was on three floors with various small fusty rooms where Tom imagined many a shady deal had been struck. He found a seat near the entrance so he could rendezvous with Lorraine as soon as she came in. Tom couldn't help feeling this was not a place where a single woman should be left unchaperoned for long. The landlord was a tall, middle-aged man in a shabby cardigan and comb-over hair à la Bobby Charlton. He had a world-weary expression and a hacking winter cough. The only other people in the pub were two youngish men in zip-up fleeces and baseball hats, which appeared at least two sizes too big for their heads; they were drinking cheap German lager from the bottle. Somewhere at the back of the pub a dog howled balefully. Another young man in a hoody and bobble hat came in and went up to one of the shadowy cubicles on the first floor.

After ten minutes, Lorraine Schiller appeared at the door in a full length sable fur coat and Russian bearskin hat. She looked for all the world like an extra from the set of *Dr Zhivago*.

'Well look what the cat dragged in!' said the laconic publican.

'Hello, laughing boy, long time no see,' said Lorraine.

'I thought you was in Germany, Lol.'

'Flying visit, sweetheart.'

'Oh hello, Tom! I didn't see you there.'

'Mrs Schiller, now I hear?' said the landlord.

'Yes, that's right. I finally got someone to make an honest woman of me.'

132

'What can I get you, on the house?'

'I tell you what. I will have a port and lemon, for old time's sake.'

'So, you've been in Hannigan's before,' said Tom, stating the obvious.

'It's Lorraine, by the way. Yes, this was one of my haunts when I was on the cabaret circuit, wasn't it, Moray? Sorry, Tom Bradshott, meet Moray Sykes.'

'Pleased to meet you, Moray,' said Tom holding out his hand.

'Likewise,' said Moray shaking Tom's hand, then quickly wiping his own with a bar cloth.

'So, Lol, where did you meet this sugar daddy of yours?'

'Otto met my eyes over a crowded beer tent at the Oktober Fest in Munich,' explained Lorraine.

'What took you to Munich?' asked Moray.

'A singing job. Do you remember Heidi the au pair? Well she had a group of Kellar singers and one of them fell pregnant and dropped out, so she gave me a call.'

While Lorraine and Moray caught up, Tom became increasingly aware that the two young men at the other end of the bar were taking an interest. They had heard the name Tom Bradshott and had been chuntering on for some time.

It was obvious that they had been on a marathon drinking session as neither seemed capable of sitting on their bar stools. They kept slipping off and holding onto each other for support. After a bit more sniggering, the man nearest to Tom turned round and called across the bar.

'Alright, Tommy boy, who's this, your latest slag?'

Tom studiously ignored the remark, not wanting a repeat of the chip shop debacle.

'Hot and tasty I bet,' said the other man.

'A right fucking bike by the look of it,' interjected his chum.

'Alright you two mind your Ps and Qs,' said Moray sternly.

Tom had, despite his best intentions, decided on direct action and marched towards the two men.

'It's alright, Tom, really,' said Lorraine taking him by the arm and pulling him back. Unfortunately, this emboldened the nearest drunk who landed a blow to the bridge of Tom's nose. At this point, Moray went to the back of the bar and unlatched the door to his living quarters, where upon two of the largest Rottweilers Tom had ever clapped eyes on entered the fray and his assailant and his companion fell over each other repeatedly in their efforts to make a smart exit from the bar, followed closely by the young man from the first floor, who stopped, smiled and gave Tom the thumbs up. It was only then that Tom noticed the man had an expensive looking camera hung round his neck.

After a couple of large whiskies, Tom began to feel a little better.

'I'm really sorry, Tom. Are you okay?' said Lorraine.

'Why? It's not your fault. I really don't know what's happening to this country; it's going to the dogs. Oh thanks, Moray. Your hounds were magnificent, by the way,' said Tom.

'Soft as butter, they are really. Killer, Fang — here, boys.' The two dogs lolloped back in, pleased with their evening's work.

'Oh God! Look at the time,' said Tom. 'I'm sorry to rush you, Lorraine, but I have a big day tomorrow. What was it you wanted a word about?'

'The thing is, Tom, I have certain gifts which manifest themselves in dreams or premonitions, if you like.'

'Gosh, Lorraine, I'm really sorry but I don't really buy into any of this.'

'Well let me just tell you what the dream was and then you can make whatever you will of it. I dreamt you were walking through a kind of maze made out of swastikas, taking the wrong turn all the time. Then this deep voice, you know like that Morgan Freeman, says you'll find what your searching for, but not where you expect. The next thing I see is you stepping out of the maze holding a little child's hand.'

'Was it a boy or a girl?' asked a sceptical Tom.

'I couldn't be sure; it all went fuzzy. Here, Moray, get us another of those port and lemons.'

'Ah there you are.' It was the professor. 'I see you've been having fun,' he said, surveying the upturned bar stools and Tom holding a bag of frozen peas, provided by Moray, across his battered and bruised nose.

CHAPTER 34

'Well good morning everybody and thank you for coming and apologies for the short notice. My name's Rhian Morgan Powell and I am Senior Prac. with the Children's Disability Team, this is Nikki Hooper from the SCAMP team and most of you will know Mr Parks, Evie's headmaster.'

Tom Bradshott's head, which was already tender, began to spin. Bonnie was sitting opposite him, barely able to hide her fury. Not only had Tom turned up late but he was sporting a very obvious black eye and possible broken nose.

'So, for those unfamiliar with the concept of person-centred planning, it is based on the premise of placing the person at the centre of any decisions that are made about their life.'

'Sorry, I have a question,' queried Bonnie. 'If that's so, why was Evie not allowed to come to the meeting?'

'I assure you, Mrs Bradshott, it was not a case of not being allowed; she was uninvited, in part because of the challenging nature of some of her issues. It was felt that the meeting might be distressing to her.'

Now it was not just Tom's head that was spinning but the whole room. He attempted to pull himself together.

'Well, first of all, since I've yet to be introduced, I am Tom Bradshott and secondly can we rewind a little here? May I ask Nikki what exactly the SCAMP team does?'

'So,' said Nikki Hooper. Which got her off to a bad start already. Tom hated the current fashion of starting every explanation with 'So.' Nikki couldn't have been twenty-five, if she was a day. An enormous pair of dark glasses perched on her expensively coiffured hair, she was dressed in a well-tailored, tight, herring-bone pattern skirt and blue blouse, with a necklace made up of golf ball size grey beads. As she talked, she paused to dig a desultory fork into her kiwi fruit and lychee salad.

'So, SCAMP, or to give it its full title, Signalled Children's Anger Management Pod, does exactly what it says on the tin,' said Nikki, rather unhelpfully, thought Tom.

'I hope you were able to sort out childcare for today's meeting without too much difficulty?'

'Oh yes; it wasn't a problem.'

Bonnie had left Evie with Gerard for the afternoon doing patchwork collages, neither of them aware that what they were cutting up, were some of Tom's favourite shirts. It was not in Bonnie's nature to be vindictive, but when she got the call to say he was running late, she couldn't resist getting a little revenge.

'So, shall we start? Our first topic is "what we like about Evie". Mr Parks, could we have your input?'

Mr Parks gave his input; it didn't take long.

*****

Chloe Whiting read the coroner's report from the fatal plane crash in which Sir George aka Gunther had been piloting his own plane.

Date: June 1969
Type of aeroplane: Piper P.A. Navajo
Number of occupants: 2
Weather conditions: Fair
The name of deceased: Surname Brecht
Christian name: Gustav
Cause of death: Multiple fractures/shock/heart failure
Verdict: Open

Her next avenue of research would be local papers, printed in the vicinity of where the crash had occurred, near Selby in North Yorkshire. There was very little coverage in the national papers at the time, given that Sir George was already quite a high-profile figure. Callum had thought that the 'cat with nine lives' aspect of Tom's grandfather's life might be the hook on which to hang the programme, the fact that he fought on the wrong side in both World Wars didn't seem to matter in 2016, which was overall a year of shifting political alliances.

'Nice one, Chloe,' said Callum encouragingly. 'See if there's anything else you can dig up from the local press, a picture of the lucky survivor, alongside his bashed-up plane would be good. Remember, we've still got gaps to plug.'

'Okay, boss,' said Chloe. 'By the way, have you started house hunting yet?'

'No, not yet. I'm not sure Oliver is so keen on a country retreat. Whenever we get west of Richmond Park, he says all he can smell is the muck spreader and I caught him looking in the paper at houses in Finsbury Park the other day; hardly the bucolic idyll, darling.'

CHAPTER 35

Back in Berkshire, the multi-agency network person-centred planning meeting had turned into a marathon; everyone had been given a piece of flip chart paper and told they must fill it with words that describe Evie. Tom was not up to this, a fact that the chair of the meeting, Rhian, hadn't failed to notice.

'Are you sure you are quite well, Mr Bradshott? Your face looks very swollen to me?' enquired Rhian Morgan Powell.

'It's nothing,' said Tom. 'I have a mild, allergic reaction to felt tip pen, that's all.'

Bonnie gave him a withering look and handed in her sheet of paper on which she'd written, 'ADORABLE' two hundred and fifty times. Mr Parks looked at his watch and Nikki Hooper of the aforementioned SCAMP team was updating her electronic diary.

'Well, I hope we all enjoyed that,' said Rhian. 'Moving on to more sensitive areas, I hope you will understand, Mr. and Mrs Bradshott, that although our priority must be Evie, at this stage of any suggested intervention your views our vital. Can I ask you both what you know about Cromer?'

'Is that another acronym?'

'No, Mr Bradshott, it's a town in Norfolk.'

'We want to put an option on the table,' explained Nikki.

'Yes; it's in the light of several incidents where we feel Evie's and others' safety may – and I mean may – have been put at risk,' said Rhian.

'May I ask what you mean by that?' snapped Bonnie.

'We received a call from a concerned member of the public regarding an RTA in which they were suggesting Evie was involved.'

'What kind of accident and where exactly was it?' asked Tom.

'Outside Evie's home address.'

'The caller said they had witnessed Evie alone at the steering wheel of a vehicle in collision with another vehicle,' explained Rhian.

'And there was no sign of a responsible adult at the scene,' said Nikki looking up from her mobile phone.

'Excuse me, but have you somewhere else to be, because you appear more interested in your emails than my daughter's welfare,' said Bonnie.

'My apologies, Mrs Bradshott, but I need to be in contact with my pod at all times,' said Nikki.

'Could we get back to the matter in hand?' pleaded Rhian.

'From the school's point of view, of course, there is the matter of Evie's disciplinary record,' said Mr Parks.

'And, of course, what some may see as an abdication of parental responsibility,' added Nikki.

'I beg your pardon?' said Bonnie.

'Placing a vulnerable child under the care of an unvetted adult,' explained Nikki.

'I've lost you now,' said Tom.

'The caller, who I can reveal rang in on several occasions reported Evie being regularly in the sole care of a Mr Gerard Casey. Now from our records, we have no registered qualified childminder under that name,' explained Rhian.

* * * * *

Barry Goldwing was nothing if not decisive and the pulling of the episode of *Family Matters* was one of his easier decisions. It was, after all, by definition a family show. The picture in the showbiz page of *The Sun* showing Tom leaving Hannigan's bar with a bright shiny black eye and a brassy blond on his arm and the accompanying headline 'BRADSHOTT CAUGHT BRAWLING AGAIN' sealed the deal. In Goldwing's mind, it also called into doubt the whole idea of using Tom to host his programme on the eccentricities of the British States-side. Stephen Fry might be more expensive, but he'd be a safer pair of hands.

He called Callum to give him his decision regarding *Family Matters*.

'But we are almost there with it, Barry.'

'I'm afraid this Bradshott guy is finished. Now, if he'd been a professional footballer or a politician for that matter, but Joe public don't like to see their chefs brawling and carousing. The papers have got his number now and they are not going to let go. I'm sorry, Callum, but my decision is final.'

* * * * *

'Cromer Residential Community College offers a complete educational and Social Orientation Experience,' explained Rhian. 'And we feel Evie would be ideally suited to such an approach,' said Rhian, who felt Evie's person-centred planning meeting was moving towards a satisfactory conclusion.

'So your plan is to send my daughter nearly two hundred miles away to some dead-end seaside town and incarcerate her for what remains of her childhood,' said Bonnie.

'Over our dead bodies,' said Tom. 'Evie will continue her education locally. Her mother and I will place both our careers on hold to continue to ensure she has a full and normal life experience and we will fight you all the way in the courts if you and your inattentive colleagues attempt to deprive us of a proper family life,' said Tom.

Bonnie was almost as startled as the rest of the attendees at the meeting by her husband's intervention.

'Well thank you for speaking so frankly. I suggest we reconvene in a week to give us all a cooling off period and a time for considered reflection,' said Rhian, seeing that she might have met her match.

Perhaps all this officialdom and red tape around Evie was what Loraine Schiller had seen in her dream. Perhaps Tom was leading Evie out of a maze by the hand.

CHAPTER 36

'You know sometimes, I feel like packing it in,' said Callum.

'Oh, come on, you love what you do,' said Chloe.

'Sorry I just feel so shitty today; Oli and I had two friends over to dinner last night – Rick and Tony. We had a fab evening. They are making the move out to the sticks; they've bought a small holding near Sittingbourne. Well anyway, we got a call this morning; apparently at the end of the evening, they got out of their minicab and were attacked by a gang of about five teenage, yes teenage, kids. Rick had his mobile phone pinched and Tony got a nasty kicking for trying to stop them. They said that they should be honoured as they'd been done by Queer Bashers Anonymous.'

'Oh God! What is this country coming to? I'm so sorry Callum,' said Chloe.

'Well let's hope they fare a little better in Sittingbourne, but I tell you what, it really shook us up.'

They were sat in Starbuck's across the street from the studio of Janus Films. It was full of other media types, working on their laptops and a gaggle of schoolgirls shrieking at each other like a colony of over excited seabirds.

'And now the show's been pulled. I ask you! After all the work we've all done, the research, the trips to Germany in the bloody, freezing cold, all a waste of time.'

'I don't think it's been a waste of time. I've learned more about what utter bastards the Nazis were, how the Berlin Wall destroyed lives and that drinking too much wine and eating chocolate bars doesn't in fact make me totally irresistible to men,' said Chloe.

'Come on, give me all the gruesome details,' said Callum, pulling up his chair in the way his mother did, when the wrestling came on the telly.

The gang of girls poured out into the street and the sound level dropped by about a hundred decibels.

'A girl has to have her secrets you know,' said Chloe.

A woman in the window seat gave Chloe an old fashioned look and the waitress closed the door firmly to keep the cold out and dissuade the schoolgirls, who were jumping up and down on the bench in the bus shelter outside, from coming back in. For this, she received an impromptu round of applause from all those working on their laptops.

'Anyway, I suppose we are the ones who are going to have to tell Tom that the show's been pulled. I know he was hoping that this was going to raise his profile.'

'I think his profile's pretty high at the moment anyway,' said Callum showing Chloe the picture of Tom in Hannigan's bar from the day's edition of *The Sun*.

'I will do it; I need to return the suitcase anyway. I will run it down tomorrow.'

'A little birdy told me he's staying at his mother's at the moment.'

'Oh why's that?'

'Apparently, she's not very well, but I think the real reason is that Bonnie has called time on all his philandering.'

Chloe turned a delicate shade of pink.

'Oh, I'm sure it will all sort itself out.'

'You know he'd been bonking his ex-agent Kat Kawalski, before she scampered off to the States.'

'Well you are a little mine of information,' said Chloe.

'And she is an ex of the late lamented Prairie Dog.'

'God, I loved some of his early stuff. What was that album called, *Cactus Nights*.'

'Well I'm not one to speak ill of the dead, but to me he always sounded like a kitchen waste disposal unit in meltdown.'

'More of an Inglenook Fumbledick fan are you?'

'Here, I could fire you for that, sexual stereo typing, if ever I heard it.'

'So, tell me more about this Kat woman.'

'Well, according to my sources, she was left a fortune in Prairie Dog's will, much to the chagrin of all his ex-wives and girlfriends.'

'So poor old Tom. His wife kicks him out; his hot mistress is now a rich hot ex-mistress and his TV career is on the skids,' said Chloe.

'Just about covers it, but in addition, he's staying with his mother. You saw her in the rushes for the show. She makes Joan Crawford look like Mother Teresa; I found her adorable by the way.'

'That seals it. I'll drive down this afternoon, drop the suitcase off, give Tom the bad news about the show and hopefully get a glimpse of this medusa of whom you speak.'

One of the more raucous of the schoolgirls from earlier came back into the coffee shop. Her demeanour was much changed, as she was dragging in behind her a bemused, spotty-faced youth, much as a female sabre tooth tiger might do with an unfortunate gnu en route to her cave. The only sound to be heard from the girl was a kind of quiet purring.

Chloe and Callum started to giggle in a very juvenile way and decided it was time to make a move.

CHAPTER 37

'So that went well,' said Tom.

'Misplaced irony, Tom, given that your black eye seriously undermined that passionate speech you made right at the end,' retorted Bonnie.

'Do you want to grab a bite to eat, or a coffee?' asked Tom.

'I need to catch my train.'

'What happened to the car?'

'Well, you heard them talking about it in there. It was a minor shunt, but hard to take for my little old Citroen. Us old girls get a bit fragile you know.'

'Look let me give you a lift,' said Tom.

'I'm not sure that's a good idea,' Bonnie replied.

'We need to talk and I'm really running short on shirts.'

Bonnie had a vision of what was happening to Tom's shirts, probably right at that moment.

'Okay let's go and grab a coffee, I can always send the shirts on to your mother's,' suggested Bonnie.

'Whatever you say,' said Tom.

'Tom, there's something I need to tell you,' said Bonnie.

'Sounds ominous.'

'It's about your mother.'

'What's she said now?'

'She's made me an offer, a financial offer.'

'What kind of an offer?'

'If I take Evie to the States, for at least the next two years, she'll pay me ten thousand pounds.'

'She'll what!' said Tom.

'Help us all have a new start apparently,' Bonnie continued, 'I turned her down.'

'Christ the woman is pure evil,' said Tom, shaking with anger.

'Tom, I'm sorry. I know you're going through a tough time. But I just thought you had a right to know.'

'Listen, can we talk again another time? There is something I need to do.'

'Tom, for God's sake, she's not going to change now and you know she'll probably deny the whole thing.'

But it was too late, the red mist descended over Tom as he made his way to the car park, tears stinging his bruised and reddened cheeks.

* * * * *

Otto and Lorraine Schiller had extended their trip to England on the grounds that they had not managed to have a proper honeymoon yet. Otto had been in touch with Monika at the Bundersarchive and asked her to hold the fort. She had been busy, but still found time to email him with more background to the Rohmer case.

They had booked into a health spa, as Lorraine had decided Otto needed to lose some weight. After a short courtship, she didn't want a short marriage as well and the colour black was not a good look for her.

'So Otto, you cunning old devil! How did you know I was going to meet Tom at Hannigan's the other night? I deliberately didn't tell you because I wanted to see him alone.'

They were in bed, enjoying a post coital cup of tea, watching news of President Elect Trump appointing his team.

'When will the world ever learn? It's like a form of mass short term memory loss!' said Schiller.

'You haven't answered my question.'

'Does it matter?'

'Yes, it does. I'm the one with the psychic powers.'

'I looked at the email you sent him.'

'But you don't know my password.'

'Some of the qualities you need to have to be one of the top archivists in Europe is good observational skills and attention to detail. I watched you entering your password the other day and made a note of it.'

'Otto, if this marriage is going to work, you're going to have to trust me.'

'I do trust you, my dear, but when marrying a beautiful woman, a man should take out a little insurance to protect his assets, don't you think,' explained the professor.

'Put that cup down and come here and give us a kiss, you daft old bugger,' said Lorraine.

Lorraine Gittings had had her first 'dream' aged eleven, when staying with her Aunty Vi. She had been unable to travel with her mum and dad to Marbella, as she had contracted chickenpox and one of the worst cases their family doctor had ever seen. Her mum had said her back had looked like an overdone Welsh rarebit. Her dad added with all those scabs in her hair, she could have been that kid from the *Exorcist*. Anyway, Aunty Vi had stepped into the breach.

Aunty Vi's house had remained much as it was when she and Uncle Monty had bought it. A vision in red whirling circle wallpaper, room dividers with strategically placed bits of Troika ceramics and various rather sickly houseplants. Monty had been a travel agent and one day in the long hot summer of 1976, had taken advantage of a generous thirty percent staff discount to buy a one way ticket to Kos, where he took over a taverna and took up with Lexie, a local girl ten years his junior.

Vi was distraught and wouldn't leave the house for three months living of Valium, Hirondelle wine and Findus crispy pancakes. She snapped out of her depression almost as suddenly as it had begun, after being persuaded to attend an Encounter Group and discovered what she called 'The real me'. Since then, she'd given up almost everything and devoted herself to a string of worthy causes. Lorraine adored Vi, but she adored Vi's wardrobe full of clothes even more, spending her time donning

Vi's cast-offs from the sixties and seventies. There was the aquamarine kaftan that buttoned up the front and the blanket material poncho à la Clint Eastwood, not to forget the green, felt floppy hat and reefer jacket.

It was the night before her parents were due to return from Marbella and Lorraine had found it difficult to sleep, when she dreamt that her father was walking towards her with his head on fire.' When she told her aunty in the morning, Vi said it was probably the 'special' mushrooms, which she'd added to the ratatouille they'd had for supper the night before. The next day, she learnt that her father had had a stroke on the flight home and was now in intensive care. Although he made a partial recovery, he was unable to speak for the rest of his life.

* * * * *

Chloe arrived at Pink Cottage, Phyllis Bradshott's house, just as two of the ladies from Downstairs Downstairs Domestic Agency were leaving.

'Hello there,' said Chloe.

'Evening,' said the older of the two women.

'Am I right? Mrs Bradshott lives here doesn't she?'

'That's right, dear.'

'Is now a good time to call, do you think? I understand she hasn't been very well.'

'Oh, I think you'll find her fighting fit dear,' said the other woman, with a hunted look in her eye. She had good cause to be wary of Phyllis, who was in the habit of following her around the house, checking to see that each wastepaper bin had been emptied to her satisfaction and every ornament dusted with due diligence. If things were not up to scratch, she would arraign the offender with comments such as, 'I don't know in which particular farmyard you spent your formative years but here we like scrubbed to mean scrubbed, polished to mean polished and beds to be of the made variety, which does not mean just tossing the duvet down as St Peter might have done a net on the sea of Galilee.'

Chloe knocked the door in trepidation with the suitcase in hand.

'Hello, Mrs Bradshott. I'm part of the team that's been making the programme *Family Matters* with your son, Tom.'

'Oh yes, come in come in, my dear, a little late for tea. May I offer you a sherry?'

'Oh, thank you, but I'm driving.'

'Oh, I know! I have just the thing; some elderflower cordial.'

'Sounds delicious, thank you.'

'Right I'll pop and get it and then you must give me all the details. Have you got a transmission date yet?'

'No not exactly,' said Chloe hesitantly.

After couple of minutes Phyllis returned with the cordial.

'I did enjoy that bit of filming. I haven't had so much fun since I played the Maid of Orleans in the school play.'

'The main reason for coming was to return this suitcase to Tom.'

'Well I'm afraid, my dear, your guess is as good as mine as to my son's whereabouts,' said Phyllis. 'I only seem to find out when one of my domestics shows me some lurid picture, purporting to be Tom coming out of some low-life establishment in Soho. The trials of motherhood, my dear; they never truly grow up.'

'I expect he's shared all the stuff in the suitcase with you. After all, much of it belonged to your father,' said Chloe.

'Yes, from such a sad time. I prefer to remember happier times. He and I were like two peas in a pod you know.'

'How lovely, after all that happened.'

'So, my dear, our little film. When might we expect to see it? There will be people in the village, who wouldn't want to miss it.'

'Well actually, Mrs Bradshott, the thing is, it's not going to be shown.'

'Oh and why's that?'

'Well it's all come as a bit off a shock; the producers have scrapped the whole project.'

'I knew it; it's Tom's recent antics isn't it? Brawling in the street or in pubs. The trouble is, he's got no consideration, none at all,' said Phyllis.

'Well, we are really not sure of the whole story yet.'

'You don't have to shield me, dear. No one knows my son the way I do, wilful, headstrong and inconsiderate!'

'Look, I mustn't keep you, but I did want to ask you a little bit about Tom's father, if it's not too painful,' said Chloe.

'Not at all, dear. It all started at The Annual Totteridge Tennis Club Dance. My papa was away on business and my poor mother had taken to her bed. I was chaperoned, of course, by Poppy Benbow, an old friend of the family, whose husband had been a Desert Rat. No protection against dysentery, I'm afraid. Poppy had been a widow for many years; her looks let her down, poor darling. Where was I? Ah yes, Roger was staying with a friend and had been asked to step into the doubles team after one of the team turned his ankle. Anyway, Roger used to say he fell in love with me the moment he clapped eyes on me over the finger buffet. He waited until Poppy went off to 'do her face', which you can imagine, my dear, was a longish job and then seized his chance and led me onto the dance floor. The orchestra were playing 'Smoke gets in your eyes' and the rest, as they say, is history.'

'Oh, how romantic,' said Chloe.

Phyllis could feel herself becoming a little breathless and the heart palpitations she'd been having on and off for several weeks were growing a little stronger.

'Well it's good of you to come all this way, but I understand you'll want to get going. My late husband used to say driving at night is like taking over a company without seeing the books.'

CHAPTER 38

Bonnie's train was late and when she got back to the house, Evie and Gerard had both fallen asleep, Evie curled up on the sofa and Gerard snoring away in Tom's old armchair. On the kitchen table, the patchwork collage was coming on nicely, while on the floor were the remains of Tom's shirts. She trod softly so as not to wake the two sleeping beauties, picking up the cast-off bits of material. They began to evoke such memories for her that she realised the shirts were not just important to Tom.

Gerard began to stir.

'I'm so sorry; I must have dropped off there.'

'Evie too, by the looks of things.'

'Yes, I was reading her Oscar Wilde's *The Selfish Giant*. Must have sent myself to sleep as well. How did the meeting go?'

'Very, very, badly I think,' said Bonnie.

'Did your husband show up in the end?'

'Yes.'

'Good.'

'Not really; he'd been in a fight and I think he's gone off to murder his mother.'

'Well now, why would he want to be doing a thing like that?' asked Gerard.

'You haven't met his mother; otherwise you'd know,' explained Bonnie.

'Is Daddy really going to kill Granny?' said a newly awake Evie.

'Were you not listening to the story, Evie? The old selfish giant was in a real bad temper with his mother; he didn't kill her, but he made a dreadful smell and sent it to her in an airtight parcel the very next day,' explained Gerard.

'Oh wicked!' cooed Evie.

'Listen, thanks for everything,' said Bonnie. 'I don't know what I would have done without you. But now my book is with the publisher, I won't be needing Evie's favourite babysitter so much – though you know you're always welcome here.'

'I'm not a baby, Mummy!'

'Oh, right you are, I get the message,' said Gerard.

'Sorry that was clumsily put.'

'Look, Bonnie, Evie is the most important person by miles in all this.'

'Thank you.'

'No, thank you,' said Gerard. 'Now remember, Evie, next time the postman comes, hold your nose just in case.'

* * * * *

Tom passed Chloe in the lanes on his way to his mother's, but he was in too much of a temper to notice her despite her frantic waving. He, of course, was harder to miss in the Jensen.

'Oh! Look what the cat dragged in,' said his mother.

Tom said nothing; he went up to his room, collected his clothes, threw them in his holdall, then marched into the sitting room and took the wedding photo of himself and Bonnie from the mantelshelf.

'Oy! What do you think you're playing at?' said Phyllis, who was just pouring herself a large gin and tonic.

'This was a present to you, which I'm appropriating. You're to have nothing of ours to show off to the village worthies.'

'That knock on the head has sent you do-lally, Thomas. Sit down and I'll get you a drink, even though the doctor says I shouldn't have to deal with any more stress.'

'I know about the grubby little deal you tried to do with Bonnie and this is the finish, Mother, do you hear me, the finish!'

'I have no idea what on earth you are talking about.'

'God knows, since Dad died I've tried to make allowances. But whatever the reason, Mother, you are poison, pure poison.'

'I shall call the police if you don't stop shouting,' said Phyllis, her glass trembling in her hand.

'Don't worry; I am done. Oh and about your funeral arrangements, you'll have to find someone else, as I won't even be in attendance. It would be a bit hypocritical, I feel.'

'Just go will you and when you've had time to think, you'll see that whatever I may have done was for your benefit. Bonnie was never right for you and then poor little Evie came along. Too much responsibility for someone like you, Tom; you see if I'm not right.'

By this point, Tom had already gone. He threw the holdall in the boot of the car and laid the wedding photograph carefully on the back seat, swearing never to return.

* * * * *

Tom had no idea where to go. He'd been so incensed by his mother, he hadn't made a plan. He phoned Bonnie, who sounded relieved when she heard that no blood had been spilt and agreed he could stay the night in the spare room. The weather was foul; it was like driving through a perpetual car wash. Raindrops were leaping back up from the tarmac like popcorn from a pan and tree debris festooned the road. Tom had cut across country and wished he hadn't. He arrived at the house just before midnight. Bonnie was still up; her publisher had emailed requesting various changes to the manuscript, so she was working on her laptop.

It felt odd knocking on the door of his own house, but that's what Tom found himself doing.

'Sorry I'm so late. The roads are a nightmare.'

'No problem. Do you want tea or something stronger?' said Bonnie.

'Whisky, I think.'

'Well you know where it is, help yourself.' Bonnie perched herself back on her stool and returned to her work.

Tom came back in with whisky in hand.

'Do you know that woman tried to deny it at first?'

'That woman?' said Bonnie, who was only half listening, while trying to make the adjustments to one chapter her editor wasn't happy with.

'My mother; anyway I've disowned her. From now on, I am an orphan. I should have done it years ago: controlling, selfish, manipulative old woman.'

'I am sorry, Tom, but I need to get this done.'

'No problem. Anything I can help with?'

'Not really,' said Bonnie. 'You look bushed, the bed's all made up for you.'

'Oh right! I'll turn in then shall I?'

'I'll see you in the morning.'

'We'll have a chance to have a real talk then.'

'I guess,' said Bonnie looking at her laptop studiously.

CHAPTER 39

The next morning, Tom woke drowsily to find he was not alone; his daughter was lying beside him, her arms around him as he lay on his side.

'Evie; hello, darling. How did you know I was home?'

'Well, Daddy, I heard your voice last night, but I thought it was a dream. So I got up this morning and looked for you and as soon as I smelt your coat in the hall, I knew you must be home.'

'Smelt?'

'Yes, it smells of beer and cigarettes and sort of cabbagey things.'

'But how did you know I was in this bedroom?'

'Mummy has been leaving her bedroom door open. Besides, the only thing she's been sleeping with at the moment has been her laptop.'

Listening to Evie, Tom realised how much he'd been missing her. That slow rather deliberate delivery and her wheezy chest, her telling it like it is, just her general 'Evie-ishness'.

They got up as quietly as possible and made breakfast together. This was something that Evie had always adored, but somehow Tom had never noticed her adoring it; they put a pot of strong coffee on ready for Bonnie when she surfaced and croissants in the oven, again for Bonnie. Then, together they made Eggs Benedict, which Evie always referred to as Benedict Egg.

This was their favourite dish.

* * * * *

Chloe had two hard copy photographs in front of her on her desk. She peered at one and then at the other through a magnifying glass.

'They could be, you know,' she mused out loud.

'Could be what?' queried Callum, who was looking at estate agents' websites.

'The same person.'

'Chloe, I think you need a holiday. We know that Gunther Rohmer and Sir George Roberts were the same person. Anyway, we are not working on that programme; remember it's on the scrap heap. Now who do you think we should do next? Barry wants ideas. How about Piers Morgan or Andy Murray?'

'I'm not talking about Tom's grandfather. I've just received more information from Professor Schiller, including a group picture of the staff at one of the clinics of the Charitable Foundation for Curative and Institutional Care where Dr Albrecht worked and where Freddy died in 1941 in a supposed Allied bombing raid. There, large as life, although a little out of focus, is someone named as Dr Albrecht. Then in an email this morning, I get this picture from *The Yorkshire Post* no less, with this in the column inches under the picture.' Chloe showed Callum the text.

Distinguished psychiatrist Dr Gustav Brecht (see picture) killed in an aeronautical accident. Miraculously the pilot, eminent civil engineer and businessman, Sir George Roberts, survived.

'Chloe, forget Bradshott,' said Callum, who'd just come across a small holding in West Sussex with five acres of land on one of the estate agents' websites.

'Sorry, boss, but it's you who need to focus. This may be really important, if not to us, to the Bradshott family.'

'Okay, Sherlock, let's hear it again.'

* * * * *

At Pink Cottage, Phyllis Bradshott was nursing a hangover of considerable proportions, when at 9am the ladies from

Downstairs Downstairs arrived. This did not auger well for domestic relations. They started busying themselves around the house.

'Kindly switch that hoover off.'

'Sorry, Mrs Bradshott.'

'But you were remarking yesterday that your carpet looked like a yak master's stable floor and inferring that we'd failed to cleanse the offending article,' said the braver of the two women.

'Don't you get on your high horse with me, young lady. That was yesterday, this is today!' bellowed Phyllis. This made her head hurt all the more. 'I'm retiring to the turret room, as I cannot stand your noise anymore. One of you may bring me a cup of tea at ten, is that clear?'

The turret room was rather grandly titled as it was merely a small, circular space with a witch's hat roof that Tom's father used to refer to as 'his eyrie'. Since his death, Phyllis had made little change to the room, apart from the introduction of a chaise longue. She had four similar such pieces of furniture dotted around the house. They provided both a dramatic focus and, in three out of the four cases, excellent viewing points to keep an eye on the domestic staff. Ten o'clock duly arrived and with it the tea.

'Put it where I can reach, it if you please,' barked Phyllis.

'There's just one other thing, madam.'

'Where were you wanting this suitcase put?'

In Tom's anger the previous night, he had not taken the case containing Gunther's wartime records, medals, etcetera. In fact, he had not seen it and Phyllis was so taken aback by her son's outburst, she had thought no more about it.

'Oh, it can stay up here, I suppose,' said Phyllis. 'I wouldn't want any of you accusing me of overworking you.'

'Thank you, madam, we'll be finished in a few minutes.'

'Thank the lord for small mercies,' said Phyllis.

She must have nodded off for quite a few moments as all was quiet and her tea was cold when she came round. The turret room was the coldest room in the house, made colder it seemed by all her late husband's possessions on the wall. There were a variety of photographs: his school photograph, his army regimental photograph, various pictures taken at Haslemere Rotarian's charity dinners, a photograph of him and some of his golfing chums teeing off at Carnoustie and in pride of place on his desk was a framed photograph of Silas, his late lamented (not by Phyllis) golden retriever. Phyllis had made a decision, it was near twenty years ago since her husband died for goodness' sake. Time for a fresh start; she would have the room completely redecorated from top to bottom and she might consider advertising in *The Lady* for a companion. Heaven knows when she would see Tom again. She felt confident it wouldn't be long before he got himself into a big hole; then he'd be sorry for the cruel, hurtful things he had said last night.

She was about to go downstairs and plan the advert she would be placing for a companion, when she remembered the suitcase. It could stay up here for the moment, she thought, but perhaps she would just see exactly what it contained. The first thing she found was a photograph of her father in 1914; he was nineteen at the time, very handsome.

During the First World War, his hair had turned prematurely grey. When he came to England, some thirty-five years later, he very sensibly found a discrete hairdresser and had it returned to its original black. Phyllis looked at the photo and thought how much like a young Dirk Bogarde he looked. She moved the picture of Silas to one side and put her father's picture in its place. This seemed to her to be making a start of her new life. However long she had left, she didn't know, but she was determined to make the most of it. Next, she took out the copy of *Mein Kampf* and replaced it quickly, remembering her father's little rhyme that he used to recite to her when she was a little girl.

If I was a belittler
The first person
I'd belittle
Would be
Herr Hitler.

As she did this, the rest of the contents fell out, including Gunther's Iron Cross and his small notebook, which appeared from a cursory glance to be a wartime diary. She didn't think she would read it, because she herself had always lived her life by her strongly held, pacifist views.

CHAPTER 40

'You two look like you've been having fun,' said Bonnie looking at the state of her kitchen.

'Your coffee and croissants await you, madam,' said Tom.

'Sorry, Mummy, we couldn't wait and we've had ours.'

'So I see,' said Bonnie. 'Right, I'm on my way. I just need to check my emails, see if my editor approved my final chapter rewrite.'

'All work and no play makes Jill a dull a girl,' said Tom.

'Don't push it, buster!' said Bonnie with feeling.

'Mummy, can we all go to the park pleeease,' said Evie.

'Well I don't know; your father's probably got some place to be.'

'Nope, lead me to those swings.'

'Well let me just check for those emails and take a shower and maybe I'll catch you up.'

Tom watched as Bonnie went back into the bedroom in her bath robe, her slow walk, the curve of her back, her natural blond hair, done up in an unruly pineapple. She was so delightfully unmanufactured and so resolutely un-American in her attitude to the passing of the years and he had lost all this, just because he couldn't keep it in his trousers.

'Come on, Daddy, let's go,' said Evie.

'Okay, darling, last one to the top of the slide is a frightfully bad egg, what!'

Evie loved it when Tom pretended to speak even posher than he actually

spoke.

'Tally ho,' she cried and off they ran.

Bonnie checked her emails there was nothing from her publisher, but there was an email from Rhian Morgan Powell asking whether it would be possible for her to call round in person. She wanted to put their minds at rest regarding yesterday's meeting and any misconceptions about outcomes there may have been and would this afternoon be convenient.

How very odd, thought Bonnie as she showered a little more quickly than she normally would.

* * * * *

'Seren! Seren!' Evie called, spying her friend on one end of the seesaw in the play area behind the cricket pavilion.

'Hi Evie,' said Seren.

'Who's that man?' said Seren, staring at Tom.

'That's not a man; that's my dad,' said Evie emphatically.

'Perhaps he'd like to talk to my mum; she's having one of her cross days.'

'Seren really!' said her mother.

'Kids do say great stuff, don't they? We might not like it, but wow,' enthused Tom. 'I'm Tom Bradshott, by the way.'

'Morning, I know who you are, Mr Bradshott. My name is Pamela Richards.'

'Seems our two girls really hit it off,' observed Tom.

'Seren is like me; she sees the good in everyone.'

'Great quality to have.'

'So, are you staying in the village for long this time?'

'Sorry, I thought you knew. I live here.'

'Oh, we've been aware for several years now that we've had a celeb in our midst, but of course we don't seem to see you in person much. The village fete, for instance, or church once in a while. We seem to get to know you more through our national newspapers.'

'I know, tell me about it. They've made me out to be a cross between Rambo and John Prescott. But things are going to change. Looks like I will be last week's news pretty soon. So hopefully Willows End will be seeing a lot more of me.'

'It's not just the village though is it? Eve needs to see a bit more of you.'

'I beg your pardon? And it's Evie, actually.'

'Look I don't want to talk out of turn, but the word in the village is that your wife's not really coping.'

'Now wait a minute.'

'I know how hard it must be for you both, with a child like her. But Tom, may I call you Tom? A firm hand at home is what's required and when I read in the papers your grandmother was a Tweedside, one of the oldest and most aristocratic families in the country and your grandfather no lesser person than Sir George Roberts, I just thought how sad you've been cursed in the way you have. Of course, I know even the royal family have produced unfortunate children.'

'You're her,' said Tom.

'I'm who?'

'You are her, aren't you?'

'I'm sorry. I don't follow you, Tom. By the way, I did used to enjoy your *Let's Do Lunch* shows; they really used to brighten up my day when the old man was away on business,' she smiled coquettishly at Tom.

'I've just escaped the clutches of one small minded, vindictive, mean-spirited woman to find myself getting the come on from another.'

'I beg your pardon?' said Pamela.

'Come on, Evie. I think we'd better go and find Mummy and we will take the Jensen out for a spin, see if we can find any nosey old parkers to knock over.'

'Are you threatening me?'

'Are you a nosey old parker? Then possibly, but thinking about it, I wouldn't want the bumper of my beloved classic car damaged by any old muck spreader.'

'You realise, I hope, that I will be relaying your remarks to the relevant authorities.'

Tom leaned towards her, keeping his voice low so the children wouldn't hear.

'Look, lady, if you do, I will tell of the passionate affair you and I have been having while your old man's been away and how you've been bad mouthing my wife to get me to leave her for you.'

'Who'd believe that?' said Pamela.

'People believe I am capable of anything at the moment. One paper apparently said my life was in free fall. I tell you now, the press will just love another titbit concerning the sordid adventures of Tom Bradshott and you'll have a starring role. There may be a bit of collateral damage. I hope, by the way, your husband's the understanding type.'

'Your wife knows this is utter nonsense. I'm in the church choir for God's sake. I was only doing my duty in reporting my concerns,' Pamela spluttered.

'And you think my wife, whatever she might think of me, would deny our affair? After all, you have done your best to destroy my family. We might as well have been having an affair. But on looking at you, Pamela, you've been hanging around in the store a bit too long for my liking, so I think I'll pass.'

'Daddy, are we going for that drive or what?' said Evie. 'Because look! Here comes Mummy.'

Tom and Evie ran down to meet Bonnie as she came around the side of the pavilion.

'Is that who I think it is?' said Bonnie furiously. 'I need to speak with her.'

'No, you don't,' said Tom. 'I think her days of anonymous calls to the authorities might be over.'

'Oh yes? Well I think her days are over, period,' said Bonnie glaring over at Seren's mother.

'Seriously, Bonnie, she won't be bothering us again. I think we should quit while we're ahead and Evie's been very patient. I said we'd go for a drive; maybe get some lunch out?'

'I still might kill that woman,' said Bonnie furiously.

'We are not in Texas now, dear,' chided Tom. 'By the way did your publisher get back?'

'Yes, they're going to publish! The blurb will say "A must read for any parent with any sense". Only thing is, they want me to use a pseudonym. Anything but Bradshott. Apparently you're a toxic brand for the type of reader that we're after.'

'How about Annie Oakley?' said Tom.

Bonnie smiled as they both grasped one of Evie's outstretched hands.

'We will be having proper lunch, won't we?' said Evie.

'Proper lunch?' queried Tom.

'You know, a real blow up.'

'I think you mean blow out, sweetie,' said Bonnie.

'What? Splendid! Sounds an absolutely spiffing idea,' said Tom, putting on his silly posh voice again for Evie.

CHAPTER 41

At Pink Cottage, Phyllis had made a discovery. On picking up her father's wartime diary, a sheet of paper that had been tucked between the front cover and dust jacket had fallen to the ground. Her father's small and precise handwriting was all too familiar to her. Phyllis, who had forgotten most of her German, had a struggle to translate what was written. When she eventually was able to translate it, large salty tears began to run down her cheeks.

12th Sept 1941

Today I was given the worst news. The two people I hold dearest in all the world are dead; I know who is responsible. I believe this crime against my family was perpetrated to punish me. My son, who has lived his life in a world I was never able to enter, has died and my beautiful wife, who tried so hard to understand her darling Freddy, has found it impossible to continue. I know of her fate through one of my neighbours in the Alexanderplatz. She jumped from the third floor of our house in Berlin; her broken body was found in the street. The full names of my two beloveds are Ingrid Christina Rohmer and Frederick Heinrich Rohmer. Should I not survive the war and as I very much hope the Third Reich has been squashed under foot, I ask that all steps be taken to investigate fully the circumstances of their deaths. In particular, a man called Albrecht, who worked at The Charitable Foundation for Curative and Institutional Care and SS Officer Pieter Von Geysell. Should I survive, whatever the outcome of the war, I put on record my intention to avenge my wife's and son's deaths.

I will never, can never, love in the way that I loved my Inge and Freddy. All that is left for me now is to wait for death, whether it comes sooner or later is of no concern, once I have justice for my family. From this day forth I am a mere animated corpse.

Gunther Rohmer.

Phyllis put the piece of paper down, blew her nose and dabbed the tears from her eyes. She went down to her desk in the sitting room and began to write her advert for a companion to be placed in *The Lady*.

Seeking live-in companion, aristocratic English lady in poor health. Single well-bred female required, non-smoker in good health, with excellent conversation skills, able to do a little light dusting. The advertiser has a busy social life and a variety of interests. References required.

* * * * *

Callum and Chloe were in discussion with Barry Goldwing regarding who was to be the next subject for *Family Matters* when Chloe couldn't help chipping in:

'Well it will have to go some way to meet all the strands of Tom's family.'

'Chloe, quit while you're ahead. Bradshott's dead and buried. He's yesterday's news, the Galloping Gourmet of our age.'

'Who the hell was the Galloping Gourmet?'

'Exactly.'

'What if I told you that I think Sir George Roberts deliberately crashed his plane to kill his passenger?' said Chloe excitedly.

'I'd say you're nuts and who cares. Now can we move on?' said Goldwing. 'I fancy Piers Morgan,' he continued changing the subject.

'Do you really, Barry?' said Callum smirking.

'For our next show, idiot!'

'I can't believe you two. Where's your journalistic nous?'

'Chloe, it's time to move on, I think,' said Callum. 'Thinking about it, I'm not sure digging up all that unhappiness serves any purpose now.'

'Not on a Sunday night when all the viewers want are "Bodices and cocked hats", or heart-warming stories about a family from Norfolk entitled: "How I discovered my husband was really my sister and then how we made it work,"' said Goldwing.

'I disagree; I think Ingrid and Freddy's story should be told. The whole T4 project was, after all, a dress rehearsal for the holocaust.'

'Okay, okay we have work to do, people. I think I just happen to have Piers Morgan's number in my contact list.'

Chloe made a decision; she wasn't going to let it drop. After all, what she did in her own time was her business. She would speak with Tom, tell him what she was beginning to suspect.

* * * * *

Rhian Morgan Powell needed to get all her ducks in a row before her meeting with the Bradshotts. She had been dealing with bolshie parents ever since she'd become Senior Prac. with the Children's Disability team. These people – even if he was high profile – were obviously, seriously dysfunctional.

She'd received all the relevant reports from Mr Parks and Nikki Hooper from SCAMP. Cromer Residential Community College was very obviously the best option for little Evie and once she had the go ahead from her bosses, it could be ticked off her 'to do' list.

* * * * *

Tom had thought about taking the family to his restaurant, The Nosebag, to check out how things were going, but at the same time he knew the press were still sniffing round him, so decided to find a country pub instead.

He had made a momentous decision and put his Jensen Interceptor up for sale. So, they all piled into the battered old family Volvo.

'So what do you think this Morgan Powell woman wants to see us about now?' queried Bonnie.

'Probably wants to come and tell us what wonderful human beings we are.'

'Seriously, Tom I'm frightened. I feel Evie's future may be being taken out of our hands,' said Bonnie.

'I wouldn't worry too much about that school in Norfolk. I have a feeling that might be a non-starter. Anyway, don't worry about that now; let's eat!'

They settled for The White Hart Inn; three hundred years old and showing its age nicely, with a cavernous inglenook fireplace, beams that might have come out of Noah's Ark and walls without a right-angle to be seen anywhere.

They all went for the Sunday roast. Evie had treacle tart and ice cream, Tom had the apple crumble and Bonnie picked at her cheeseboard.

'Penny for them,' said Tom.

'Penny, for what?'

'Your thoughts.'

'I was thinking this is the kind of stuff we used to do, before everything got kind of ruined,' said Bonnie.

'Mummy, why is your cheese sunburnt?' asked Evie.

'It's called Edam, honey and it always comes that colour.'

'Excuse me are you Tom Bradshott?'

Immediately Tom thought, Oh no here we go again.

'I made Queen of Puddings the way you suggested on telly the other night. It were reet grand.'

Tom turned around and there was the biggest Yorkshireman he'd ever seen.

'The name's Brian and I won't disturb you. I just want to say those bastards in the press, they need to do one. You're alright, you are.'

'Thanks, Brian,' said Tom.

'No problem, pal,' replied Brian.

Bonnie and Evie were giggling conspiratorially, when Evie looked up and saw the outsized northerner.

'How did you get to be that big?' asked Evie.

'Well you see, sweetheart, I live in best county in Britain and biggest. So, we are all big up there. My great Uncle Amos were nigh on seven foot tall and he were a Methodist to boot. Anyway, nice to meet you all.'

'And you and thanks, Brian,' said Tom. 'What a nice man.'

He looked around but Bonnie was nowhere to be seen.

CHAPTER 42

Chloe was like a woman possessed. She'd taken a day's leave and told Callum that she was having boyfriend trouble, which, for once, wasn't true, as her man from the treasury was being very attentive. He had declared his undying love, telling Chloe that once he'd put the kids through university, he would leave his wife for her. The fact that his little girl was nine and he had a son aged ten suggested wedding bells weren't currently in the offing.

Chloe had arranged to meet Professor and Mrs Schiller for lunch, on her, at the health spa where he and Lorraine were staying. She wanted to run past him her theory, too see what he had to say. Chloe brought the photograph from *The Yorkshire Post* of Gustav Brecht and the picture of Dr Albrecht and the staff at the clinic. She waited in reception and after about ten minutes the Schiller's arrived.

The professor had been for a work-out in the gym and judging by his reddened complexion and the veins on his cranium appearing like large earthworms, he had somewhat overdone it. Lorraine Schiller, on the other hand, looked chilled and glamorous and 'out there' in a way Chloe could only admire.

'Professor, there are two reasons I wanted to meet up before you go back to Germany,' Chloe explained. 'Firstly, I have a great big apology to make; it appears we are scrapping the programme about Tom's family, due to adverse publicity. Of course, we will still pay for your flight and any out of pocket expenses from the day of filming.'

'My dear Chloe, don't give it another thought. Lorraine and I have had a ball, I can assure you and I have learnt more about the darkest recesses of my country. So do not concern yourself. Now, what was the second thing you wanted to talk to me about?'

* * * * *

In the lounge of The White Hart, Tom was getting anxious. After an initial panic, he'd assumed Bonnie had gone to the ladies but now he was worried as ten minutes had gone by.

'Evie, can you do Daddy a favour and see if Mummy is in the ladies?'

'Well she wouldn't be in the gents would she, Daddy?'

'When you've had a look, come back and tell me and if she's not there, we will go and find where she is.'

While Evie was gone, Tom asked for the bill.

'Well,' said Evie, 'if she is in there, she's a good hider. There *was* a lady in the toilets and I asked her if she'd got Mummy in there with her, but she hadn't.'

'Right! Okay Evie, we'd better go and find where naughty old Mummy is hiding.'

The White Hart was miles from anywhere. Tom tried Bonnie's mobile but it was turned to ansaphone and he texted her but with no response. He went up the lane leading from the pub, turned left and continued up for about half a mile. He then they drove back, turned right and went on for a mile.

'Daddy.'

'Yes, Evie.'

'Mummy's good at this game, isn't she?'

Tom drove back to The White Hart to check if anyone had seen her leave. When they got back, Bonnie was sat at their table drinking a large glass of sauvignon blanc.

'Where the hell have you been?'

'You checked the ladies right and quite rightly assumed I wasn't in the gents, but nobody checked the disabled toilet.'

'You frightened Evie,' said Tom crossly.

'No, Tom, I frightened you. I told Evie that we were going to play a little trick on Daddy and she played her part very well.'

'Did I, Mummy? Thank you.'

'I've never known anything so childish in my life and just when we were having such a great day!'

'Oh, Thomas, be magnanimous. After all, I think you have great expectations of me in that direction.'

'Come on! Let's go home, before I have any more trouble out of you two.' He pretended to look sternly at Evie. 'I've had more than I can handle and we have still got that bloody woman from social services to deal with this afternoon.'

* * * * *

At the spa, raw veg was the order of the day and Chloe, who didn't feel she could be a party pooper, dived into the celery selection with as much gusto as she could muster. She wasn't a great one for this obsession with personal fitness regimes. She was, of course, fortunate in being someone whose svelte-like beauty remained immutable, regardless of any lifestyle excesses.

Otto Schiller liked the fact that he had not one, but two beautiful women at his table. Chloe cut to the chase.

'It's concerning this character, Dr Albrecht, in the Rohmer case.'

'A vile, unpleasant, yet highly intelligent individual from what I can gather,' said the professor.

'Who, from what you were saying, escaped justice.'

'He sounds a proper little bastard from what I've heard,' chipped in Lorraine.

Otto Schiller gave his wife a look as if to say 'butt out, I am the expert here' and continued.

'Or was silenced by Von Geysell or one of his associates? While he remained free, we know Von Geysell did much to cover his tracks.'

'What birth sign was this Albrecht geezer?' queried Lorraine.

The professor gave his wife another hard stare and continued.

'He was extremely cunning and had links with residual Nazi sympathisers both home and abroad.'

'Professor, do you think there is any chance at all that when Albrecht escaped, if he did, whether with Von Geysell's help he could have come to England?' asked Chloe.

'Well, Chloe, as an historian, unlike my dear wife, I like to deal with the facts of the past rather than visions of the future. There is, you will be interested to know, some circumstantial evidence around Von Geysell which could support your theory. It does not concern Albrecht however, but a young scientist called Erik Wessels, who had been working on the V1 and V2 rocket systems. He was twenty-one years old and a mere junior research assistant. However, his brilliance was noted among others such as a certain Werhner Von Braun, who as you will no doubt be aware went on to the States and was chiefly responsible for developing the rocketry required for the Apollo manned lunar landing programme.'

'Yes, one small step for man and all that.'

'My dear Chloe, for us at the time it was a big deal. Your generation has superseded it all with science fiction. But for us on a planet broken and threatened by the Cold War, this offered hope on two fronts. One that the superpowers could compete in a relatively harmless way and two that there might be hope for future generations of escape from mutual annihilation on some other celestial body.'

'I've always thought that would make a good stage name you know,' mused Lorraine Schiller, 'Celestial Body.'

'So this Erik Wessels; what happened? Did he go to America with Von Braun?' asked Chloe.

'Well no, actually; they wanted him apparently, but he ended up in England.'

'What did he do over here?'

'Well he landed on his feet really. Started working for Lord Dampling, who was developing his own motor racing team and needed a chief engineer. Dampling was a multi-millionaire who had bought himself into the British aristocracy through his father's fortune. He had a coterie of titled friends who all thought the sun shone out of his – what is it you say over here, oh yes, arse.'

'Really, Otto, you're making me blush, you really are,' chuckled Lorraine, pretending to be shocked.

'So Wessels prospered under this guy Dampling's patronage?'

'It would appear so. You see it was known by many that Dampling had always admired the Third Reich for its professed industry and sense of purpose. He held enormous garden parties in the early twenties after the first war. He invited 'down on their luck' Germans across for country weekends, amongst whom were a certain Herr and Frau Geysell and their young son Pieter. The Von was added at a later date,' explained the professor.

'We know that during the Second World War, Dampling wrote to Von Geysell and when Von Geysell's parents were both killed in bomber command raids, he became like a surrogate father to Pieter.'

CHAPTER 43

For once Rhian Morgan Powell looked like she might get away with a relatively stress-free Friday afternoon due to a decision taken by her superiors, which although with potential for storing problems for the future, meant less hassle today. The only fly in the ointment was that her sat nav had packed up and finding her way around the twisty ill-disciplined lanes of mid Berkshire to the village of Willows End was proving something of a trial.

It was around 4.15pm when she eventually reached the Bradshotts' house.

Evie answered the door.

'Hello, you must be Evie,' said Rhian.

'Why must I?' said Evie.

'Are your mother and father around?'

'Yes, they're in the office, would you like to come through?'

Tom and Bonnie had been slowly making their peace that afternoon, after her turning the tables on him at The White Hart at lunchtime by doing a bunk.

He said he understood that he needed to be punished. She said she was not trying to punish him but wanted him to get an idea of what having an unfaithful untrusty partner was like. She said it was based on stuff she'd seen tried out in the judicial system, called Victim Impact Experience. She had taken him into Evie's room to show him the patchwork collages made so lovingly by his daughter from his favourite shirts.

He smiled wanly at her.

She told him the next step would be her sleeping with someone, as yet to be decided. She may have to look further afield than Willows End and was putting feelers out in both Newbury and Basingstoke.

'Okay, okay,' Tom had said. 'Whatever it takes. 'I'll even come and watch while you are doing it.'

'No, you won't,' said Bonnie.

'Why's that?'

'Because you'll be outside taking ticket money.'

'Look I can't say it enough; I've been a selfish shit.'

'Wrong, Tom, you just haven't said it enough,' explained Bonnie.

'I will do anything, Bonnie,' pleaded Tom.

'Well let's just start with one thing, shall we, you being a stay at home daddy with Evie. If they don't try to ship her off to Norfolk, that is.'

'Why, what are you going to be doing?'

'I've got a book to sell. Remember, your career is all washed up. Your inheritance is up the swanee and I noticed all the remainders of that two-bit recipe book *Zest of Life* in the back of your car.'

'I'm waiting for a new agent and publicist from Stalky and Co.'

'Listen! Let's face it, Gordon Ramsey, you ain't and you certainly ain't no Philip Roth.'

'I didn't know he was a chef.'

'So listen up, big shot. Someone has got to go and earn this goddamn family some money.'

Tom couldn't stop himself. He rushed towards her clumsily, embracing her and then found himself kissing his wife with a passion that overwhelmed him to such a degree that he wasn't sure whether he was going to pass out and lose control of most of his bodily functions. Thankfully, Bonnie calmed him down by kissing him back in such a tender way that he found himself gradually returned to a state of some calmness.

Evie and Rhian Morgan Powell had been watching events for the last five minutes. Rhian was rather hoping that Evie would inform her parents that she had arrived, while Evie was just delighting in watching her mum and dad getting on better than she could remember for a very long time.

'Did you know my mother's written a book? It's called *Parenting: It's Child's Play*?'

'Oh, there we are then,' said Rhian Morgan Powell.

* * * * *

Upcountry Health Spa was one of those places, where in the old days it would have been quite easy to run to fat. In the hands of the country gentry, it had been a place where one would go down for breakfast in the morning, look at the ornate Jacobean sideboard and immediately come out in sympathy with its groaning, under a ton of kedgeree, several hundredweight of bacon and the odd sheep.

Now the place was run on very different lines. Corridors were decorated with portraits of today's sporting heroes like Jennifer Ennis Hill and Mo Farrah, whereas in previous times, the corridors would have been the preserve of well-nourished squires in over filled scarlet waistcoats and their equally substantial good ladies.

Chloe and the Schillers were finishing their lunch in the enormous oak panelled, entrance hall.

'Professor, I just feel so awful you have done so much in helping us find out all the background to Tom's family in Germany and all for nothing.'

'I think it may be time for me to make a little confession, Chloe my dear.'

'Oh, this should be worth hearing,' said Lorraine pulling her chair a little closer and dipping a carrot into a ramekin full of not very much.

'The work I have been doing around this case has not been entirely on behalf of *Family Matters*.'

'There was me thinking it was something really kinky,' chuckled Lorraine.

'You were saying, Professor.'

'Well the point is, my dear, I have a personal interest in a certain Pieter Von Geysell.'

'In what way?' asked Chloe.

'I believe he was responsible for my father's death. When I saw your programme concerned Gunther Rohmer, I already knew there was a link to the SS and Von Geysell, who were keeping him under surveillance, suspicious about his loyalties to the 'glorious' Fuhrer.'

* * * * *

Back at the Bradshotts' in Willow End, coffee was being made.

'I'm sorry I was a few minutes late,' said Rhian Morgan Powell.

'Oh, don't apologise: you timed it just right, Ms Powell Morgan,' said Tom.

'It's Morgan Powell; Mrs Morgan Powell actually, but Rhian will do just fine.'

'Well do have a seat, make yourself comfortable.'

'I'm sorry to bother you, without much notice. I expect you're both very busy, but I just wanted to fill you in, on the go forward part of yesterday's meeting.'

'Excuse me, the what?' queried Bonnie coming in with the coffees and teas.

'Oh, just the action points we agreed yesterday, Mrs Bradshott.'

'I don't recall agreeing to a great deal yesterday.'

'Well that's really the point; you see on reflection and after due consideration the out of county placement we discussed for little Evie is now felt inappropriate at this stage.'

'Oh, so the agreeing in the end was done by you and your colleagues, but you agreed with us, which is the important part,' Bonnie smiled sweetly.

'Evie tells me you're writing a book,' said Rhian.

'Written it,' said Bonnie. 'While I was neglecting her, apparently,' she continued acerbically.

'There was never really, any suggestion...' protested Rhian weakly.

'I know what was being implied, Rhian,' said Bonnie.

'Well looking to the future,' said Rhian brightly, 'We feel that by making certain adjuncts to the family dynamic, Evie's future educational, social and emotional needs can be best met by an interface, where all agency co-produce, Berkshire-based solutions.'

'So she's staying here is what you're saying, Rhian and continuing to attend the village school?' Tom sought clarification.

'Yes, Mr Parks has agreed to this with some further teaching assistant hours to go in.'

'Bet he was delighted about that,' said Bonnie.

'Well I have some news on that, hot off the press, isn't that what they say? Mr Parks has decided to take early retirement. I believe he intends to move to the Scilly Isles to grow geraniums.'

'Well I wish him well. I hope those geraniums don't get chopsy on him mind, you' said Bonnie.

'Forgive my wife,' said Tom. 'She's suffering a little from sleep deprivation.'

'Tell me about it,' said Rhian. 'Well I'm so pleased we are all sorted out.'

Evie came in. She'd made a plate of peanut butter and damson jam sandwiches.

'I thought if I made some sandwiches, you'd stop talking about me and start eating, they're delicious, by the way.'

CHAPTER 44

It was 5pm and a coach party had just arrived at Upcountry Health Spa. Many of the arrivals were obviously health spa virgins, judging by the apprehension in their eyes and their bulging luggage. They were blissfully unaware that luggage-checking for contraband packets of Hobnobs and secreted Mars bars was as rigorous as anything you got put through by security at JFK or Heathrow.

It may not have been a large lunch for Chloe and the Schillers, but it had certainly been a long one involving many courses each as equally insubstantial as the last.

'Do you, I wonder, know the Nazi's attitude to people of mixed German North African descent?' said Professor Schiller as the chicory and Sea Kale surprise arrived at their table.

'Not great, I imagine.'

'Well in some respects they got off comparatively lightly. They were not incarcerated or executed en masse. However, in terms of military preferment, their ethnic impurity barred them from high office.'

'So where does Von Geysell fit in?' asked Chloe.

'Perhaps we better begin at the beginning and we will get to the individual concerned a little later. In fact, let's begin with me, one of my favourite topics, as you may have noticed,' chuckled the professor. 'I was born in 1943.'

'Here, you told me you was early sixties, when we met,' said Lorraine.

'What's ten years between friends, my beloved.'

'So you were a war baby,' Chloe observed.

'Yes and sadly my dear mother was by then a widow.'

'How dreadful for you,' said Chloe.

'Much worse for my mother. But I never knew my father.'

'What was his profession?'

'He was an archivist and genealogist, like me.'

'No one quite like you, Otto my darling,' said Lorraine.

'He worked in Berlin for the Reich under duress, as I understand it.'

'Do you know what they made him do?'

'He worked as part of an ethnicity verification programme, weeding out those considered to have an impure bloodline in the military and other government departments. It was essential to ensure only those of pure Aryan lineage were promoted to senior positions.'

'How was this done?' asked Chloe.

'Pretty crudely by today's standards, through birth, marriage and death certificates and limited census records from the late nineteenth, early twentieth century.'

'Fascinating! And how odd that you should have chosen the same profession.'

'Odd yes and actually very fortunate for me in trying to find out exactly why my father died. You see, we know the 'how' and 'when': 12th December 1942. He was involved in a hit and run incident, not far from the government building where he worked.'

'Could it not have been an accident? It was wartime remember; the Germans must have had the black-out like us, the bastards. Oh, sorry; present company excepted, of course,' said Lorraine.

'It could have been, but I have all my father's records from the time back in our little house in Templehof and his diary entries for the week in which he died make pretty interesting reading.'

Chloe had a date that night but was hooked by the professor's story.

Lorraine, in contrast, had wandered off and was chatting up the young man at reception, who looked as if he was quite relieved to have a substantial desk between them.

'Isn't she magnificent!' observed Schiller. 'Am I not a lucky man?'

'Absolutely; so, your father's diary?'

'Yes; underlined on the day after he died was an entry stating that he was to have a meeting with top brass regarding proposed promotions within the SS.'

'And you think this meeting that he never attended was connected in some way to his death.'

'Let's just say, a person of interest to both you and I, had a lot to lose if my father had ever reported to that particular meeting. You must remember, the Nazis were riding the crest of a wave in 1942; the war was going well, there were opportunities for advancement for ambitious young men of the right type.'

'And that person of interest was Von Geysell,' said Chloe.

'In my father's notes for the meeting, he concludes that Von Geysell's grandmother was born in Somalia and therefore not acceptable for any senior post, due to his "racial inferiority"; his notes suggested it would be more appropriate for Von Geysell to be demoted in rank.'

CHAPTER 45

At Willows End in the Bradshott house they were tucking into Evie's peanut butter and damson jam sandwiches, all except for Rhian, that is, who suddenly announced that she needed to leave, but insisted that she'd touch base with them about the extra support that they would receive for Evie, including psychology and low arousal techniques.

At this point, Bonnie whispered into Tom's ear, 'Now that sounds kinda fun.'

'Well, I'll be on way, got to get home, clean the house, you know! Quite frankly I couldn't keep a dog in my house let alone kids!' With it being Friday, Rhian was perhaps a little demob happy. 'Nice to meet you both. Good luck with the book, Mrs Bradshott and er good luck to you, Mr Bradshott.' And with that she was gone.

'Shall I make some more sandwiches just for us?' said Evie.

'I think we've probably had enough honey, but they were scrummy,' said Bonnie. 'You could take some of the cups to the kitchen for me though, sweetheart.'

Once Evie was out of the room, she whispered, 'Tom, how come you were so confident they weren't going to ship Evie off to Norfolk?'

'I looked up this place in Cromer, found their website and gave them a call. I pretended to be a social worker with a hard-to-place client, who had been excluded from school. They gave me all their spiel about the quality service they provided and then told me that, unfortunately, due to staff costs, they had just had to raise their fees to £80,000 per year. I happen to know Berkshire Council are expected to make God knows how many zillion pounds cut to their social services budget.'

'Your deviousness and duplicity actually comes in handy at times.'

Tom's mobile rang.

'Hello, Tom. I'm so sorry to bother you; it's Olive Finch here.'

'Hello, Miss Finch. What can I do for you?'

'Well, the thing is, I have no children.'

'I'm not sure how I can help there,' said Tom making faces as he spoke, which made both Bonnie and Evie giggle.

'Sorry, I'm not making myself clear.'

'Please take your time.'

'There's something your grandfather gave me when I retired and well, I want it to return it to the family. Will you come and collect it tomorrow? You see, I think it won't be long before I kick the bucket.'

'Oh, I'm sorry to hear that! Are you ill?'

'Not physically dear, no. Come tomorrow and I'll explain.'

'Let me just check my diary, Miss Finch.'

He put the phone on hold.

'She wants me to go down tomorrow. Wants to give me something before she pegs it: probably the cat!'

'You must go!' said Bonnie.

'Right, Miss Finch, I should be with you by late morning.'

CHAPTER 46

Chloe got back to her basement flat about eight and found a note from her man from the treasury to say he'd had to take one of the children to hospital with suspected appendicitis. Chloe mused that the trouble with being the mistress of a married man was that their excuses were always so bloody noble!

She decided to make herself a large, gooey chocolate cake: comfort food for the long lonely night ahead. She felt exhausted after her lunch with the Schillers and all that stuff about the professor's father. She couldn't get his final throwaway remark as she left Upcountry Health Spa out of her head:

'My dear Chloe. If you can prove conclusively that Von Geysell was responsible for my father's death and that he was given shelter here in England by Lord Dampling, I will be grateful till my dying day. You see, I believe my father was basically a good man: he may not have been a brave man but he didn't deserve to die in the way he'd did. *Auf wiedersehen*, dear Chloe.'

In the end, she'd quite forgotten to do what she had gone down to do, which had been to show the professor the two photographs both of which she believed were Dr Albrecht. What an airhead! Still it was the weekend tomorrow; no chance of seeing Mr Upstairs and plenty of time for some more detective work; elementary, Dr Watson.

There was a plaintive knock on the door. It was Callum.

'Can I come in? I feel like jumping of Hammersmith Bridge. Have you got any vodka?'

'Noooo, but I will have cake shortly,' said Chloe.

'Well, that'll do I suppose,' said Callum.

'So, what's up, Chuck?'

'Oliver has thrown me out; he says he's sick and tired of me banging on about becoming self-sufficient in the country. Says that if I wanted to be Worzel Gummidge he certainly wasn't going to be my Aunt Sally. He also said my beard could do with a good trim. He was really, really horrible!' Callum started to weep.

'Oh sweetie, I am so sorry. Come through; you'll never guess who I had lunch with today,' said Chloe.

'Betty Boop, Joan Crawford and the Aga Khan, for all I care,' said Callum.

'Actually it was Professor and Mrs Schiller.'

'Oh God: it's at this point I should be reading the riot act to you.'

'Why, what for?'

'Well apparently it wasn't just Tom doing his best to get his name in every paper that got the programme scrapped. We were warned off apparently.'

'Who on earth by?'

'Well, let's just say "from on high" shall we?'

'This whole business is getting weirder by the minute.'

'Where's this cake then?' said Callum, taking in Chloe's living room.

'Very Tenko,' he observed.

'Oh yes. Sorry about all the washing. I've got nowhere else to dry stuff.'

'Are you telling me that someone in the British establishment doesn't want us to make a programme about a down on his luck TV chef, which mostly covers events from over seventy years ago? Professor Schiller has a theory you know,' said Chloe.

'That's the trouble with professors; they usually do,' said Callum, plumping up the cushions on Chloe's sofa.

'Do what?'

'Have theories,' replied Callum.

'No seriously: he reckons his father was bumped off by that SS guy Von Geysell,' explained Chloe.

'And what evidence does he have?'

'He's a historian, Callum and so was his father; they record everything!'

They tucked into Chloe's chocolate cake, with abandon. Chloe's afternoon at Upcountry Health Spa was a distant memory. Callum then popped around to the convenience store and bought a cheap bottle of vodka.

'I'd love to know who it was who leant on Barry Goldwing,' said Chloe.

'He was quite prominent, old Sir George; he was a rising star within the Tory Party by all accounts. They do have a habit of closing ranks,' observed Callum. 'They also have a habit of stabbing each other in the back these days,' countered Chloe.

'Not back in the late sixties pre-Thatcher, however much they hated each other in private.'

'What are you saying? Someone from back then doesn't want too much digging around?' said Chloe.

Callum's phone rang.

'Oh hello. I was hoping it was you – Chloe I'll take this in the kitchen, if that's okay.'

'Yes, that's fine,' said Chloe. 'I'll just polish off the vodka while you're gone.'

Forty minutes later Callum came back into Chloe's lounge.

'That was Oliver. Apparently, we're back on. He's sorry he was such a bitch. If I want to be a yokel, he says that's fine and he'll even design a smock for me.'

'I'm really happy for you,' sobbed Chloe. 'I on the other hand have just been dumped for the second time in a week and this time by text.'

'Tacky or what?' said Callum. 'Looks like I might have to pop out for more vodka.'

* * * * *

Tom chugged down to Eastbourne in the Volvo. It was like driving an ancient tank after the Jensen. He'd brought the CD that Kat had sent him; Prairie Dog's rusty, razor-blade voice seemed well suited to the slow progress he was making.

I find myself at the last bend in the creek
My eyes are weak and my voice is hoarse
I've been through the white rapids
And where the river flows slowly.
I must return to the first bend
And seek my love at her source.

When Tom reached Miss Finch's flat, she came to the door to greet him and he was glad to see her looking hale and hearty.

'Oh Tom, I'm very grateful to you for coming. I know your weekends must be precious.'

'Gosh, absolutely no problem. How are you feeling this morning?'

'We are in pretty good shape aren't we, Augustus. How are you?'

'Fine, perhaps a bit tired; things have been pretty full on. You know how it is.'

He was exhausted. He and Bonnie had spent most of the night making love. He had forgotten how she knew every way possible to please him in bed. The skill with which she'd undressed him put the clumsiness with which he had undressed her to shame. He still had that public-school boy hang up that all women were in essence breakable, like fine porcelain. She had no such inhibitions, as the teeth marks on his shoulder bore witness. They were a little deeper than those left after such nights when they were younger. Apparently, she still needed to punish him. But otherwise, it was a night to be added to the list of memories that brought an involuntary smile to his face and aroused him like the major aftershocks in the first few hours after an earthquake: a reawakened intimacy that slated passion in a way that nothing else he'd experienced did.

189

'Earl Grey or perhaps shall I put the percolator on?' said Miss Finch.

'Coffee would be fantastic,' Tom replied.

Tom loved Olive Finch's flat; it seemed so ordered. One wall full of book shelves, the books all carefully arranged by topic and then alphabetically and the other walls, duck egg blue; the high regency ceiling; the ornate plasterwork around the light fittings; the well-worn Persian runner by the side of the baby grand, with all those pictures of his grandfather on it. The exquisite arrangement of dried flowers on the mantle shelf. A house well lived in, yet not affronted by excess or drama, nor out to impress anybody. Just designed to bring pleasure to its owner and solace to weary travellers, like him.

'I'm sorry you must think I am a bit of a drama queen all that talk of popping my clogs.'

'Not at all, Miss Finch. It's just that I was worried about you.'

'I suppose I am a bit of a bridge to your past Tom, aren't I?'

'That's not why I was worried, I can assure you. I really enjoyed our time together the other day.'

'You see the thing is, as you may have gathered, I do like to be organised.'

'You put me to shame; I seem to live in permanent chaos.'

'Augustus will be the main beneficiary of my will, of course.'

The cat looked particularly disinterested at this point, yawned and returned to his mid-morning nap. Tom wondered whether he would stay awake long enough to enjoy his inheritance.

'You think I'm mad, don't you, Tom?'

'Not for a moment.'

'Don't be under any illusions! I'm aware that my will means nothing to darling Augustus. There is also, of course, a small bequest to The Royal Opera House on the basis that Augustus could have first refusal on a box should he chose to go.'

'Excellent,' said Tom.

'You're just like your grandfather. He never quite got it, when he was having his leg ever so slightly pulled,' chuckled Miss Finch. 'Augustus will be getting most of my money, but he's not one for the opera, as far as I know.'

'You had me going there for a minute,' said Tom.

'Would you like to come through to my sewing room and I'll show you what I'd like you to have?'

Miss Finch led Tom to the back of the flat.

'This was Mother's room when she was still with us. She liked to watch the children in the next-door garden. I offered her the front bedroom of course with the sea view, but she said the ocean frightened her: "too deep by half", she used to reckon. I do miss her. Ah here we are.'

The room was full of works in progress. Half-finished pieces stretched in frames, embroidery projects and a table obviously just for lace making and repairing.

'Gosh how do you find the time to do all this?'

'Single people often have an extra supply of time, Tom.'

She took him over to a small painting of a medieval looking young woman peering out from a castle interior towards distant parkland, populated by half a dozen deer: on her lap was a piece of incomplete needlework.

'Sir Edward Burne-Jones.'

'Yes, I think I've seen the original in a gallery or museum somewhere,' mused Tom.

'Well actually you won't have, Tom, because this is the original,' said Miss Finch, removing Augustus from a ball of wool.

CHAPTER 47

Chloe was picking her way through the debris of last night's binge session with Callum. She couldn't help feeling that it served as a telling metaphor for her life. Mr Upstairs had got cold feet and a cold heart for that matter. Anyway, she was giving up men for the foreseeable future and if she took up with one again, she'd go for her usual type: left-wing poets, full of angst and fury, with such large chips on the shoulders, they walked with a stoop. Bad tempered and often rather smelly, they were subsumed by their art, which meant they neither had the energy nor the money to stray far.

But for now, she would concentrate on the mystery of 'The Real Dr Albrecht'. She rang Professor Schiller and told him about the two photos.

'I don't doubt they are one and the same person. I came to the same conclusion some time ago,' said Professor Schiller.

'What? You mean that you have seen both photos?'

'Yes my dear. As I say, my interest is in Von Geysell, but he and Albrecht's fate after the war appear in some way conjoined. I know both came to England, helped almost certainly by Lord Dampling of the Dampling motor racing team. Remember, he had known Von Geysell as a boy. He may even have known of the business of his mixed ethnic heritage. Anyway he took pity on him.

'Albrecht, who we believe to be Dr Gustav Brecht, set up in private practice, possibly with some of Dampling's money, but Von Geysell is the man who I believe murdered my father. Well, then the trail goes a little cold. As I've said, Lord Dampling had been a patron of Pieter Von Geysell, but I have no real evidence of what became of him.'

'God, I don't know where to begin with all this.'

'Well of course there is the present Lord Dampling, the grandson of the founder of the motor racing team.'

'Where does he hang out?'

'Coldmere Castle, down in your county of Kent, I believe,' said the professor.

* * * * *

In Eastbourne, Miss Finch had brought the coffee into the living room. She'd asked Tom to bring the painting from her sewing room.

'I very much want you to have it.'

'But it must be worth many thousands of pounds,' said Tom.

'Yes, around one hundred and twenty actually, although the Pre-Raphaelite brotherhood come in and out of fashion, you know.'

'It's very beautiful; she looks so sad though.'

'It used to hang in his office and when I really had the hots for him, silly chump that I was, I used to think he'd bought it because it reminded him of me, waiting lovingly in the wings. There's an inscription on the back.'

Tom turned the picture over. The inscription read:

A small token of appreciation for all your hard work in helping me create a company of which we should both be immensely proud.

Signed: Sir George Roberts
February 1969

'A bit formal for someone you'd worked with for best part of twenty years,' commented Tom.

'That was your grandfather, Tom. He was very much of the old school with his way of doing things.'

'So it would seem; it certainly fits in with what his brother said about him. Forgive me, but by my maths, that makes you only forty-two when you retired.'

'Well it was really more of a change in role. My mother had become very frail by then, so I became her full-time carer.'

'You said my grandfather helped you buy this flat.'

'That's right, he could be hugely generous: hence the picture. He gave away so much in terms of money and possessions, but very little of himself. Good form was everything, from opening doors for women to sacking any of his staff for swearing on site, when a female was present, which in those days wasn't that often – the female, not the swearing?'

'Very buttoned-up then.'

'Oh yes, until the days leading up to his death, that is.'

'You visited him?'

'Regularly in those last few weeks.'

'How did that work? Did you share visiting with my mother?'

'Your poor mother found it all a little upsetting.'

'She seems upset by most things,' said Tom.

'No, you see your grandfather was very confused by then. Kept telling your mother she wasn't his child and that he wanted "his child". It's thinking about those last hours, that got me in such a state last night. Firstly, I was having nightmares about being entombed and when I awoke in the middle of the night, I remember Sir George crying out like that towards the end of his life. "I can't breathe," he kept saying, "I can't breathe."'

'Oh God, that must have been awful!'

Olive became unsteady on her feet and rested on the arm of a small, beautifully crafted, occasional chair.

'I thought it must have been some wartime experience at first, but then I remembered the construction site tunnel.'

'What happened? You have told me but just remind me.'

'Oh, it's all a long time ago, Tom and I shouldn't be bothering you with it. It was a length of tunnel Roberts Road Builders had constructed on a road somewhere in the south Midlands. I think it was more of an extended underpass really, but quite innovative at the time.

'The project was mothballed and nearly sunk the company before it began. I can't remember why; it was a long time ago, but I remember that Lady Elspeth had to help the company from her own private fortune. Where was it now? Just outside Oxford or Banbury. I really don't recall.'

Miss Finch looked particularly frail. Her voice trailed off but she seemed on the point of saying something else, when Augustus (a cat with prospects, if ever there was one), ambled through the room on the way to his favourite window seat.

'Please don't distress yourself, if it's all too difficult,' said Tom who had become aware of the toll the story seemed to be taking on Olive.

'You're very like Sir George, you know, Tom.'

'Was it peaceful for my grandfather at the end, Miss Finch, I wonder?'

'Well yes, Tom. In fact, he looked relieved to be dying.'

'You were there then.'

'Yes. I sat with him on that day, he let me hold his hand and that was that.'

CHAPTER 48

When Tom got home to Willows End, Bonnie had news.

'I am going to America,' she announced.

'Oh God, Bonnie, what have I done now? I can't believe I've cocked it up again. I love you so much, you know.'

'Hey honey, it's all good! My publishers want me to go on a tour of America to promote the book. It'll be published out there after Christmas. Is that okay with you?'

'Of course! America, Land of the Free,' said Tom. 'Are they paying your expenses?'

'You bet they are. Will you and Evie be okay? I'll only be gone a couple of weeks. I'll try and see my folks while I am out there. It'll be three weeks max.'

'We will be fine, won't we, Evie?' said Tom.

'Don't worry, Daddy, I'll look after you,' said Evie who was mixing herself a cocktail of lemon barley juice and cocoa powder.

'My flight is this Sunday. By the way, that asshole Parks said Evie can start back at school next week,' said Bonnie.

'He still there?' queried Tom.

'Finishes at the end of term, apparently,' replied Bonnie.

'Do you want to try some?' said Evie, handing her father a beaker of her concoction.

'Not really, darling... not sure, you should either,' said Tom.

'Perhaps it needs a bit more cocoa powder?' said Evie.

'Are you sure you'll be okay?' said Bonnie.

'Yes, we will be fine,' said Tom. 'It's funny though. I was just thinking a few days ago that it was me who might have been going to America for that show Barry Goldwing wanted me to be in.'

'What show?' queried Bonnie.

'Oh, it never came to anything.'

'Anyway, why are you worrying about whether I get expenses or not? Didn't you say that the picture Miss Finch gave you was worth over a hundred grand?'

'Well, I've been thinking about that.'

'Wow, that sounds ominous.'

'I'll tell you more when you get back from the States,' said Tom mysteriously. 'How are those cocktails coming along, Evie?'

* * * * *

Now is as good a time as any, thought Chloe as she travelled into work on the Tube. The man opposite her was on his Kindle while absentmindedly scratching his crotch. He looked about sixteen but was dressed in expensive 'city fatigues' underneath a camel hair coat. The woman next to him had six carrier bags around her feet that mostly appeared to be full of magazines and quiz word books; the contents of one, however, clinked suggestively every time the train pulled into her station. The woman's breath confirmed the contents. She wore a woolly hat, secured by a scarf made out of netting, with numerous cigarette burns in it.

Chloe wouldn't miss the daily ordeal of the Underground, where both the self-assured and the lost, sat cheek by jowl, buttock to buttock and yet for all that connected them, they could be in different universes. She had her letter of resignation in her handbag. She had made sure she had bigged up Callum as the best boss she could possibly have had, but then went on to say that recent events had made her feel artistically compromised as a programme maker and that she felt she needed to move on to fresh challenges. In the cold light of day, she realised for someone who'd only been doing the job for a year, that it probably sounded rather pompous: after all, she was only a researcher. She'd written it after three glasses of wine last night; hence its grand eloquence, but she couldn't be arsed to redraft it now.

Changes had to be made in her life and this was a start and besides, she had a case to solve. Perhaps that was her destiny: to become the Miss Marple of the Northern Line and die a virgin, although thinking about it, she was a trifle late for that.

'So, what the hell are you going to do for money?' said Callum. 'Your looks will soon start to fade, you know.'

'Cheeky beggar,' admonished Chloe. 'I shall become a female private detective and failing that I'll set up a cake-making business.'

'Well you will certainly get my custom.'

'Sorry to hear you're leaving us Chloe. Was it something we said?' enquired Barry Goldwin, on his way through to his office.

'It's all in the letter, Barry.'

'Well don't be a stranger. Callum, has that car for Piers Morgan been organised? Remember this next show has got to be a belter.'

'Right, Madam! You better clear your desk,' said Callum.

'Oh Cal, I love it when you re masterful,' giggled Chloe.

* * * * *

When she got home, Chloe had a 'missed call' on her ansaphone. It was from Tom, so she returned the call.

'Hi Tom.'

'Chloe! How are you?'

'Okay. Hey listen, I've jacked my job in with Janus Films, so you might be better talking with Callum.'

'Yes, I heard you'd resigned. I hope it wasn't anything to do with the programme.'

'No, I just fancied a change,' said Chloe.

'I don't expect you're interested now, but if you remember, I was going to meet Grandfather's PA the other day.'

'Oh! What was she like? I bet she had some stories to tell.'

'I've actually been down a couple of times. She's a darling and very refined, don't you know.'

'Did you find out much about Sir George?' asked Chloe.

'Not much more about his character that we didn't know already. But she did confirm that the bloke who died in the plane Grandfather was flying was German and I tell you what, old George/Gunther was a lucky bugger to live as long as he did. He went through both World Wars, then later the plane crash and apparently before that he was nearly killed inspecting some tunnel outside Oxford when it partially collapsed. He was like a cat with nine lives.'

CHAPTER 49

It was two weeks now since Bonnie had set off for the States and Tom and Evie had settled into a generally happy routine. There had been a few ups and downs. Evie had had to comfort her father when a buyer arrived for the Jensen and Tom had had to have words with Mr Parks about Evie being sent home from a nature walk, apparently for being stubborn. She'd stopped halfway up a hill, just outside the village and sat down in the middle of the road, saying she wanted to find out what it was like to look through cats' eyes.

'You are aware that Evie has a heart condition?'

'Yes,' said Mr Parks. 'Quite common in children with Down's syndrome.'

'Did it not occur to you that the "cats' eyes" stuff was just an excuse because she probably didn't want her classmates to know that she couldn't keep up?'

'Well I know she's high functioning for a child with Down's syndrome, but I really don't think she would be able to make up such a story.'

'Mr Parks, may I just say how appropriate it is you are retiring to the Scilly Isles.'

'Well really I have a good mind to...'

'And I have a good mind to take you to court on the grounds of negligence and putting my daughter's health at risk,' said Tom.

* * * * *

Otherwise they had had a good time together, preparing food, walking on frosty weekends either to the playground, or to see Gerard, who was always delighted to see them. Evie would sit on his sofa and they would share a huge bag of chocolate peanuts and raisins, looking through photograph albums and then Gerard would put on his records, well more accurately, his record.

It was a 'best of' album by The Dubliners and they would jig about to 'The Irish Rover' and pull Tom up from the armchair to join in. Rather than two left feet, Tom had feet that seemed incapable of any kind of dance step. Occasional tables went flying and fireside rugs took flight. Eventually, to avoid further damage they had allowed him to sit down.

'Daddy, wherever did you learn to dance like that?' Evie asked.

'I don't think anyone taught your father, it's just a God-given gift,' said Gerard.

One day, while Bonnie was away, Tom and Evie ran into Pamela and Seren Richards at the swings. Tom gave Pamela a lascivious wink and she scuttled off sharpish.

On Sunday evening, Tom cooked a small pheasant in red wine with roasties. They were just settling down in front of *Strictly Come Dancing – the results*, when there was a knock at the door.

On the doorstep stood a very elderly man, but still ramrod straight: he towered over Tom. He was dressed in an expensive looking three-piece tweed suit under a full length, wax coat and bush ranger type, leather hat.

'I'm awfully sorry to bother you. You probably won't even remember me. It was so long ago that you would have seen me last! I am Alexander Tweedside, your great uncle and I've come to beg your mercy.'

* * * * *

Chloe had a plan. The key to finding the truth both about Dr Albrecht and Von Geysell, she concluded, was buried deep somewhere in the British establishment. She was eager to establish whether Albrecht and or Von Geysell ever faced justice and to know what part Gunther/Sir George played in it. She felt she owed it to poor Heinrich, who had so adored his sister-in-law and to Professor Schiller who never saw his father and in a strange way to Tom Bradshott, who seemed so disconnected from his forebears. She was young, free and single and had a bit of time on her hands; she did like a good mystery and it would be nice to be actually using her degree in some way.

There was one particular family that might be able to shed some light on events from all those years ago. Chloe was going to go to Coldmere to try and interview the present Lord Dampling, the grandson of the Nazi sympathiser, who had taken such an interest in the young Pieter Von Geysell, to see if he had any answers. First of all she had to think of a cover story. Coldmere was known as one of the finest Palladian, country houses in England. She decided she would say that she was a journalist doing a piece on the stately homes of England for one of the glossies.

In the meantime, Chloe had to find herself new accommodation; seeing her ex-lover arrive home from work each night was a little much, although the pain was starting to ease. She was beginning to remember more of his imperfections: the way he would leave her bathroom in a state, something he was probably never allowed to do upstairs; that look he would give her when as well as giving him a second slice of cake, she would cut herself one too.

There was a meanness to the man as well. On the few occasions when they'd eaten out somewhere on the other side of the city, he would always give in, when she suggested they go Dutch. The man must have been on a hundred grand a year, for Christ's sake!

She had seen a couple of possible flats around the Edgeware Road, but they were mostly out of her price range. In fact, she hadn't quite worked out how she was going to fund staying in London. She had given Mr Upstairs a month's notice of her giving up the flat. So life might involve a bit of sofa surfing for a while. She would ring around some of her girlfriends to see what she could work out.

CHAPTER 50

'Yes, yes of course I remember you. I think, though, I must have been very young,' said Tom.

'I was unable to make your father's funeral, so heaven knows when it was that we last met but it's very good to see you now.'

'Come through, won't you: you must be frozen.'

'Well I live in Perthshire, so this is really like a balmy summer's evening for us.'

'Can I offer you a cup of tea, something to eat or perhaps a wee dram to keep the cold out?'

'I am driving, so a cup of tea would do just fine.'

'This errand of mercy – you've come a very long way,' said Tom.

'Well the thing is, I'm kind of killing two birds with one stone. I have fished all the rivers in the United Kingdom apart from the River Tested, which is where I am on my way to,' explained Sandy.

Evie was glued to the television, oblivious to the new arrival.

'Evie, this is Sir Alexander Tweedside,' said Tom to his daughter.

'Great Uncle Sandy will do fine.'

'What makes you great, Uncle Sandy?' asked Evie.

'Well actually, he's your great-great-uncle,' explained Tom.

'Don't worry your head about it, lassie.'

Tom made the tea and dug out some shortcake biscuits.

'You said something, about an errand of mercy?'

'It's your mother, Tom. She is distraught at how affairs have been left between you.'

'I didn't know you and my mother were in regular contact.'

'We are not really, though besides you I am probably the only bit of family she's got left. We send Christmas cards etcetera, that kind of thing and an annual phone call. You see,

Tom, your mother never forgave me for moving up and out from our estates in the Borders. "Giving up the family birth right" she said. As for me, I couldn't get out of that draughty, old mausoleum fast enough. I live in a two-bedroom gillie's cottage now, happy as a sand boy.'

'What's it like being very, very old?' asked Evie, keen to get in on the conversation.

'Evie!' admonished Tom.

'Well now, I think it may be like being very, very young. People try to tell you what's good for you and try to stop you from doing stuff, because they say it'll be bad for you, or it's dangerous, or some such twaddle as that.'

'Oh, I see,' said Evie. 'So, it's only the bit in the middle when you can do what you like.'

'Evie, Great Uncle Sandy's come a long way...' explained Tom.

'Don't worry, Tom. Evie and I are getting on famously, aren't we?'

'Yes,' said Evie. 'But I'm going to bed now. I am shagged out.'

'Evie!' admonished Tom.

'I know; I am a bit pooped myself. Goodnight, Evie, it's been a pleasure to meet you,' said Sandy.

'So, Uncle Sandy, as I understand it, you're here as an emissary on behalf of my mother?'

'That's about the long and short of it, Tom.'

'Can I ask you, where does my mother get her character from? I know her own mother wasn't like her in character.'

'Your grandmother, my sister, was an intelligent, vivacious, caring woman, before she became unwell.'

'Yes, I thought that, so she wasn't an embittered, twisted, old snob then?'

'Oh, Tom, you mustn't be too hard on your mother. She's been through a lot, one way or another.'

'Sorry, but so have lots of people, but they don't turn into Medusa. Are you sure you won't take a wee dram, to keep the cold out?'

'Well as long as it's a wee, wee one.'

'I wanted to ask you what your memories of my grandfather were.'

'George? Well he was a very driven man; he worked every hour of the day and night to build that business up.'

'And forgive me for asking, but his marriage to my grandmother – were they happy?'

'Well, yes, certainly in the beginning; my sister doted on George and he was a very dutiful and considerate husband. Though the business hit a tough patch and some of Elspeth's money had to be used to shore the whole thing up.'

Tom poured Sandy and himself a whisky.

'And when my grandmother became ill?'

'No expense spared, dear boy. The best medical supervision money could buy.'

'And then there was the plane crash?' said Tom.

'Absolutely. This chap Gustav had come highly recommended. Your grandfather was so delighted he thought this would be the answer to everything.'

'Do you by any chance remember who recommended Brecht?'

'Well as a matter of fact, I do. I wasn't very happy at the time. But once your grandfather met him, he showed utter faith in him.'

'Why were you not happy?' asked Tom.

'Well, Tom, despite what you might think by my appearance, I have been a life-long socialist and the person who recommended Brecht was someone for whom I had the upmost contempt: a chap called Dampling, a quasi-Nazi who would have been quite happy to see the jackboot stride across our green and pleasant land.'

Tom and his great uncle ploughed through the rest of the bottle of whisky.

Tom insisted that Sandy Tweedside stay that night and they chatted 'till the early hours. Both were nursing sore heads in the morning. Evie wasn't, however and she was still intrigued by her great-great-uncle.

'How long have you been my great-great-uncle?' she asked.

'Since you were born, Evie.'

'Why have I just met you, then?'

'Evie!' said Tom.

'It's okay, Tom. You see, Evie, I live a long, long way away.'

'I know; you could move to Willows End and then you could see me every day until you die, which won't be a very long time anyway, will it?'

'I don't suppose it will be, Evie, but when I do die, I intend to come back as one of the great stone pillars of the Scottish coast.'

'Oh,' said Evie.

'Do you want to see a picture of one?' said Sandy getting his mobile phone out, much to Tom's surprise.

'What's the matter, Tom: did you not know we had phones in Scotland? Perhaps you thought it was all done through pipers sending messages across the glen. Here Evie, away and take a look at this: it's the Old Man of Hoy. Well that'll be me when I go, the Old Man of the Tweed, that's what they can call me,' chuckled Sandy. 'Now, Tom, I think I'd better be on my way. Any chance you'll reconsider about your mother? She's very distressed.'

'I'm sorry, but no. My mother never shows much contrition and what she did is only just about forgivable, in any case. I will, of course, discharge my filial duties; should she require full-time care, I will help fund it. But see her again? No, I don't think so.'

'Well having heard what you've told me, I can't say I blame you, laddie. Evie, it's been a pleasure to meet you, a fine specimen of a Tweedside female you are, to be sure.'

Evie flung her arms around the old man's knees.

'Hope the fish are biting for you,' said Tom.

'Remember, if you're ever up my way, come and see me.'

'Will do.'

'One day you know, Tom, the red flag will fly over Balmoral. I won't live to see that day, but you might.'

'Gosh there's a thought,' said Tom.

'Goodbye now,' said Sandy putting his battered old Land Rover in reverse.

Tom went back into the house and the phone rang; it was Bonnie ringing from Los Angeles.

CHAPTER 51

Chloe was shocked to receive a positive response from Coldmere Castle. The present incumbent, Sir Nicholas Dampling had granted her an interview. She hadn't quite worked out what her tactic would be as she drove through the wintery Kent countryside. It was all very well asking him about the Addams interior and the Van Dykes but how could she get on to the subject of Sir Nicholas's grandfather and his alleged dubious connections to Nazi Germany.

She'd chosen an alias for herself, Amanda Feltham, found an old pleated skirt at the back of her wardrobe and bought herself a sleeveless padded jacket, so she would look the part.

Sir Nicholas greeted Chloe at the door; he was short and stocky with receding hair and in his late fifties. He wore tinted glasses and was dressed in a blazer over a blue striped shirt of the type that can only be found in Jermyn Street these days and cavalry twills. Two black Labradors lolloped behind him, looking distinctly miserable.

'Miss Feltham isn't it? Welcome to my humble abode,' said Sir Nicholas.

It didn't look all that humble to Chloe: twin flights of steps led up to an enormous portico supported by four marble columns.

'The house is a bit of a hotchpotch of styles unfortunately, but I'll take you through room by room, give you the guided tour. This is Parish by the way, my right-hand man in all things.'

Chloe looked up and then looked up a bit further. Parish was built like a rugby lock forward and then some. He was perhaps a little past his prime, but the muscle beneath his impeccable double-breasted suit showed that here was a man ready for anything. Chloe gave an involuntary gulp.

'Very pleased to meet you, Mr Parish.'

'Good morning, madam. May I take your coat?'

Parish took her coat before she could say yea or nay and then moved off like a creature from one of Ray Harryhausen's stop frame animations.

Dampling showed her into the Great Hall. It had one or two modernish family portraits. 'Graham Sutherland captures my mother rather well we think,' said Dampling.

Most of the other pictures were vast landscapes or animal pictures.

'Of course, you'll recognise Landseer. My grandfather picked that up for a song. By the way, I'm surprised you haven't brought a photographer down with you, if this is for the glossies.'

'Oh, I'm so sorry. I meant to tell you the photo shoot will be happening separately, if that's okay?'

'A bit of an odd arrangement: there may be a problem if your cameraman requires me to be here, as I'm up in town a lot at the moment on party business.'

'Yes! I read in the paper that you're a bit of a rising star in the Tory Party at the moment.'

'Well that's very kind! Bit of a late starter but anything one can do for the cause.'

'The cause?' said Chloe.

'The Conservative Party.'

* * * * *

Two hours later, the tour of the house was complete.

'So there you have it: that's Coldmere for you.'

'Tell me about Dampling's motor racing team?' said Chloe. 'I have always been a bit of a petrol head. Your grandfather was by all accounts an extraordinary man,' said Chloe.

'Yes, I think he was in his own way,' said Sir Nicholas.

'He founded the family business, didn't he?'

'Yes, we were the best precision engineers in the country for a time.'

'And then along came the cars. It must have been such an exciting time.'

'Well for a comparatively short period in the fifties we were competitive. I tell you what, if you're a bit of a petrol head,' said Sir Nicholas giving Chloe a curious look, 'let's take one of the cars out for a spin.'

Ten minutes later, Dampling was burning rubber in his Dampling Marauder sports car with a rather nervous Chloe at his side. The rear drive to Coldmere Castle provided a straightish bit of road.

'Considering this car was built in the fifties, still got a bit of poke in it.'

'Absolutely, I'm having a ball,' said Chloe (who wasn't).

'I'll just show you what she's like coming out of a bend.'

Chloe gripped the edge of her seat.

'By the way, Ms Feltham, or should I say Ms Whiting, I'd appreciate it if you would leave this family alone. We have enough problems with the genuine gutter press. Having some amateur trying her luck is not something I appreciate.'

'I don't know what you mean. My name's Feltham, Amanda Feltham,' said Chloe.

'Look I don't know what your angle is, Ms Whiting and I don't really care. But I agreed to you coming as I like to take a look at the enemy first-hand. At the risk of being ungallant, I don't think much of what I see but be assured, I will use all means at my disposal to protect the Dampling reputation.'

He pulled the Marauder up outside the great house.

'I don't know how you found out who I am but I'm not sure your family has much of a reputation to protect, Sir Nicholas.'

'I can assure you any skeletons you feel you've uncovered – real or in this case imagined – belong many years in the past. What this country needs is modern leadership, for a new age and if the call comes to step over the white line, I will step up to the plate: the old certainties are dead in the water, Ms Whiting – another golden age of opportunity beckons. For those of us who believe Britain was and can be again Great Britain. What it can do without is people hardly more than children going on crusades into a history they neither lived through or understood.'

'I haven't finished you know, not by a long chalk,' said Chloe defiantly. 'We know about your grandfather's links to people like Von Geysell.'

'Good afternoon, Ms Whiting, safe journey home.'

CHAPTER 52

'Hi Tom, honey, how are you? How's Evie?'

'We're fine. How are you?'

'Well I'll be home in a couple of days. If I have to sit through another dumbass radio interviewer asking me dumbass questions on English nannies and whether the royal family still have wet nurses, I'll scream.'

'Never mind; back to the cold old UK soon,' said Tom.

'Hey, you'll never guess who I bumped into the other day.'

'Who was that? Martin Scorsese, Steven Spielberg?'

'No, Kat Kawalski,' said Bonnie.

Tom could feel the back of his throat dry up. His hangover kicked back in with a vengeance.

'Oh and how was she?' said Tom.

'She was just fine. We had lunch together.'

'Lunch!' said Tom.

'Yes, you know, the meal you Brits have between breakfast and afternoon tea.'

'Well, so is everything okay? I mean...'

'Everything's fine, Tom. I needed to talk to her.'

'I don't quite understand why,' queried Tom. 'I made a dreadful mistake and I hurt you and I am so sorry.'

'This was not about you, Tom. It's about me making Kat aware of how she'd hurt my family.'

'I didn't realise you were going to LA.'

'It's the last leg of the book signing tour.'

'Well, I don't see what purpose your meeting served.'

'Remember me talking about victim impact programmes? I needed Kat to know how her sleeping with you had hurt me.'

'Why?'

'Because I hate leaving things unsaid. We did far too much of that when Evie was born, never sharing our feelings.'

'So how did Kat take that?' said Tom.

'Very well as a matter of fact. She said that she knew what she'd done wasn't right and was glad to have the opportunity to clear the air. Once we'd done that stuff, we had a great meal. She told me about Jo Jo and her hopes for the future. I told her about going to a Prairie Dog concert in Sacramento, when I was seventeen.'

'You never told me.'

'I was invited backstage afterwards.'

'Don't tell me you went.'

'As a matter of fact, I did!'

'Oh God, I don't think I want to know anymore.'

'As a matter of fact, he was an absolute 2tleman.'

'So, you and Kat had a lot in common,' said Tom feeling like one of the husband's in *The First Wife's Club*.

'Well, let's just say we found we had a lot more in common than just you. And I have to say, I admire her for trying to help Jo Jo, the poor mixed up boy. So, what else's been happening at your end?'

Tom told Bonnie about his run in at the school with Mr Parks and the surprise visit of Sandy Tweedside.

'Okay honey, lots of love to Evie, see you in a few days' time.'

* * * * *

As Chloe drove away from Coldmere Castle, through twisty little B roads, she could not have been more angry. Pompous, arrogant, patronising were only a few of the adjectives she could use to describe Sir Nicholas Dampling. In fact, she was so angry it was only at the very last moment that she saw the Range Rover pull out from a crossroads straight in front of her little Fiat. For a split second she had sight of a vast form at the steering wheel, before her little car careered into the hedge.

She must have lost consciousness for a few seconds. When she came round, there was no other vehicle to be seen. The car was nestling some way into the hedge, but after a bit of wheel spinning on the wet grass verge, she managed to get the car back on the road again. There was a slight dent to the bumper and a crack to the windscreen, but it was driveable. When she eventually got home, she started to shake. She didn't want to be on her own, so she phoned a couple of her girlfriends but all were either out of town or in some cases out of the country on pre-Christmas breaks. It comes to something, Chloe thought, when you have to go on holiday to prepare for another holiday. She rang Callum. He said he'd be there in quarter of an hour.

'I still say you ought to go to Accident and Emergency. And why haven't you phoned the police?' said Callum bringing in the tea from Chloe's kitchen.

'You managed to find everything?'

Chloe was lying on her sofa under a throw in a foetal position.

'Chloe, I am serious.'

'I couldn't give them a clear description, it was icy, there was no collision with another car. No CCTV in deepest Kent. I think I'd feel rather foolish.'

'So, what are you going to do?'

'Make some more cake and find myself somewhere to live,' said Chloe.

'So that little shit, Dampling, goes on his merry way. You know he's in line for a cabinet position don't you? The way the wind's blowing that man could pull the Tory Party to the far right and make his late grandfather proud of him. I tell you, Chloe, look what's happening in France, Austria and Italy.'

'I think I'll do a lemon drizzle this time,' said Chloe. 'Can you stay here for a bit this evening, Callum?'

'For a bit of what may I ask, Ms Whiting?' said Callum.

'Lemon drizzle cake, if you're lucky.'

CHAPTER 53

The week before Bonnie returned from the States dragged for Tom. He had been unnerved by her description of the summit meeting she'd held with Kat. But then everything else went pear-shaped. Firstly, he got a call from his manager at The Nosebag to say there'd been a fire. Thankfully nobody had been hurt and damage had been minimal. The fire brigade said the fire had started at the rear of the building among the bins. It could have been kids messing about or an alchy trying to keep warm but there was some indication that it had been started deliberately.

Tom had gone over to reassure the staff, but in his own mind, this was a further reason for him to sell the place. The other call he got was from Sandy Tweedside, to tell him that his mother had died.

* * * * *

Otto Schiller felt a terrible sense of responsibility when on ringing to get a progress report from Chloe, she told him about her ill-fated meeting with Sir Nicholas Dampling and being forced off the road.

'I should never have encouraged the girl,' he said.

'Look, Otto, she's a grown-up able to make her own decisions,' said Lorraine.

They were back in their house in Templehof and Lorraine was feeling a little tetchy, picking her way through the professor's pile upon pile of books.

'I tell you, Otto, living in this house is like living in a giant game of pick up sticks,' Lorraine complained. 'I'm afraid to bloody well move.'

Right on cue, a column of books and magazines about four feet high toppled over right in front of her. It was a random collection, including works by, Ovid, Schumacher, Rommel and

Erasmus with a few copies of *National Geographic* and *New York Literary Review* thrown in.

'We either get a skip, or we're moving to somewhere where your office is right at the bottom of the bleedin' garden.'

'I think I ought to go back to London, before something awful happens. What do you think, my sweet?'

'I think, Otto, you are a seventy-three-year-old overweight man, who has spent his working life on his derrière. What can you honestly do to help?'

'I don't know, my darling, but I still think I should go. Chloe sounded really frightened.'

* * * * *

One of the ladies from Downstairs Downstairs had found Phyllis's body. She'd died in bed, probably painlessly; her heart had given out as she had been told it eventually would. Phyllis had left strict instructions that Sandy Tweedside was her next of kin and Tom wasn't to be contacted.

Having met and liked Tom, this was not an instruction Sandy could follow and they arranged to meet at Pink Cottage on the Monday.

Tom phoned Gerard the night before Bonnie was due to arrive at Heathrow. Gerard agreed to stay with Evie the next morning, while Tom drove to pick Bonnie up.

* * * * *

Bonnie ran up to Tom and threw her arms around him.

'I'm so sorry, Tom. I can't pretend I was fond of Phyllis, because I wasn't. But I give her credit for one thing and one thing only, successfully giving birth to you. The fact that she then proceeded to fuck you up emotionally is, of course, unforgiveable.'

216

'It was her heart, they said.'

'A bit on the small size was it?' said Bonnie pulling no punches.

'Hey that's my mother you're talking about.'

'Sorry honey. You know me. I can't pretend to have liked the woman. In fact, there have been times when I found it difficult not to hate her.'

When they got back to Willows End, Evie was still awake; she and Gerard were watching Disney's *Dumbo* and tears were rolling down Gerard's cheeks.

'Mummy, Mummy, hello! How was the good old US of A? He'll be alright in a minute. It's the bit where they lock up Dumbo's mother,' explained Evie. 'Come on, Gerard, cheer up. They're not real elephants you know, like the ones on the telly that the poachers shoot.'

'You see! I told you all us Bradshott women just tell it like it is,' said Bonnie.

* * * * *

Sandy Tweedside greeted Tom at the door of Pink Cottage.

'Thank you for coming, Tom. I know how impossible this must be for you. But I really don't think I can sort all this out at my age.'

'Why the hell should you have to? I'll help, of course. If you'll allow me to.'

'Tom, I know things were not good between you, but you're still her son and there's not just her things here; there's all your father's stuff upstairs which never really got sorted out.'

'I'm just so sorry you've had to come all the way back down from Perthshire.'

'Well as a matter of fact, I was only back home for about an hour when I got the call.'

217

'Now I have asked the nice ladies from Downstairs Downstairs to box up all your mother's clothes and take then to the local charity shops in Haslemere. If it's easier, I'll deal with her correspondence and um, notify her friends etcetera from her address book.'

'That won't take long. There'll be a lot of crossings out. She fell out with most of her friends.'

'Tom, I just want to say that you can contest the will you know. I'd support you. It seems very wrong that you should not get a penny.'

'Thank you, Sandy, but it wasn't her money I ever wanted.'

'I realise that, son, but something made your mother the way she was, you know,' said Sandy. 'Remember, the dead can't harm you.'

'Don't worry, Sandy. I don't believe in ghosts.'

'Did she leave any instructions for the funeral, Tom, do you know?'

'No not that I know of,' said Tom sweetly.

CHAPTER 54

Chloe felt a lot better in the morning. Callum had stayed till just before midnight; they'd eaten cake and drunk too much once again. She was determined not to give up trying to find answers to the questions that had been thrown up in Tom's grandfather's life. But for the moment, she really needed to concentrate on finding a new flat. She'd seen an advert for a tiny basement flat just off Duncan Terrace in Islington. It was described as mega bijou, which didn't sound too promising, but she made an appointment for that evening. She set about clearing up the mess she and Callum had made the previous night. She had been given more of an insight into Callum's life outside of work. Apparently, he was an active member of the Anti-Nazi League and had been involved in many marches against groups like the English Defence League and Britain First and in his youth the National Front.

Callum talked about how the far right as distinct groups were finding it difficult to recruit members. UKIP had had an effect, but most of the extremists saw them as flaky and after the Brexit vote something of an irrelevance. Having observed a successful tactic by the far left to take over the Labour Party using social media and other means, they were now trying to swing the Tory Party behind a hard line on immigration, welfare and anti-gay marriage amongst other things using the same techniques. The strategists behind this according to the Anti-Nazi League were a group called the KOA (Keepers of Albion).

'Good God, it's all very scary really, isn't it?' Chloe had commented.

'Well yes, kiddo, it is. That's why I wanted you to go to the police after what happened. You see, we are pretty sure that Sir Nicholas Dampling had links with KOA before he became an MP and went mainstream and his advisors and supporters have been very keen to distance Dampling from his past.'

* * * * *

Tom was in the turret room at Pink Cottage, sorting his late father's stuff out from nearly twenty years ago; not that it actually needed much sorting. Everything had been carefully filed, from his old school reports, right up to his pension plan statements, along with a file with his completed golf round cards in it and a box full of receipts for the numerous expensive gifts of jewellery he'd bought Phyllis over the years. His books were all neatly arranged including a complete set of *Wisden* up until his death and *A History of the English Speaking Peoples* by Winston Churchill. His cassettes and records again were alphabetically arranged; mostly light classical, Gilbert and Sullivan, Rossini, some comedy including The Goons and Bob Newhart.

Most of the stuff Tom put in bags to be shredded and it was only after he had been doing this for some time that he noticed the picture of his grandfather, where the photograph of his father's old dog, Silas, used to be. In front of the photograph was the note left by Gunther, which Phyllis had found when it fell from the front cover of his notebook.

Tom, whose German wasn't great, could make out various phrases:

I will never, can never, love in the way that I loved my Ingrid and Freddy...Avenge my wife's and son's deaths.

This was the man of action speaking, a man with a cause. The name Albrecht appeared but not that of Von Geysell. The note confirmed one thing for certain. Gunther, if he survived, was not going to let matters lie. It also showed the intensity of feeling he had for his first wife and young son Freddy and that he could never feel that way for anybody else.

Tom slumped down in his father's old office chair. It dawned on him that this might go some way to explaining the way his mother behaved.

He went downstairs and found Sandy sifting through more paperwork.

'Thinking about it now, I do remember my mother having some thoughts about her own funeral.'

'Thank goodness for that. I was beginning to feel at a loss as to what would be appropriate,' said Sandy.

* * * * *

Chloe had just got back from viewing the Flat in Duncan Terrace. Had she been one of *The Borrowers* it would have done just fine, but as a full size, real person, she was unimpressed with the details of the place as described online. Phrases like 'easy to keep clean', 'ergonomically designed' and best of all, 'galley kitchen' for a room two feet by four feet. It would be easier, if a little less hygienic, to do one's cooking in a portaloo. In addition, the flat stunk of skunk and got no natural daylight; it was a place to grow rhubarb but not a place to live, concluded Chloe. She knew that it would be snapped up straight away as the urban single's equivalent of refugee standing space at the back of the food aid lorry; every morsel is grabbed however meagre.

The phone rang; it was Barry Goldwing.

'Hi Chloe, I wonder whether you might meet me for a chat tomorrow. I've been reflecting on a few things and wanted to talk them through with you.'

'Well, yes, of course, Barry.'

'Okay, that's great. See you at my office around 10am, or would you like me to send a car?'

This struck Chloe as very odd as the firm's cars were usually made available to celebs or wealthy potential investors, not petulant ex-employees.

* * * * *

'I can't thank you enough, Tom and this lunch is on me by the way,' said Sandy.

The two men were sat in a pub just off the A3 in Hindhead. They'd both tucked into steak and ale pie, chips, peas, carrots and cauliflower.

Tom always felt slightly more kindly disposed towards his food if someone else was paying. When he was paying, he felt responsible, almost more responsible than when he was cooking food in his restaurant.

The small talk lasted until they'd both partaken of the strawberry cheesecake.

Tom went to the bar and returned with a pint for Sandy and a half for himself, as he had quite a drive still in front of him.

'Tom, there's something else I need to tell you about your grandfather, said Sandy 'Whether it was his wartime experiences – after all he was in the first war as well, as we know. I tell you, the Somme in 1916 wasn't a pretty place to be. George suffered what we now would call post-traumatic stress disorder. He had terrible waking dreams. I remember when he was up with us in the house in the Borders. Elspeth and he were already sleeping in separate bedrooms and she wasn't really in a fit state to help, so I went to him. He was in one of the guest bedrooms. Four-poster bed and all that nonsense. Well, he was staring up at the canopy, appeared wide awake, screaming "Let me out, let me out!" or it might have been "Get me out, get me out! It's too late for him... where he belongs..." Then all this "get me out" stuff would start again.'

'When was this?' queried Tom.

'I would say in the mid-fifties. He was still a comparatively fit and able man. His business was just beginning to take off. Roberts Road Builders were winning contracts all over the place. So his working life was not being unduly affected.'

'Do you know whether these dreams continued?'

'He never acknowledged them, but there were a couple of other occasions when I heard him call out.'

'Can I ask where they were living in those days?'

'Well, in the early days George rented a house in London and they would split their time between there and the Borders. Then, when the money started rolling in, he bought a house in Totteridge, north London but Elspeth hated the place and spent most of her time up north.'

'You talked about this chap, Dampling, who you loathed. How much do you think my grandfather had to do with him?'

'He didn't care for the man, but they did do business. Dampling's business was engineering. Engine parts that kind of thing; your father had quite a lot plant bulldozers, tipper trucks that kind of thing. But they didn't have a great personal relationship, as far as I know.'

CHAPTER 55

After a few cold and frosty days at the beginning of December, when they'd been able to get on with the project, the rain had started to bucket down and all Fran Burrows and his crew could do was sit tight in their caravans on site, play a bit of three card brag and watch *Flog It* on the telly. It was too wet for the JCBs to move across the uneven ground. This looked like a road widening scheme that was going to be put on hold till the spring at this rate. There was a tunnel that had been made obsolete once the motorway had been built that would have to go so the builders could access the site for a new 120-house estate to be built just by the side of the M40 north of Oxford.

Ryan, one of Fran's crew, had opted to brave the wind and rain and go for a pee in the great outdoors rather than use the very blocked portaloo arrangement. Fran used to call it the Tardis because you were usually in for a big surprise when you got inside it.

After ten minutes, Ryan hadn't come back and Fran peered out the window to see Ryan transfixed by something by the side of the old tunnel.

'Ryan, you pillock, you're getting soaked. Come on get back inside,' said Fran, who looked out for the lad in paternalistic way, having not seen his own kids since Maureen took them off to her mother's in Killarney.

What had mesmerised Ryan and made him oblivious to how wet he was becoming, was the very gradual appearance through the runnels of mud, rainwater and his own urine of a pair of skeletal hands bound together with what looked like bailer twine. There was an air of supplication about the bones that made Ryan instinctively scrape away the mud around them, as if rescue could be performed, but when the dome of a skull, like some obscene fungi, began to appear from the ground, Ryan turned and ran for all he was worth back to the caravan.

* * * * *

Chloe arrived at Goldwing's office in good time for her meeting. Barry was bustling around, mobile phone to his ear talking to someone about future programme making.

'Well, I'm sorry you feel that way, but as Lord Grade said when asked about the cost of the film he made called *Sink the Titanic*, it would have been cheaper to raise the Atlantic. That's how I feel about your idea; quite frankly it stinks like a year-old unemptied cat litter tray. Come back to me when you have a good idea. No, on second thoughts it's a good idea if you don't come back to me.'

'Chloe darling, thank you for coming. Come through, let's talk. Chloe, listen, I heard what happened down in Kent. It sounds like you had a narrow escape. So there are two things: firstly, I wondered whether you'd consider coming back on the team. We need you, someone with real balls.'

'I thought you said Sunday night TV should be Ovaltine TV.'

'I did and I stand by that, but I'm talking Tuesday evening Channel 4 hard-hitting political, with Callum as your director, you researching and doing pieces to camera. What do you say?'

'Channel 4? Not your usual style, Barry.'

'Look, what can I tell you? They're good payers and never let it be said I let my politics get in the way of a good story.'

Chloe thought about the miniscule flat in Islington that she couldn't afford.

'Well, thank you, Barry. I'll give it serious consideration. What was the other thing you wanted to talk to me about?'

'I just wondered if you'd seen the red top papers this morning?'

'No! I haven't had a chance,' said Chloe.

'*The Mirror* led the way,' said Barry handing her a copy. The headline read:

DAMPLING'S GRANDFATHER 'FIXER' FOR NAZI KILLERS

Then Barry handed Chloe *The Sun*. It was a little more direct:

NAZI SIR NICK AND THE KEEPERS OF ALBION.

'Well this won't help him get that cabinet position. I wonder who broke the story,' mused Chloe.

'Let's just say that if a certain well-connected TV personality should leave his phone unlocked with his contact list open when in "make-up" for one of our shows, it was too good an opportunity to miss. A certain esteemed newspaper editor received an anonymous tip-off and his million-circulation red top lapped it up.'

'You mean, it was you!'

'Listen, when Callum told me about what happened to you and then I read about that suspicious fire at Tom Bradshott's, something clicked for me. No one puts the frighteners on my staff, past or present, or Tom for that matter.'

'Do we know that Dampling was behind the fire at The Nosebag?'

'No, but subtle pressure was being applied from let's say "on high". That's why I pulled the plug on the programme. I thought it was because Tom was being a pillock with the women and the brawling in public and the powers that be weren't impressed. Well, to be honest, I thought fair enough because I wasn't impressed by Tom's public schoolboy gone bad antics. But now it makes more sense that it was about the politics. The Damplings have a dodgy history going back three generations that they've done their best to cover up.'

'But if Dampling knew I wasn't who I said I was, why did he agree to the interview?' queried Chloe.

'First rule of politics: Get to know who your enemies are. He wanted to take a look at what he was up against and how much of his family's unsavoury past you might have known about.'

'But then why send his goon to frighten me like that?'

'I have to tell you, Chloe: it may be they intended to do more than frighten you.'

'Oh, come on.'

'You're too young to remember the Jeremy Thorpe affair; politics can be a rough business.'

'Blimey!'

'Probably something you said really put the wind up him. You see, I've had my doubts about Dampling before and I tell you I don't want that little shit having anything to do with the Tory Party that I love.'

'Wow, you don't take prisoners do you?' said Chloe. 'A bit of a White Knight really.'

'Well, I think Dampling will crawl back under the stone from where he came for a while,' chuckled Goldwing.

'Well thank you and thank you for the job offer, I'll let you know asap,' said Chloe.

* * * * *

Later that day Barry got a call from the Conservative Central Office to let him know that they would support his application to become the prospective Tory candidate for East Didcot and wished him every success in his interview with the local party membership. Barry's world was one governed by two axioms. One was 'Nobody owes you a living' and the other was 'You scratch my back and I'll scratch yours'.

CHAPTER 56

The day of Phyllis Bradshott's funeral arrived. It had rained solidly all morning and now the rain had that icy component in it. So when each nugget of cold slipped down between Tom's collar and neck as he stood outside St Joseph's church waiting for the hearse to arrive, he shivered like an eel on a bent pin.

It appeared the event wasn't exactly going to be a sell-out. Bonnie had stuck to her word and stayed home but Evie had insisted on coming, saying that loving Grandma Phyllis was hard, a bit like eating celery or maths homework, not much fun, but it had to be done.

'Would you like to say a few words about Grandma in church today?' Tom had asked Evie.

'Oh I don't think I better had, Daddy. They wouldn't be the kind of words you should say in church,' Evie had explained.

It has to be said that Evie's opinion of Phyllis had been coloured somewhat by Bonnie's feelings about her mother-in-law.

Two of the ladies from Downstairs Downstairs arrived and sat at the back of the church. While an elderly partner of Jarrett, Hargreaves and Miller Chartered Accountants, came to represent Roger Bradshott's old firm. A handful of the regular congregation of St Joseph's filed in.

Sandy Tweedside was there of course. As he took his seat beside Tom, he whispered, 'When you get to my age, you're hardly out of these togs. This is my third funeral this month. People try and hang around till Christmas, of course. But when the weather is like this, I wonder why they bother.'

Much to Tom's surprise, Olive Finch arrived carrying a small but exquisite wreath, which she handed to one of the undertakers. She took a seat several pews behind Tom and acknowledged him with a nod and a smile.

The service began with 'The King of Love My Shepherd is' as Phyllis's coffin was wheeled in on one of those utilitarian trolleys that they seemed to use these days, with three of the funeral directors' staff either side in suitable beribboned hats and full mourning dress. Tom had remembered one of his mother's instructions that the undertakers were not to look like 'bookie's runners, taking shelter from a shower of rain'. The service was taken by a young and very pious clergyman, who seemed incapable of projecting his voice beyond the lectern. Hence, most of the elderly congregation caught very little of what was said. Sandy gave a reading from 'Romans'. Towards the end of the service Tom got up to give a eulogy. It was remarkable, purely on the basis of its brevity, suggesting everybody would remember Phyllis in their own special way, before inviting everyone back to Pink Cottage for light refreshments.

The ladies from Downstairs Downstairs had arranged the seating in Phyllis's large downstairs lounge. Although a kind of sunroom, today the rain beat down on the partially glass-covered roof. The staff at Downstairs Downstairs would have been saints not to take a modicum of pleasure in bringing down all Phyllis's sofas, settees and day beds, from the observation posts where she daily harangued them, to use as extra seating for the funeral attendees.

Olive Finch perched herself on the end of one of the settees, sipping a cup of lukewarm and very stewed tea without wincing once, which, given her strongly held beliefs around tea making, showed a great deal of self-control.

'Miss Finch, you really should have at least let me come and collect you from the station.'

'Oh dear, I couldn't possibly. There's always so much to think about at times like this. You have, of course, my deepest sympathies, Tom.' She proffered a consoling, beautifully gloved hand.

'Thank you. I am sorry it's not very warm in here.'

'Oh, it's fine. What a lovely home your mother had,' observed Miss Finch.

'Have you not been here before?'

'No, your mother and I lost touch really in recent years. I hadn't seen much of her since her father died. You know how it is?'

'Absolutely,' said Tom

'Tell me, is that who I think it is?' said Miss Finch glancing across at Sandy Tweedside.

'If you mean my great uncle Sandy, I would say yes,' said Tom.

'Oh, Olive my dear, how wonderful to see you again,' said Sandy striding across the room towards her, much as he would when attempting to land a salmon on the River Dee, only without the waders.

'Sir Alexander, it's got to be over forty-five years.'

'Tell me, Olive, have you kept yourself just for me?'

'Oh, go on with you.'

'You haven't changed a bit, you know.'

'Either you've gone blind, or you think I've gone senile,' said Olive sternly.

'Don't be cross; you know you were the only one for me.'

'Sir Alexander, I hardly think this conversation is appropriate to the occasion,' said Olive using one of her gloves to slap Tweedside gently on the wrist.

Tom walked off smiling and proceeded to pour himself another largish whisky. He felt mildly sloshed and was glad Bonnie had agreed to come and pick him and Evie up from Pink Cottage.

The ladies from Downstairs Downstairs were handing round cheese straws, de-crusted cucumber sandwiches and mini pork pies.

Evie was helping by plying people with sweet sherry, exclaiming as she did so:

'I don't know how people drink this stuff. It's DISGUSTING!'

'Thank you for coming to the service, by the way. She would have been very touched,' said Tom to the two ladies from Downstairs Downstairs.

The two women, who knew very well of Tom's womanising reputation, both blushed. Tom resisted the temptation to ask whether they'd come to the funeral to make sure she was dead, having witnessed the way Phyllis used to treat them.

CHAPTER 57

Chloe and Callum were sat in a pub not far from Janus Films, catching up on the gossip.

'So you still haven't given Goldwing an answer. Keeping him dangling for an extra few thousand on the salary, is that the plan?'

'No, Callum, that is not the plan! These last couple of months have been so bizarre. Heinreich's death, Tom getting into not one, but two punch-ups and then this business with Dampling.'

'Well, he is a piece of work,' said Callum.

'Then there was that fire at Tom's restaurant and now his mum's dead.'

'Yes, but apparently she's been on death's door for a while.'

'So she told me. I feel a bit guilty about not going to the funeral. But I know things weren't good between Tom and his mother,' said Chloe. 'Anyway, tell me more about this series of yours.'

'The thing is, Chloe; I want to make programmes, but not just any old programmes; ones that really shake the political tree. Have you heard of John Pilger?'

'Of course I've heard of John Pilger.'

'Well I want you to be his female equivalent. Well if not Pilger, Jeremy Bowen at least.'

'Orla Guerin, as you seem to be having difficulty coming up with any women.'

'Oh that's it is it? Serious journalism. In that case, I don't want you going for the dolly-bird look like that girl on the telly now. What are you having? It's my round.'

'Large vodka please?'

'You're not as cheap as you look, lady, are you?' said Callum scuttling of to the bar.

Chloe looked over at one of several screens positioned around the bar. A young female reporter was quizzing a police officer.

'Detective Inspector, can you comment on reports circulating locally that the victim had his hands and feet bound?'

The DI shuffled from foot to foot. He was not dressed for the weather in shirt and tie and a thin well-tailored suit, which was gradually being darkened by the rain.

'I am not in a position to add to my statement: the body of a male, possibly aged between fifty and sixty, has been found at a road improvement scheme just north of Oxford. A full post mortem is being carried out to establish the cause of death. We do, however, believe the deceased has been in situ for some considerable time and a murder enquiry is ongoing. Specialist officers are on the scene supporting members of the public who found the human remains.'

'Thank you, Inspector.'

The young reporter turned to the camera.

'So, there we have it. A gruesome discovery, which has left police with many unanswered questions. We will, of course, update you should there be any further developments.'

* * * * *

The Bradshotts returned to Willows End in the old family Volvo. The journey was undertaken in comparative silence. Evie slept most of the way and Bonnie felt it best to allow Tom to be alone with his thoughts.

When they got in, Bonnie got Evie snugly tucked up in bed. Outside, snow had started to fall; it was the duck feather type of snow, billowing down through the night sky as if each flake was making a decision exactly where to land.

'Bonnie, you know the Burne-Jones picture? If it's okay with you, I've decided what to do with the money when we sell it.'

233

'You are going to sell it then?'

'Yes. I'm not a great fan of the Pre-Raphaelites; it's not just "Bubbles", they all have such soapy expressions on their faces in my eyes. I want to put half the money in a trust fund for Evie and half I want to give to research into autism, in memory of my uncle Freddy.'

Bonnie came over and kissed Tom on the forehead.

'Now I remember why I love you.'

* * * * *

Earlier that evening, Sandy Tweedside had driven Olive Finch to the station in his noisy old Land Rover.

'It's odd how we've both got to know Tom a little over the last few weeks,' said Sandy. 'What do you make of the lad, Olive?'

'Well I don't actually think it's my place to give an opinion,' said Miss Finch.

'Place be damned, Olive! You were always the brains behind old George's business. Oh, he was driven and a hardnosed negotiator of contracts, but I reckon without your organisational abilities and emotional intelligence about other people, prospective clients etcetera, Roberts Road Builders wouldn't have been half the success it was.'

'You always had a sweet way with words, Sir Alexander.'

'So how about Tom? Does he cut the mustard?'

'He suffered I think from getting too much success at a young age, but there's a fine man there in my opinion.'

'My thoughts entirely.'

'Mrs Bradshott must have been very proud of him.'

'Sadly, if she was, she kept it well hidden,' said Sandy. 'You never married then Olive?'

'No, it was not ordained to be, shall we say.'

'What a waste,' chuckled Sandy as they turned into Haslemere station car park.

* * * * *

Chloe had just got through her front door when the telephone rang.

'Oh Chloe, hello this is Otto Schiller. I have been worrying about you and this whole business with Dampling. There has been no more trouble, I hope.'

'No Professor, no more trouble, but there have been developments.' Chloe told the professor about the body found outside Oxford. She'd done a bit of research and it was the same spot where Roberts Road Builders had been working.

'So, do you think there is a tie to Sir George and the tunnel collapse?'

'Chloe, you have helped me such a lot, but I don't want you to get into any more danger,' said Schiller.

'You've found out something else, haven't you?' said Chloe.

'Well, yes.'

'Come on, Prof, spill the beans!'

'You remember Von Geysell had been recommended for promotion? Well with my father's report on Von Geysell's mixed race heritage not being placed before the committee, his promotion was confirmed and his star was certainly in the ascendancy. Oberscharfuhrer Von Geysell was a Senior Officer in the SS. He continued working in Berlin organising slave labour, rounding up any dissenters and having them summarily shot.'

'He sounds like he was a sadist, actually took pleasure in what he was doing,' said Chloe.

'Who is to say, dear Chloe? He was certainly psychopathic,' said the professor. 'However this is the piece of information that I found most interesting. Apparently America and the United Kingdom conducted bidding wars for high value scientists and engineers. There was a protocol where the newly formed War Crimes Commission would vet these people.

'They, of course, wouldn't have a real problem with Wessels, the young engineer being brought over by the British through Lord Dampling. After all, Wessels had no direct blood on his hands. As part of the deal, it was agreed that AN other would be allowed to go with the expert, whether it be a scientist or engineer. We know that Wessels wasn't, shall we say, the marrying kind, so could it be that Von Geysell came over to Britain with Wessels. After all, he'd arranged several such transfers to the UK including Albrecht's, although we believe he came on his own.'

'Well that certainly strengthens the case against Dampling,' said Chloe.

'Yes, but it doesn't really have any direct connection to your body in the tunnel being Von Geysell. What I can tell you is that Sir George was not only useful to the Allies when he was still in Berlin but also when he came over here. In fact, it may well have been with the help of British Intelligence that he was able to gain a new identity in the UK. You see, Rohmer Road Builders would not have been so acceptable to the general public in Britain.'

'There seems to be a lot of bits of information that seem to be leading that way.'

'So, what now, will you go to the police?'

'I don't know.'

'If you are thinking about me, Chloe, it's enough for me that my father's murderer might be that corpse and that he was buried alive. But there are other people to consider here.'

'I know, Professor. I won't do anything stupid and thank you for all that additional information. One more question; do you think British Intelligence may have turned a blind eye to whatever Sir George's private agenda may have been as a kind of "quid pro quo?"'

'I'm sorry; I'm not with you,' said the professor.

'There was some kind of deal done?'

'I can only speculate, my dear, but from what I understand from those who work in that line, it is much simpler to let others do your dirty work for you. After all, they had caught all the big fish.'

'Big fish?'

'Oh, people like Dr Karl Brandt, who until he fell out with Hitler for trying to smuggle his wife to America during the final weeks of the war was part of the inner circle. Brandt was the chief instigator of the euthanasia project and Tiergartenstrasse 4. He was tried at Nuremberg and put to death.'

'How on earth did you get hold of all this information?' asked Chloe.

'We know a great deal about the Nuremberg trials of course at the Bundersarchive and for that matter Tiergartenstrasse 4.

'But some of it came when I was over in England at the National Archives in Kew; we didn't spend all our time honeymooning you know. The rest came from information kept by the War Crimes Commission and one or two very old contacts, who perhaps know a little too much than is good for them. By the way, Chloe, it is I, who must thank you.'

CHAPTER 58

The sale of Tom's restaurant, The Nosebag, had been agreed in principle and he had decided to hold a farewell pre-Christmas lunch there for staff, family and friends. The restaurant was closed to the general public and the tables had been pushed together to form one enormous dining room table. The guests included a couple of Tom's school friends, one or two from the cricket club, Gerard Casey, Olive Finch, Chloe and Callum and Great Uncle Sandy, who still in his more fanciful moments carried hopes of whisking Olive off up to Perthshire.

'We may not have long, but we'd have a ball,' he'd confided in Tom.

Roast turkey and all the trimmings were the order of the day, preceded by parsnip and butternut squash soup and finished off with Christmas pudding, a lemon sorbet, coffee and mince pies. Tom had called in favours from other chefs, so that his staff all sat down with the other guests. He sat at one end with Bonnie, while Evie held court at the other end having donned a chef's hat and apron.

Tom got to his feet, it has to be said, a little unsteadily, after everyone had sated themselves on the turkey.

'I would just like to propose a toast to my adorable girls, Bonnie and Evie and the rest of my family, represented today by my incomparable Great Uncle Sandy and other dear friends round the table, but especially my loyal staff here at The Nosebag who have paddled, or is it piddled, no, no paddled like crazy to keep the old place afloat. Seriously, I can't thank you enough. So, here's the toast, The Nosebag!'

After the sorbet, Tom popped out into the backyard by the bins. You could still see the scorch marks on the whitewashed walls and even the air maintained an acrid quality that when breathed in nestled in the back of one's throat.

Chloe joined him. She was an occasional smoker and Christmas time was one of those occasions. Being basically a cheerful person most of the year round apart from when she had boyfriend trouble that is, she found going up a gear in jollity stressful and reason enough in her mind for lighting up.

'I feel very honoured to have been included today,' said Chloe, taking a light from Tom.

'I don't know why that should be. You've become a real friend over all this business.'

'Tom?' said Chloe.

'Yes.'

'That business of the tunnel collapsing in on your grandfather.'

'Yes. Awful thing; shook him up really badly apparently.'

'You don't think there's possibly any connection to that body they found near the M40?'

'Yes, as a matter of fact I do. Do you?'

'It might have all been a coincidence.'

'Apparently, whoever it was had sand deeply embedded in one or two fingernails, which suggests he was alive for some time in there.'

'Who told you that?'

'A chap called Fran Burrows. He'd been site foreman there: one of his boys had discovered the body.'

'You mean you went all the way up there?'

'From Willows End, it's not far. I'd seen the reports on telly. So, I went up to take a look. They were just knocking off work, so I followed Burrows to the local pub that night.'

'Didn't he recognise you?'

'Of course he did. He's a *Sun* reader for God's sake. Thankfully he's a fan. I bought him a few pints and he was a bigger fan and it loosened his tongue. Gave me all the gory details.'

'Wasn't that a bit of a foolish thing to do?' said Chloe.

'Chloe, all we've been going on is hearsay and conjecture. And all this happened, if it did happen, over sixty years ago and quite a long time before I was born, so it would be a bit of a leap to accuse me of being an accessory after the fact.'

'It just worries me. You've been through quite a lot recently, Tom,' said Chloe drawing on her cigarette.

'So have you by the sound of it,' said Tom. 'The tunnel business – I wonder whether Olive Finch saw it on the news.'

'Well there's one way for you to find out.'

They went back in; some of the guests were beginning to look for Tom to say their goodbyes. He exchanged hugs and merry Christmases with his friends from the cricket team. Then he made his way over to Olive Finch, who was deep in conversation with Gerard Casey.

'Saint Augustine said, "Faith is believing in something, we don't yet see."'

'How fascinating, Mr Casey.'

'I am a humanist you know,' said Miss Finch. 'My faith is only in the things I do see.'

Tom looked over at Sandy Tweedside standing at the bar and for once looking a little forlorn.

'Very good, Miss Finch,' said Gerard. 'Tell me have you ever been in love?'

'Oh yes.'

'What did it look like,' said Gerard.

'The difference surely is that love is usually a temporary aberration replaced in time by companionship, shared interests and a common history. While faith is often a permanent affliction.'

Gerard chuckled. 'You may have a point there.'

'May we borrow you for a few moments, Miss Finch,' said Tom. 'And may I get you a drink, a cognac perhaps?'

'Thank you, Tom. What I would really like is a cup of tea.'

'It's a bit of a delicate matter. There's a small staff room we could use, if you don't mind the mess,' said Tom. 'This is Chloe, by the way. She has been an absolute brick keeping me going through the whole programme making.'

'I thought you told me the whole thing has had to be shelved.'

'Yes, that's right.'

'Miss Finch,' said Chloe, who could see that Tom was flagging. 'Have you by any chance seen the piece on the news about the body they haven't been able to identify that they've found just outside Oxford?'

'Tom darling, some more of your guests are going.' It was Bonnie.

'Your wife is so beautiful, Tom. Come and sit with me, dear.' Olive patted softly the seat of the chair next to her.

'This is all a bit awkward,' said Chloe. 'You see the less people involved the better.'

'Chloe, I may not know all the ins and outs of Tom's family skeletons and which particular closet they're in, but for us now, it's really important there are no secrets,' said Bonnie

'Quite right, my dear. Now, Chloe, you were saying,' said Miss Finch. 'Ah yes the body near Oxford. What about it exactly?'

'Do you think there is any possibility that it is the body of a man called Von Geysell?'

'I don't think it's a possibility. I know that the corpse or what's left of it is that of Pieter Von Geysell.'

'So, my grandfather confided in you?' queried Tom.

'Not exactly.'

'How do you mean?' asked Chloe.

'Tom, I'm sorry I didn't tell you the whole story about the accident in the tunnel when you visited me at the flat the other day. You see, my dear, it was no accident and your grandfather's injuries were not as a result of any collapse.

'Your grandfather was so good at so many things but there was one thing he just never got the hang of. I was a girl guide you see, so I was taught how to tie knots that would not, excuse the pun, come undone. When you asked had your father confided in me, well yes. Sir George, or for this purpose shall we refer to him as Herr Rohmer, told me the whole story of Ingrid and Freddy and the Charitable Foundation for Curative and Institutional Care, what Albrecht had done to Ingrid, how Freddy had been murdered by Albrecht on Von Geysell's orders and how Von Geysell had gone on to execute Herr Rohmer's best friend. So when the opportunity arose for, shall we call him Sir George now – I really never did take to the name Gunther – for Sir George to obtain some justice, I was only too pleased to help.'

Tom couldn't avoid looking down at Miss Finch's delicate piano playing, lace-making hands, holding the bone china teacup so demurely.

'How did Von Gesell come to be re-acquainted with grandfather?'

'Lord Dampling had taken him on at the same time as a man called Wessels, a brilliant engineer by all accounts. Dampling can have had no knowledge of Sir George and Von Geysell's previous dealings with each other. Thinking all Germans must still have sympathies with the Reich, he started doing business with Roberts Road Builders and sent Von Geysell over as a glorified rep to try and sell Sir George engine parts. Well of course, as soon as he walked in the office door, your grandfather recognised him. The office in those days was a small industrial unit and the staff consisted of me. He came into my little den, on the pretext of ordering tea and told me who it was that was in his office. We both knew it was too good an opportunity to miss.

'Whether Von Geysell recognised Sir George as General Major Gunther Rohmer, I'm really not sure. As I understand, Sir George had altered his appearance when he originally came to England. But while he was being subdued by your grandfather, we made sure. Von Geysell knew who Sir George was and he knew why we were doing what we were doing.

'Of course, your grandfather was at the business end of Von Geysell and that's where he received his injuries. The man flailed about. Sir George had him in what I believe is called a headlock, but I bound his hands and feet. I remember him kicking out at me, but I was quite nimble in those days and he didn't catch me once.'

'So, he wasn't dead when grandfather put him in the tunnel?'

'Oh no, dear; Sir George assured me he was not. You see, we both felt he should have a little time to reflect on his misdemeanours. Sir George, because of his underground exploits in the First World War, reckoned that once he had blocked the tunnel, which he did with one of those little digger vehicles, Von Geysell would have had about twenty-four hours before the oxygen ran out.'

'And after Sir George came out, no one else went in to check?'

'Why would they, dear? The land was owned by the company. Sir George

barred any of his men from going near the tunnel as it was "unsafe". People had better things to do with their time. Bombed-out houses still needed pulling down. Spears into pruning hooks, as my Christian friends would say.'

'But what about Dampling? Did he not report one of his sales reps as missing?' asked Tom.

'No, he didn't; not really surprising. It wouldn't have gone down well with post-war Britain, that Dampling had a former Senior SS officer wanted for war crimes on his books.'

'So why didn't Grandfather just hand him into the authorities?'

'What's the expression they use these days? Ah yes, I think he preferred to "keep it in-house."'

'And how about Dr Albrecht or should I say Gustav Brecht?' asked Chloe.

'Sir George spent a long time tracking him down. Albrecht was also very twitchy, when he heard on the grapevine of Pieter Von Geysell's disappearance, but providentially, Sir George was able to use Lady Elspeth's illness and the prospect of a fat fee as a lure. He knew for some time that Gustav Brecht was his man. It was, I believe, your grandfather's intention to kill himself and Brecht, fortunately for me, he didn't succeed.'

'But Von Geysell! Why, Miss Finch, did you risk everything for Sir George?' said Chloe.

'You sure got some balls, honey,' said Bonnie.

'Thank you, my dear,' Olive replied

At this point, Evie burst through the door.

'It's alright, Daddy. I've said your goodbyes for you. Gave them all a hug, but as their friend, Daddy, you need to tell one or two of them to have a wash a bit more often. Phewey!' she said holding her nose.

'Evie?' said Gerard, who could see that something was up and Evie had interrupted. 'Am I going to give you your Christmas present now or will I send it to The Little Sisters of Mercy?' With that Evie was gone. Gerard winked as he closed the door.

'Sorry about that, you were going to tell us why, Olive?' said Tom.

'Two reasons, firstly my tutor at secretarial college taught us that a good PA should think of her boss as a high wire act. However good they might be and particularly when learning a new routine, they will always need a safety net and secondly, as I once intimated to you, Tom, I was deeply in love with your grandfather. He meant everything to me.' Miss Finch looked directly into Tom's eyes. 'Once I realised that, everything became much clearer.'

Bernard Pearson